Praise for
KATE EMERSON

"No one knows the unusual customs and dangerous characters of the Tudor court like her."

—*New York Times* bestselling author Karen Harper

"Captures the pageantry and the politics of the Tudor court, portraying real-life characters who negotiated turbulent times, and giving historical fiction fans a first-rate read."

—*Booklist*

⇺ *The King's Damsel* ⇻

"An engaging tale of loyalty, love, and treachery in the court of King Henry VIII."

—*Fresh Fiction*

"Basing her latest novel on a letter relaying that Henry VIII claimed a mistress while wed to Anne Boleyn, Emerson cleverly captures their affair and the woman who caught the king's eye. Emerson's handling of the tumultuous period, and rendering of Henry's personality, enables readers to believe they are there."

—*RT Book Reviews* (4 stars)

"Kate Emerson proves time and again that she knows her stuff regarding the Tudor period. She is able to write clear, vivid descriptions that make it seem as if you are right there at court with the characters. . . . Easy to get caught up in."

—*Always With a Book*

"A real treat."

—*Historically Obsessed*

⤳ At the King's Pleasure ⤶

"A wonderfully absorbing novel that is full of enough historical detail to satisfy even the most hard-core Tudor fan. Emerson beautifully depicts the difficulty of living in a treacherous period in which one had to do what the king's pleasure demanded, in spite of the risk of losing one's head."

—*Library Journal*

"I continue to be awestruck by each and every book."

—*Historically Obsessed*

⤳ By Royal Decree ⤶

"Another captivating novel. . . . Emerson skillfully manages to keep Elizabeth's life as the central point and never loses track of her faith in love and happy endings."

—*RT Book Reviews* (4 stars)

"Appealing . . . a refreshingly willful, sexually liberated heroine."

—*Publishers Weekly*

"Presenting the tempestuous and often scandalous court through the eyes of Bess Brooke . . . the author paints a confident, realistic picture of the king."

—*Historical Novels Review*

⤳ Between Two Queens ⤶

"Intrigue, romance, and treachery abound in this well-researched, sensitively written book."

—*Renaissance* magazine

"Emerson's sharp eye for court nuances, intrigues, and passions thrusts readers straight into Nan's life, and the swift pace will sweep you along."

—*RT Book Reviews*

"Filled with intrigue, mystery, and romance . . . it provides Tudor fans with yet another viewpoint of the fascinating lives of those closest to Henry VIII."

—*Historical Novels Review*

✦ *The Pleasure Palace* ✦

"A riveting historical novel . . . vividly fictionalizing historical characters and breathing new life into their personalities and predicaments."

—*Booklist*

"Emerson's lively 'fictional memoir' . . . includes many vivid descriptions of the clothing, comportment, and extravagant entertainments . . . and adds to these lighter moments a subtle undercurrent of mystery and political intrigue."

—*Historical Novels Review*

"Rich and lushly detailed, teeming with passion and intrigue, this is a novel in which you can happily immerse yourself in another time and place."

—*RT Book Reviews*

Also by Kate Emerson

ROYAL
Inheritance

KATE
EMERSON

GALLERY BOOKS
New York London Toronto Sydney New Delhi

G

Gallery Books
A Division of Simon & Schuster, Inc.
1230 Avenue of the Americas
New York, NY 10020

First Gallery Books trade paperback edition September 2013

GALLERY BOOKS and colophon are registered trademarks of
Simon & Schuster, Inc.

For information about special discounts for bulk purchases, please contact Simon &
Schuster Special Sales at 1-866-506-1949 or business@simonandschuster.com.

The Simon & Schuster Speakers Bureau can bring authors to your live event. For
more information or to book an event contact the Simon & Schuster Speakers
Bureau at 1-866-248-3049 or visit our website at www.simonspeakers.com.

Manufactured in the United States of America

1   3   5   7   9   10   8   6   4   2

Library of Congress Cataloging-in-Publication Data

Emerson, Kate.
Royal inheritance / Kate Emerson.—First Gallery books trade paperback edition.
    pages   cm
1. Inheritance and succession—Fiction. I. Title.
PS3555.M414R69 2013
813'.54—dc23
2013009133

ISBN 978-1-4516-6151-4
ISBN 978-1-4516-6153-8 (ebook)

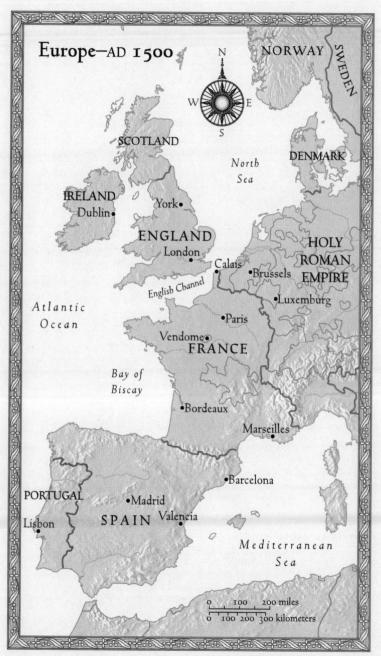

Europe—AD 1500

NORWAY

SWEDEN

SCOTLAND

North
Sea

DENMARK

IRELAND
Dublin

York

ENGLAND
London

HOLY
ROMAN
EMPIRE

Calais

Brussels

Atlantic
Ocean

English Channel

Luxemburg

Paris

Vendome

FRANCE

Bay of
Biscay

Bordeaux

Marseilles

Barcelona

PORTUGAL

Madrid

SPAIN

Valencia

Lisbon

Mediterranean
Sea

0   100   200 miles

0   100 200 300 kilometers

Map by Paul J. Pugliese

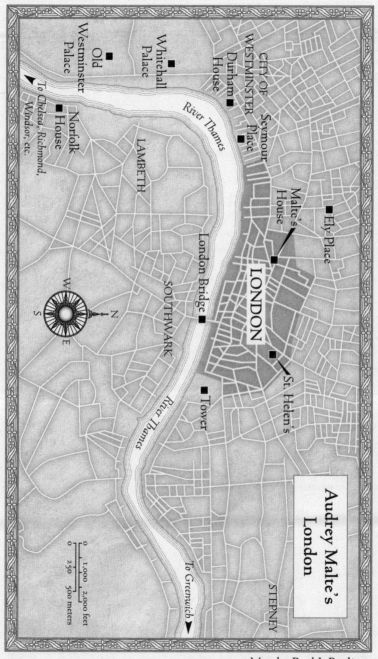

Audrey Malte's London

Map by Paul J. Pugliese

THE CHILDREN OF HENRY VIII

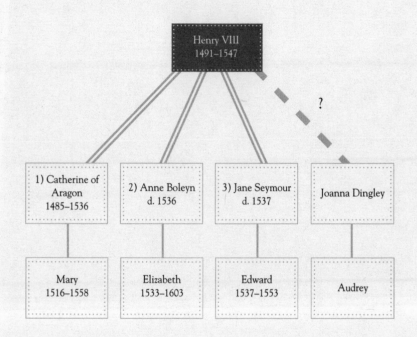

ROYAL
Inheritance

1

Stepney, near London, October 1556

he portrait painter wiped his hands on a ragged cloth already stained with a multitude of bright colors. Annoyance infused his every movement. When he spoke, his tone of voice brooked no argument: "I cannot complete this child's likeness, Mistress Harington. She will not sit still."

Hans Eworth was a master of his craft. Hireling he might be, but his services were highly prized and he was well compensated for them. However long it took him to complete a commission, while he painted he usually had only to command to be obeyed.

Audrey Harington spent a moment longer staring at the view from an upper window in the mansion that had been her husband's town house for the last six years. It was the finest residence in Stepney, barring only the nearby Bishop of London's palace. The house even boasted its own private chapel, in spite of the fact that it took only a few minutes to walk to the church of St. Dunstan, where everyone in the household went for services on Sundays and holy days.

From her vantage point, Audrey had an unobstructed view across more than a mile of flat fields and marshes to the most terrifying place in all of England—the Tower of London. Its stone walls rose to formidable heights, easily visible even at this distance. An involuntary shudder passed through her at the thought of all the poor souls held prisoner there, some of them for no more than a careless word. Some would eventually be set free. Others would be executed. Their fate would depend less upon guilt or innocence than upon the whim of Queen Mary and her Spanish husband, King Philip.

Shaking off these melancholy thoughts, since brooding about injustice would never accomplish anything, Audrey turned to address a situation she *could* remedy. Hester, her eight-year-old daughter, squirmed in the high-backed chair in which Master Eworth had posed her. It was well padded with red velvet cushions, but any position grew uncomfortable with the passage of time. The book Eworth had provided as a prop might have held her attention had she been able to read it, but it was written in Latin. The slim, leather-bound volume lay abandoned, stuffed into the space between Hester's thigh and the seat of the chair, and in imminent danger of tumbling to the floor.

"Let me see what I can do."

Audrey spoke in a genteel and well-modulated voice and rose smoothly from the window seat. That simple act, executed too quickly, was enough to betray her weakness. The first moment of dizziness was as debilitating as a blow to the head. The sensation did not last long, but by the time she recovered her equilibrium, warmth had flooded into her face. She needed no looking glass to know that hectic spots of color dotted her cheeks.

As Audrey glided past Master Eworth, she avoided meeting his gaze. He saw too much. His artist's eye was keen and she feared he had already noticed how greatly she had changed since he had painted her portrait the previous year. She had been exceeding ill of a fever during the summer just past. Thousands had been. Hundreds had died. Many of the survivors were still as appallingly weak as she was.

The woman in Master Eworth's portrait no longer existed. Perhaps she never had. That painting, hanging beside the companion piece of her husband, John Harington, in the great hall of their country house in Somersetshire, showed a tall, slender woman of twenty-seven with red-gold hair and sparkling dark brown eyes. In Eworth's rendition, Audrey wore a richly embroidered gown, radiated raw good health, and looked out on the world with confidence.

To the casual observer, aside from the fact that she now wore plain dark red wool for warmth, she might appear unchanged. But Master Eworth knew better. So did Audrey herself. Her vitality had been sapped by recent illness, and she felt at times no more than a wraith.

In spite of the effort it took to cross the room to her daughter's side, Audrey did not falter, nor did she do more than wince when she reached her goal and knelt beside Hester's chair. Illusion was more important than reality, a lesson she'd learned well during the years she'd spent on the fringes of the royal court.

Hester stared down at her mother with a sad expression that made her appear far older than her years.

"What is it that troubles you, sweeting?" Audrey asked.

"Nothing." Hester looked away, toying with the fringe on the arm of the chair.

"Is your hair braided too tightly?" The thick, dark brown tresses, an inheritance from her father, had been pulled back from her face and wound in an intricate manner on top of her head.

"No, Mother."

"Then you must keep your promise to pose for Master Eworth.

When your portrait is finished, it will hang in the great hall at Catherine's Court."

"Distract her, madam," Eworth interrupted, anxious to resume work. "She must remain motionless if I am to do her justice."

"How long?" Audrey did not look at him.

"Another hour at the least."

At this pronouncement, Hester's lower lip crept forward in a pout.

"Pick up the book and pretend to read," Eworth ordered. "For some unfathomable reason Master Harington wants the world to know he has a well-educated daughter."

"What if I read to you?" Audrey cut in before the rebellion she saw bubbling up in the dark eyes so like her own could boil over. "Then all you will have to do is sit still and listen."

Hester made a circle on the floor with the toe of her little leather slipper. "What will you read?"

"You may choose any text you like, so long as the book is written in English." The Haringtons owned a respectable library, but some of the volumes were in Latin or Greek or French and beyond Audrey's ken.

"Tell me a story instead. Tell me a true story about King Henry."

Audrey sighed. She should have anticipated her daughter's request. Of late there had been no curtailing Hester's curiosity about the late king. His portrait—a copy of one Master Holbein had painted—had always been displayed at Catherine's Court, but Hester had shown no interest in it until, one bleak and stormy winter evening, her father had entertained her by recollecting the days long ago when he had been a gentleman of the king's Chapel Royal.

Since then, Hester frequently asked for more tales of that time. Her father had recounted a few of his adventures, carefully edited, but Audrey had been reluctant to speak of the past.

Then she had fallen ill. Coming within a hair's breadth of death had brought home to her that she had a duty to tell Hester the truth—all of it. But the girl was still so young. Could she even comprehend what Audrey had experienced? She wished she could wait until her daughter was a few years older, but she feared to delay too long lest the opportunity be lost forever.

Master Eworth scuttled forward to reposition his subject with the book. Audrey waited until he returned to his easel before she began to speak. She kept her voice low, although she was certain the portrait painter's hearing was sharp enough to overhear every word she spoke.

It did not matter. In the short time allotted to the sitting, she could not delve very deeply into her story. To tell the complete tale would take many hours, perhaps even days. A sense of calm came over her as she began to speak.

"The first time I met King Henry," she told her daughter, "I was younger than you are now."

2

Windsor Castle, 1532

*E*ven as a little girl, I remembered my mother complained often of the cold and bitter winter that preceded my birth. Even the sea froze. And then, while she was still great with child, a plague came upon the land. It was called the sweat, the same vile illness that returned twenty years later to decimate the population of our fair isle. Thousands sickened and died, rich and poor alike. A few sickened and lived. My mother, Joanna Dingley by name, escaped unaffected. On the twenty-third of June, St. Ethelreda's Day, in the twentieth year of the reign of King Henry the Eighth, she gave birth to me in a house near Windsor Castle. She named me for the saint whose day it was, the patroness of widows and those with ailments of the neck and throat.

Like most girls christened Ethelreda, I have always been called by the diminutive Audrey.

I remember little of the first few years of my life. My mother worked as a laundress at the castle. She smelled of lye and black soap and the warm urine used for bleaching. She had long, black hair and eyes of a brown so dark that it was difficult to discern her pupils. Her face was long and narrow, her coloring sallow. Her hands were strong. When she hit me, it hurt.

After she married a man called Dobson, we moved into his tiny lodgings inside Windsor Castle. He worked in the kitchen as an undercook and slept above it, which meant that the good smells of baking were as often present in our single small chamber as the less pleasant scents of the laundry. Since Dobson had little patience with me, I tried to stay out of his way. His blows were much harder than those my mother gave me. When he hit me, he always left bruises.

Dobson was in a particularly foul mood on the September Sunday in the year of our Lord fifteen hundred and thirty-two when Lady Anne Rochford, she who would one day become Queen Anne Boleyn, was to be created Marquess of Pembroke. He had to rise very early—well before dawn—to prepare food for a banquet. When he got up, he tripped over the truckle bed where I lay sleeping. I was a little more than four years old and still half asleep, incapable of moving fast enough to escape. Cursing loudly, he kicked me twice, once in the ribs and once in the face.

You may well ask how I can recall anything from so early in my childhood, let alone in such detail. In truth, I cannot explain it. Most of what befell me between my birth and the age of eight or nine beyond my mother's complaints I retain only in vague impressions. And yet, there are one or two incidents that must have imprinted themselves too vividly upon my mind ever to be forgotten. This was one such, and it changed my life.

My memory of Dobson's kicks is as fresh as if they connected with my flesh only yesterday. I can still recall how the pain brought tears to my eyes and that I did not dare cry out. If I'd made a sound, it would only have made him angrier. Instead, while he stumbled about, lighting a candle, using the chamber pot behind the screen, and pulling on his clothing, I crept out of our lodgings. Heedless of direction, still barefoot and clad in nothing more than my white linen shift, I ignored the throbbing in my ribs and ran for all I was worth.

The next part of my memory is a blur. I suppose I must have traveled for some distance through narrow passages and down even narrower flights of stairs. Windsor Castle is a great, sprawling place. It would not have taken long for me to become hopelessly lost. I ended up huddled in an alcove in a drafty and deserted corridor, sitting on the cold, flagged floor with my knees drawn up to my chest. Seeking warmth as well as comfort, I wrapped my arms around them and cried my heart out, never imagining that anyone was near enough to overhear me.

All my focus was centered on the way my cheek stung and how badly my bruised ribs ached every time I drew in a deep breath. Although sobbing increased the pain, I could not seem to stop. I was so lost to my distress that I was unaware of the approach of a company of men until one of them stopped and spoke to me.

The sound of his loud, deep voice terrified me. With one last hiccough, I fell silent and tried to make myself even smaller. I did not dare look up at the man who'd addressed me. I was braced for a blow.

After a moment, a gloved finger adorned with a gold ring set with a large ruby appeared before my eyes. It came to rest under my chin and raised it until I was forced to look upon his face. His eyes, blue-gray in color, widened when he got his first clear view of my features.

I must have been a pitiful sight, an ungainly child with scraggly red locks and a tearstained face, but he shifted his hand to lift a strand of that hair and, after a moment, used an exquisitely gentle touch to caress my bruised cheek.

He asked me my name, and that of my mother, though perhaps not in that order.

He was a big man, tall and strong, and he wore the most splendid garments I had ever seen. They were made of rich fabrics and studded with precious gems. A heavy gold collar hung round his neck and the faint smell of musk and rosewater clung to his person. Beneath a very fine bonnet, he had hair as red as my own.

The gentlemen who accompanied him were also richly dressed. One of them wore the distinctive vestments and tall hat of a bishop. They all stared at me. Time seemed to stretch out, although I've no doubt that only a few moments passed. Then the red-haired man barked an order and all but one of his party moved on.

A yeoman of the guard remained behind, resplendent in scarlet livery with the royal badge, a rose, embroidered on his breast. He took a firm grip on my arm and led me away in the opposite direction. I expected to be taken back to Dobson's lodgings. Instead he delivered me to a chamber that had been set aside as a workroom for the king's tailor.

Orders had been given, although I was unaware of them at the time. I was to be clothed and looked after until such time as arrangements could be made for me. The king—for that bejeweled and gentle red-haired man had been no other than King Henry the Eighth himself—had taken exception to my mistreatment by my mother's husband.

I was taken from my mother and given into the keeping of the king's tailor, one John Malte by name, and his wife, Anne. Malte was a little man, lean and wiry, with straw-colored hair and sympathetic blue eyes and freckles that danced across the nose and cheeks of a clean-shaven face. His speech was slow and measured—he was wont to choose all his words with care—and even before he knew who I was, he treated me with kindness and consideration. When I fell asleep on a padded bench in his workroom, he covered me with a length of expensive damask.

Many years passed before I learned what transpired while I slept. At the time, I knew only what I was told when I awoke. John Malte took my small hand in his bigger, callused one and informed me that I was to come home with him to London. From that day forward, he said, my name was Audrey Malte.

3

I settled happily into my new life and soon forgot the old. Home was a tall house in Watling Street in London in the parish of St. Augustine by Paul's Gate. The entire parish stood in the shadow of St. Paul's.

I shared this house with Mother Anne, Father's second wife, with her daughter by her first marriage, and with the two daughters Father's first wife had given him before she died. Elizabeth, at nine, was five years my senior. Bridget was six when I arrived and old enough to resent the addition of yet another sister. Muriel, at age five, welcomed a new playmate.

Time passed.

When I was eight, Father explained my origins to me. He had, he said, begotten me on my mother during one of his many visits to Windsor Castle in the king's service. I was, he said, a merry-begot, for there had been much joy in my making. I thought this a much nicer word than *baseborn* or *illegitimate* or *bastard*.

In the greater world, the king had married Anne Boleyn, Lady Marquess of Pembroke, and they'd had a daughter, Princess

Elizabeth. And then he had divorced and beheaded Queen Anne. When he took another English gentlewoman to wife—Mistress Jane Seymour—she gave birth to a son, a prince who would later ascend the throne as King Edward VI. Then Queen Jane died. That was during the autumn following my ninth birthday.

Father was summoned to court to make mourning garments for the king. Kings wear purple for mourning, but everyone else must dress in black. After Candlemas, the second day of February, courtiers were permitted to resume their normal attire. Father was inundated with orders for new clothes. He worked late into the night and his apprentices with him, squinting in the candlelight to see what they were stitching.

From the beginning, I spent many happy hours in the tailor shop that occupied the large single room on the ground floor of the Watling Street house. A stairway led down to it from the living quarters above, giving me easy access. On occasion, Mother Anne dispatched me with messages for Father. More often, I visited because my sister Bridget persuaded me to go with her. She liked to watch the apprentices work. At eleven, Bridget was already showing signs of budding womanhood. The apprentices liked to watch her, too.

Father customarily set the boys to performing various tasks appropriate to their skill. Since the fabrics he worked with were valuable and not to be cut into lightly, he personally oversaw the laying out of paper patterns traced from buckram pieces onto luxurious fabrics as varied as satin, damask, and cloth of silver.

"Match the grain lines and make certain that the pile runs in the same direction," he warned. "And the woven designs must be balanced."

More important still, the pattern pieces had to be arranged so that there was as little waste as possible. Once Father approved the placement of the pattern pieces, he used tailor's chalk to mark the pattern lines on silk or wool camlet, and even on cloth of gold, but on velvet it was necessary to trace-tack the pattern pieces instead.

Bridget wound a lock of long, pale yellow hair around her finger while she watched two of the apprentices outline each shape with thread. When they were done and Father had checked their stitches, he supervised the removal of the pattern pieces. These were made of stiff brown paper. Father kept them until they wore out, adjusting them to use for more than one person.

In addition to making clothes for the king, Father also had many private clients, women as well as men. They paid him well for his services, allowing us to live in considerable luxury. He had even made a few garments for Queen Anne and for Queen Jane, although it was our neighbor in Watling Street, John Scutt, who held the post of queen's tailor. Poor Master Scutt lost his wife at about the same time Queen Jane died. Like the queen, she did not survive childbirth. She left her husband with a baby girl he named Margaret.

"I want to help with the cutting," I announced on this particular day. I was already reaching for Father's best pair of shears when he stopped me.

"This length of cloth, uncut, must first be sent to the embroiderers. There it will be stretched taut on a frame and they will use our shapes to guide them. See there? All the seam lines are clearly marked. And from the shape, the embroiderers will know whether they are stitching on the front or the back of the garment."

"And *then* may I cut it?"

"Then I will cut it. Or Richard will. And afterward, we will make this length of velvet into clothing, with suitable linings and interlinings."

Richard Egleston was one of Father's former apprentices. When he finished his training, he married another of Father's daughters,

Mary, the child of his first wife by her first husband, and stayed on in the shop as a cutter.

"I would do a most excellent job for you, Father." Eager to prove my worth, I persisted in trying to convince him. It had not yet been impressed upon me that girls could not be apprenticed as tailors, or indeed in any other trade.

"You have not had the necessary training to work with such expensive cloth."

"I can sew," I argued. "Mother Anne taught me."

What Father might have said to that, I do not know, for at that precise moment a gentleman entered the shop. I had never seen him before, but I could tell he was a courtier by the way he was dressed. Beneath a fur-lined cloak with the king's badge on the shoulder he wore the black livery that marked him as a member of the royal household.

He blinked upon first coming inside out of the sunlight. Then his gaze fell upon me. Whatever he had been about to say seemed to fly out of his head. He stood there, silent and staring, until Father spoke to him.

"How may I serve you, Master Denny?" Father's voice sounded a trifle sharper than usual. "Does His Grace the King require my presence at court?"

Jolted out of his trance, the newcomer recollected his purpose. "He does, Goodman Malte, and His Grace bade me give you this." Reaching into an inner pocket in his doublet, he withdrew a letter bearing the royal seal.

Bridget and I stayed where we were, our eyes fixed on the stranger. He was younger than Father, but he still seemed quite old to me. He had a very fine brown beard and mild gray eyes.

"Who is he?" I whispered to my sister as Father read the king's message.

"He must be Anthony Denny, a yeoman of the wardrobe and a groom of the king's privy chamber."

That sounded very important, although no more so than "royal tailor." I was too young yet to grasp the difference between a gentleman born and a merchant whose wealth allowed him to rise into the ranks of the gentry.

When Father finished reading he tossed the missive into the fire burning in the hearth. "We will set out on the morrow," he promised.

"Is this the lass?" Master Denny jerked his head in my direction.

Bridget, sitting next to me on one of the long workroom tables, assumed he meant her and preened.

"Yes," Father said. "Audrey, come and make your curtsey to Master Denny."

I heard Bridget squeak in outrage as I hopped down to obey. She'd come to expect the admiration of males of all ages and was not accustomed to being relegated to second place.

"Tomorrow, Audrey," Father said, "at King Henry's request, you will accompany me to court."

My heart began to beat a little faster. "To court?"

He nodded. "Go along with you now. You and Bridget both. I must speak further of this matter with Master Denny."

Bridget held her tongue only until we reached the hall on the floor above, the central chamber of our living quarters. Another goodly blaze crackled in that fireplace, sending out waves of welcome warmth and the soothing smell of burning applewood.

"Why were you chosen to visit the king when I am older?"

"How am I to know? Ask Father."

Bridget pinched my arm hard enough to leave a bruise before turning to the eldest of our sisters. "Elizabeth! Audrey is to go to court with Father! It should have been me!"

Elizabeth glanced up from her embroidery, a puzzled expression on her plump-cheeked face. "Why would either of you *want* to go to court?" She was nearly fifteen and soon to marry. She cared for little beyond making plans for the household and servants she would have after she wed.

Muriel sat beside Elizabeth on the low settle, all her concentration fixed on the small, even stitches she was using to hem a linen shirt. She had the same yellow hair as Bridget but none of her vivacity. Muriel's idea of an entertaining afternoon was one spent in the garden feeding bread crumbs to the birds.

"*Everyone* wants to go to court to see the king!" The exasperation in Bridget's voice made her opinion clear—if Elizabeth had possessed even a grain of sense, she would never have had to ask.

I said nothing. Although I had not thought of the incident for years, Bridget's words brought back to me the last occasion upon which I had seen King Henry. At the time, he had frightened me half to death with his booming voice. In hindsight, I realized that he had very likely saved my life.

"It is not *fair*," Bridget wailed.

"There is no call to raise your voices," Mother Anne admonished her, entering the hall from the gallery that crossed over the yard from the countinghouse above the kitchen. "What is all this to-do about?"

Our town house, a tall, sturdy structure made of wood and Flemish wall, was so large and commodious that both a warehouse and a kitchen opened off the cobblestone-paved courtyard at the back of the shop. The family sleeping chambers were above the hall—Elizabeth, Bridget, Muriel, and I shared a room. The apprentices slept in the garret at the very top of the house.

Bridget was only too willing to repeat her complaints for Mother Anne's benefit.

"Bridget can go in my place," I offered. "No one will know the difference."

Mother Anne shook her head. She was a round little dumpling of a woman, good-natured and affectionate, but she could take a firm stand when one was needed. "I very much fear, sweetings, that the king can tell the difference between a redheaded girl and one with yellow curls. You will do as your father tells you, Audrey, and we will none of us mention Bridget's complaints to him. As for you, Bridget, remember that envy is a sin. Do not allow yourself to fall prey to it."

4

March 1538

*I*t was still early spring, with a chill in the air. Father bundled me into a warm cloak for the trip upriver to the king's great palace of Whitehall, in the city of Westminster. We went by boat, embarking from the stairs at Paul's Wharf.

Father assisted me into the small watercraft he'd waved ashore and indicated that I should sit on one of the embroidered cushions. I watched him closely as he settled in beside me. He did not seem at all nervous about venturing out onto the Thames. I was less sanguine, viewing the choppy water with darkest suspicion. It was a dirty brown in color and there were objects floating in it. I did not want to look too closely at any of them, for I suspected that at least a few were the carcasses of dead animals. I will not even attempt to describe the foul stench that wafted up from beneath the surface.

The waterman extended one grimy hand in our direction while using the other to hold his boat steady. Father gave him a three-penny piece. This seemed extravagant to me. Mother Anne had taught all of her daughters to be frugal with household expenses.

Threepence was sufficient to purchase a half-dozen silk points. Two of the small silver coins would have bought a whole pig.

The oars creaked in their locks as the waterman bent to his work and we made good speed upriver on an incoming tide. We did not have far to go, and to make the journey pass even more swiftly, Father pointed out the sights along the way. They were all new to me. Since the day John Malte first took me home with him, I had not once ventured beyond London's city walls. Even within them, I had rarely gone farther from Watling Street than the shops of Cheapside.

The south bank of the Thames was largely open countryside. We could see across it to the Archbishop of Canterbury's palace, rising up in distant Lambeth. On the London side, we first passed Blackfriars. Once a great religious house, it had in more recent years been carved up into residences for wealthy pensioners and minor lords.

"Many great noblemen have houses along this stretch of the river," Father said. "The road that runs from Ludgate to the city of Westminster is called the Strand. We might have ridden along it to our destination, but then we would not have been able to enjoy the best view."

I agreed that the riverside houses were indeed magnificent. Most had terraces and gardens that ran all the way down to the Thames. Many had their own water gates and landing stairs, too.

The river itself was crowded with every sort of watercraft, from small hired boats like our own to magnificent private barges. Sturdy commercial vessels carried goods downriver for sale in London or export to foreign lands. We made steady progress in spite of the traffic, traveling much faster than if we'd taken the land route. In the Strand, pedestrians, carts, and wagons prevent those on horseback from any better pace than a slow walk.

"Look," Father instructed as we rounded the bend in the river. I gasped with pleasure as I beheld the gleaming towers of Whitehall, the king's palace at Westminster. The waterman put his back into his work and guided the boat to the water stairs Father indicated.

A liveried sergeant porter inspected us before we were allowed to pass into the king's privy garden. He knew Father on sight but he gave me an odd look. I paid him no mind. I was too entranced by my surroundings.

March is not the most beautiful time of year in any garden, but the topiary work and the greenery in the raised beds were very fine. There were gardeners busy everywhere I looked. Some were planting. Others were digging a large, deep hole.

"That will be a pond for the swans," Father said. "When it is finished it will be bounded by hedges secured to latticework."

Overlooking the gardens were galleries. Through their large windows I glimpsed courtiers walking back and forth for exercise. I was too far away to make out their faces. It did not occur to me until much later that they could see me as well as I could see them.

We walked along the graveled paths, in no apparent hurry to enter the palace. I wondered at that, and plied Father with questions, but he just shook his head and counseled patience.

The sound of the workmen's shovels digging into sodden earth seemed loud in the silence that fell between us. In the distance I heard a boatman shout, "Eastward, ho!" And then, without warning, came a strange racket, half bark and half bay. It filled the air, heralding the appearance of a pack of dogs.

They burst out of the shrubbery only a few feet in front of me, tumbling one over another in eager play. I would have been terrified had they been deerhounds, or even terriers, but these dogs belonged to a breed I had never seen before. They were tiny, the largest no more than five inches in height at the shoulder. I counted eight in all.

First one pup, then another, caught sight of me and bounded my way. Then two veered off and began to tussle with each other. The first one bit the second's ear. Then that pup went for the first dog's tail. A third, the smallest of the lot, his fur a motley white, red, lemon, and orange-brown, lost interest in me and raced back to join the fun. All three rolled off the graveled path and into the hole the men had been digging.

"Oh, no! They will be hurt!" Alarmed, I ran toward the place where they'd disappeared, trailed by the remaining dogs.

The runt reappeared first, now colored an all-over brown. As I reached him, he gave himself a vigorous shake, spattering my skirt with mud. I could not help myself. I burst out laughing and reached down to lift his warm, filthy, wriggling little body into my arms. Ecstatic at this show of affection, he licked my face.

And so it was, for the second time in my life, that I remained oblivious to the presence of the king, accompanied by a band of his retainers, until His Grace stood not a foot away from me.

King Henry cleared his throat.

I looked up and froze. Dumbstruck, I clutched the small dog closer to my bosom. I had the mad idea that I must protect him from the king.

"Your Majesty," Father said, bowing low. "May I present my youngest daughter, Audrey Malte."

I continued to stare at the king, taking in his appearance bit by bit. He was so very splendid to look at that I did not think to curtsey until Father caught my forearm and jerked me downward.

In full sunlight, King Henry the Eighth dazzled the eye. The jewels set into his doublet and his plumed cap reflected the brightness of the day. The rings he wore on every finger glittered, too. And yet, had he been clad in the roughest, undecorated homespun, he'd still have awed onlookers with his magnificence.

Taller by a head than any man in his company, he was broad of shoulder and chest and sturdy of leg. No jewel could outshine the radiance of his nimbus of bright red-gold hair. Its brilliant shade was mirrored in his full beard. Only his eyes lacked gem-like qualities, being a muted blue-gray, but he had an intense and penetrating gaze.

He was also smiling.

"Rise, Audrey," the king commanded. Then he turned to my father, clapping him on the back as he straightened from his obeisance and causing him to stagger a little. "And good morrow to you, Malte. Well met."

They began to walk together along the same graveled path Father and I had been following when we encountered the dogs. I looked around for the rest of the pack and spotted them frolicking in one of the newly planted beds. One was digging with wild abandon. The king ignored these antics, apparently unconcerned with the destruction.

Reluctant to be left behind, I joined the king's entourage, walking behind His Grace and my father. I looked down at the puppy I still held cradled in my arms. Soft brown eyes gazed back at me, full of trust and affection. Belatedly, I noticed that he wore a decorative collar made of red velvet and kid. One of the badges King Henry used—the Tudor rose—was attached to it.

Anthony Denny, the courtier who had brought the king's message to the tailor shop, fell into step beside me. "That pup you are holding is a called a glove beagle," he said. "The breed takes its name from the fact that even when full grown, they fit into the palm of a heavy leather hunting glove."

"Are they lapdogs for ladies, then?" I asked.

"They are most commonly used to hunt rabbits. They ride along on a hunt, usually in a saddlebag, until the larger hounds run the prey to the ground. Then they are released to continue the chase through the underbrush."

I had never heard of such a thing, but then I knew nothing of hunting, with or without the use of dogs.

Ahead of us, the king continued his conversation with my father, speaking to him in a companionable way that surprised me. No man was the equal of the king. King Henry, as head of the church in England, was only a trifle less to be revered than God Himself. Surely only noblemen were supposed to be on such familiar terms with His Grace.

I considered the evidence before my eyes and came to a conclusion. Father regularly saw His Grace stripped down to his linen—in order that he might fit the king for new clothes. This enforced intimacy must have created a bond between them.

The glove beagles, tired of ravaging through the flower beds, came hurtling after the king. Although he smiled indulgently at the pack, he ordered that they be taken back to their kennel.

"I will take that one now," one of His Grace's henchmen said, reaching for the little dog I still held.

"Could I not keep him with me just a little longer?" I asked.

The pup stared up at me with a pleading expression in his dark brown eyes and my heart melted. I darted a glance at the king and quailed when I saw that he was watching me. I feared I had offended him, or broken some rule about how to behave at court, and hastily dropped my gaze.

Heavy footsteps approached, crunching on the gravel, until King Henry stood right in front of me. "Would you like to keep him, Audrey?" he asked.

"More than anything," I whispered, daring to meet his eyes.

His Grace must have seen the look in mine a thousand times before. Petitioners of all ages and stations in life flocked to court daily to ask for this boon or that. But with me the king was generous.

"Take him as our gift to you, young Audrey," King Henry said. "Feed him on bread, not meat. That will discourage him from developing hunting instincts. And keep him on a leash or in a fenced yard when you take him out of doors, lest he run off and become lost."

"I will take most excellent care of him, Your Grace," I promised, thrilled beyond measure.

Satisfied, the king nodded and straightened. I barely noticed when His Grace left us a few minutes later, along with his escort. I was too busy playing with my new friend.

5

April 1538

I named the glove beagle Pocket, since he was small enough for me to carry in the pocket I wore tied around my waist. Because this pocket was hidden beneath my skirt—reached through a purpose-cut placket—Pocket caused more than one person to start and stare when he poked his head out without warning and announced himself in that strange baying bark that was distinctive to his breed. Mother Anne dubbed it a howl.

Elizabeth and Muriel responded to the little dog much as I had, with instant adoration. He returned their affection. Winning over Mother Anne took longer, nearly a week. Only Bridget refused to be charmed. She was still sulking because I had been chosen to meet the king and she had not.

A month after my visit to Whitehall, I was sleeping soundly when a harsh whisper jerked me awake.

"They are speaking of you," Bridget hissed into my ear. "Come with me now."

Still groggy, I allowed myself to be lured from the bedchamber.

For once, I left Pocket behind. He was curled into a ball at the foot of the bed, lost in puppy dreams.

Following my sister, I crept quietly down the narrow staircase. Halfway to the lower level, when the rumble of Father's voice reached me, I tried to pull back, but Bridget was relentless. She caught my arm in a tight grip and all but dragged me the rest of the way.

I knew where she was taking me. From a young age, she had made a habit of concealing herself behind the wall hanging in the hall—an embroidered scene of a picnic in a forest glade—to eavesdrop on Father and Mother Anne.

For one terrifying moment, we were exposed in the doorway and as we scuttled toward this hiding place, our white linen smocks shining like beacons as they caught the candlelight. Then we were safe in the stifling darkness. Neither Father nor Mother Anne had glanced our way.

Father was pacing. I could hear the slap of his slippered feet against the floor as he came close to the wall hanging and then moved away again. After a bit, he spoke.

"The court is a dangerous place for a young girl."

"Then keep Audrey at home," Mother Anne replied. The whisper of fabric against fabric told me she held an embroidery frame in her lap. She was calm where Father sounded agitated.

"I have no choice. I must obey the king."

The news that King Henry wanted me to return to court surprised me. It irritated Bridget. She pinched me. Twice.

Father's voice faded as he moved away. I missed a few words. And then he was talking about a recent outbreak of violence among the courtiers. "It has been as deadly as any plague," he complained. "I do not know what spawned it, but there have been brawls, duels, and even murders, all within the verge."

"The verge?" Mother Anne asked.

"That is the ten-mile radius that surrounds the person of the king. As you know, the king and his courtiers move about a good deal, but wherever King Henry is, that is the court and the verge moves with it."

Father was always being called upon to travel to different palaces. I already knew many of their names—Greenwich and Whitehall, Richmond and Woodstock and Worksop. And Windsor Castle, where I had once lived. There were many other royal houses, too, smaller ones that the king visited when he went on his annual progress.

"Audrey is *my* responsibility," Father said.

"And you do well by her." A little silence ensued. "Whitehall is but a short distance from London," Mother Anne pointed out. "You need not remain for more than a few hours at a time."

"If the court were always at Whitehall Palace, there would be no problem."

"Surely His Grace does not expect you to bring Audrey with you to the more distant palaces. Greenwich, mayhap, but that is not so very far away, either."

"Nor are Richmond and Hampton Court," he admitted.

"From any of those palaces, you can bring her home again before nightfall. She will sleep safe in her own bed."

"And what of the times when I am obliged to leave her alone in the chamber set aside for my workroom? I cannot take her with me into His Grace's bedchamber."

"She need not be alone," Mother Anne said. "You always take Richard with you. Or one of the apprentices."

"She should have a woman companion," Father muttered. "Better yet, what the Spaniards call a *duenna*."

Offended by the very idea that I should need a nursemaid, I

nearly gave away our presence. Bridget grabbed hold of my arm. Then Mother Anne began speaking again, so softly that I had to strain to catch her words.

"The girl is a great deal of trouble," she said.

"That is scarce Audrey's fault. Nor is it her doing that the king has no queen. So long as His Grace remains unwed, few women live at court. I cannot ignore the king's wishes, but I dislike exposing an impressionable young girl to unsavory influences."

"I suppose I can spare Lucy," Mother Anne said.

"Lucy would be no help at all." The tiring maid Elizabeth, Bridget, Muriel, and I shared was a great lump of a girl and slow-witted besides. "Nor would any of our other maidservants. They are either too young or too inexperienced, even your Nell."

Nell had been with Mother Anne since her own girlhood and was getting on in years. Her fingers were gnarled with age and her knees pained her when she walked.

"Perhaps one of the other girls might accompany Audrey as a companion," Mother Anne suggested. "Elizabeth is old enough to take on such a responsibility."

Beside me, Bridget began to mutter softly. She'd hated it when I had gone to court and she had not. That Elizabeth might go, too, infuriated her.

"She also lacks the necessary experience. Bad enough," father grumbled, "to let *one* of my innocent daughters stray so near to the dangerous undercurrents at court."

That image put me in mind of the roiling waters of the Thames, but I knew that was not what Father meant. Although he'd moved off again, I caught a little of what he said next, enough to understand that he was speaking of certain crimes committed against women.

Father and Mother Anne did not say much more of interest.

Mother Anne suggested hiring a respectable London matron to accompany me to court and to this Father agreed. Then they left the hall for their bedchamber.

Bridget and I waited until we heard their door close before we slipped quietly back to our own bedchamber and into the bed we shared. Pocket had not moved, nor had Muriel or Elizabeth, although the latter was snoring softly. Bridget was not speaking to me, but she managed another pinch or two before she settled down to sleep.

I lay awake, for I had much to ponder. It seemed I was to return to court and that it was the king himself who wanted me there. At first, I could not imagine why he should be interested in my doings but, after mulling over this question for a time, I settled on the only possible explanation. The answer was obvious once I thought of it. His Grace wished to ask me how Pocket was faring in his new home.

6

*F*ather need not have worried. It was some time before King Henry summoned him to court again. Soon after our encounter in the garden at Whitehall, the king departed for his hunting lodge at Royston. His Grace fell ill while there. After he recovered, in July, he embarked on his annual progress, traveling far away from London so that he might visit other parts of the realm and be seen by his subjects in those distant shires. It was November before he returned to any of the royal palaces situated near London.

In preparation for Yuletide, the king needed new clothes. With great reluctance, Father took me with him to Greenwich. I met the king at the tiltyard, where he was overseeing construction of a new seating gallery. I duly reported on Pocket's health and well-being, but His Grace did not seem much interested. After a few minutes, he strode off to speak with two of the knights who had been practicing at the quintain.

Father said, consolingly, "King Henry has a great many very important matters on his mind."

"I thought he would want to know that Pocket is nearly full

grown now." He stood almost nine inches tall at the shoulder.

Father sighed, but made no further excuses for His Grace. He escorted me back to his workroom and left me there with Mistress Yerdeley, an old woman who lived near us in Watling Street. She'd been hired to accompany me to court and watch over me when Father could not. She sat on the window seat with her sewing, nodding agreeably as he repeated his instructions for what must have been the twentieth time.

"Audrey is not to leave the workroom. No one is to come into the workroom that you do not know. You are not to answer impertinent questions about your charge. And you, Audrey, are not to speak to anyone you have not already met."

We both promised to obey him, but ten minutes after he left, Mistress Yerdeley was sound asleep, her head resting against the windowpane. I soon grew bored with staying in one place. The mending Mother Anne had sent with me held no allure. I had been taught the rudiments of reading but I had no books. Since Father's apprentice had gone with him to the king's fitting, I did not even have anyone to talk to.

I went to the door and opened it. No one was in sight but, in the distance, I heard singing. The music had the familiar cadence of a hymn and I reasoned that it must be coming from a chapel. How dangerous, I asked myself, could it be to listen to choristers rehearse? Certain of my logic, I followed the marvelous sound of those voices.

The Chapel Royal is not a place. It moves with the court. The singers of the Chapel Royal are of two sorts: the children of the chapel—a dozen boy choristers who lodge with the Master of the Chapel—and the gentlemen ordinary of the choir. Both groups perform sacred music for church services, but they also sing secular songs to entertain the king.

On this cold December day, the gentlemen were rehearsing. As was appropriate, they were in the chapel where the king worshipped. No one noticed me creep in. I was small enough to be almost invisible and my plain, dark garments blended nicely with the shadows.

Hidden behind a pillar, I stayed very still and listened to them practice. I was moved to tears by some of the hymns and awed by others. I do not know how long I lingered there, but I did not leave until the choristers finished their practice for the day and began to disperse. Only then did I make my way back to Father's workroom.

I saw no one along the way except one yeoman of the guard and he ignored me. Mistress Yerdeley still slept, only waking a few minutes before Father returned to collect us and take us back to London.

7

1539

I accompanied Father to court a number of times during the months that followed. I saw the king briefly during each visit. On these occasions, His Grace would invariably ask after my welfare and that of Pocket. I took to bringing the little dog with me, since he fit easily into a carrying pouch. This amused King Henry but did not change the pattern of our meetings.

Mistress Yerdeley continued in her role as my companion and I continued, the moment she drifted off to sleep, to slip away to the chapel in the hope of finding choristers rehearsing. Although I remained hidden, I was soon able to recognize individuals, especially among the adult singers. These gentlemen took turns playing the organ to accompany their fellows. Some of them also composed music. As I watched and listened, I learned some of their names but I also began to absorb bits of the instruction that was given to the boy choristers in plainchant and harmony. I have always had a good ear for music. Without even thinking about it, I committed to memory almost every tune I heard.

There was one hymn I particularly liked, although I did not try to reproduce the lyrics. The words were Latin and I did not understand that language. Instead I substituted nonsense syllables into the tune. On a cold early December day just a year after my first encounter with the choristers, I was tra-la-la-ing to this piece as I returned to Father's workroom.

A bellow of rage from within stopped me dead in my tracks. I broke off singing in mid-verse. A moment later I was running toward the door, for I had recognized the king's voice. He was berating Father for losing me.

"I am here!" I cried.

King Henry stood in the middle of the workroom. He turned a fearsome glare on me, causing me to skid to a stop, throat dry and heart pounding. The yeomen of the guard and the other minions who always accompanied His Grace had ranged themselves along the walls, as far away from the king's wrath as they could manage to be without actually fleeing the workroom.

From the expression on old Mistress Yerdeley's face—pure terror—as she cowered in a corner, she had been the first to feel the lash of royal anger. Father looked only slightly less shaken, but he was quick to rush to my side. Pocket, showing his mettle, stuck his head out from beneath a bench and let out one of his baying barks before retreating to safety once more.

"Here she is now, Your Grace!" Father said in a loud voice. "Safe and sound. But where have you been, Audrey? Have I not told you that you must not roam about the palace alone?"

"Leave the girl be, Malte!"

The king's command was law. Father dropped back. Belatedly, I remembered to curtsey.

"Rise, Audrey." His Grace no longer sounded angry and when I dared look at him again, I saw that his face wore a rueful smile. Slowly it dawned on me that the king's fury had not been because

I was absent from the workroom when I should have been waiting obediently for Father to return, but because he, like Father, had been genuinely concerned for my safety.

"I beg your pardon, Your Majesty, for causing so much trouble."

"It is easy to forgive a pretty girl," the king said. "Now tell me, Audrey, what was that song you were singing?"

"I do not know its title, Your Grace."

"Mayhap I should ask you, then, *where* you learned it."

"In the chapel, Your Grace." I hesitated, then decided it would be best if I confessed the full extent of my transgressions. "I go there sometimes, to listen to the choristers rehearse. They make very fine music," I added in an earnest voice.

"And you have a very fine voice, but that particular hymn is perhaps not the best choice for a girl of your years. It is called 'Black Sanctus, or the monk's hymn to Satan.' Did you know that?"

"No, Your Grace," I whispered. "I am exceeding sorry. I will never sing it again." I wished I could crawl into a hole and vanish. I was certain that anything to do with the devil must be very bad indeed.

The king studied me for a long moment, making me tremble inside. He had been quick to go from anger to good humor. I feared he could return to the former emotion just as fast.

"You must have lessons," he announced, taking me by surprise. "A singing master. I will send young Harington to you, the very lad who wrote both the words and the music to that song you were singing. You have good taste in music, Audrey. I often sing that one myself, for it is a cleverly written antimonastic hymn." He laughed at this last comment and all his minions laughed with him.

I did not understand the reason for their amusement, but I stammered my thanks. I was elated by the news that I was to have lessons. To be taught the proper way to sing seemed the most wonderful boon anyone could grant me, even better than the king's earlier gift, my dear companion, Pocket.

"We are most grateful, Your Grace." Father echoed my sentiments, sounding sincere, but I could not help but notice that his brow was deeply furrowed. Something worried him about the idea.

"She shall have a dancing master, too," the king declared. "It will do no harm for her to learn all the courtly arts. Do you know how to read, Audrey?"

"A little," I said, bolder now. "And I can write a bit, too. And cipher."

Father placed one hand on my shoulder and waited until the king shifted his gaze from me to him. "Those are skills customarily taught to the children of merchants, Your Grace, even the girls. A young wife must be able to keep her own accounts. How else should she know when she is being cheated by the butcher?"

Unspoken was the obvious thought that such a one had no need to learn how to tread a stately measure.

The big vein in His Grace's neck throbbed. He expected unquestioning obedience from his subjects. While polite, Father's defiance rankled.

I burst into speech, hoping to avert trouble. "I will be a very good student. When I learned to cipher, my teacher said I was quick with my numbers."

Distracted, King Henry inquired further into what instruction I had been given. Satisfied that it was adequate, His Grace was about to depart when he remembered Mistress Yerdeley and recalled that her inattention had left me free to wander about the palace alone.

"We will also find a reliable woman servant to wait upon you," the king decreed. "One vigilant enough not to let you out of her sight when you visit our court."

8

December 1539

hink you're a fine lady, do you?" Bridget's taunt was delivered in a whisper but it stung nevertheless.

"I am the same as you." I kept my head bent. Pocket, who lay curled up in my lap, licked my fingers.

"Then why does Father pay for lessons for you and not for the rest of us?"

"It is not Father who hired him," I muttered, refusing to so much as glance at the cadaverous figure hovering near the doorway in deep discussion with Mother Anne. Afflicted with the improbable name of Dionysus Petre, he had introduced himself as my dancing master. His arrival at the house in Watling Street a short time ago had thrown the entire household into an uproar, but it was his flat refusal to teach anyone but me that had provoked my sister's ire.

"What do you mean?" she demanded. "Who else would be so generous? Besides, we all know you are Father's favorite."

"I am not!" Although I denied her claim, I thought she might have the right of it, but simple common sense prevented me from boasting of such a thing. "And it is the *king* who pays."

The angry expression on her face changed to one of disbelief. "Ask *him*."

Hearing the agitation in my voice and seeing me gesture in his direction, Master Petre gave a start. The sight of Bridget, fire in her eyes, stalking in his direction, had him stammering an apology, although what reason he should have to beg her forgiveness eluded me.

Bridget came to a halt a mere foot in front of him, her stance wide and her hands on her hips. "Is she telling the truth? Does King Henry employ you?"

"I cannot say, young mistress." The poor man squeaked like a terrified mouse. In an attempt to avoid meeting her eyes, his gaze dropped lower, landing on her bosom. That seemed to fluster him even more.

"Cannot or will not?" Bridget took a step closer.

Her prey threw both arms up in front of his face and backed away, nearly tumbling down the stairs that led to the shop in his attempt to escape.

I felt sorry for the dancing master. He was twice Bridget's age and no doubt the younger son of a gentle but impoverished family, forced to earn his living by giving lessons. Even more than an artificer like Father, he had, of necessity, to bend his will to that of his clients.

"Bridget, leave him be." I set Pocket on the floor, crossed the room, and positioned myself between my sister and the dancing master. "I have already told you that it is King Henry who pays him."

"First a dog. Now a dancing master. Why should *you* be so favored?" Bridget turned the full force of her outrage on me, giving Master Petre time to recover his wits. "It is not *fair*. I am older than you are."

"And Elizabeth is older than us both. Perhaps Master Petre should give *her* lessons instead."

"Oh!" he exclaimed. "I cannot—" He broke off, eyes wide, when we both turned to glare at him.

It was perhaps fortunate that Elizabeth and Muriel entered through the other door at that moment. They had been to the fishmongers and Elizabeth still carried her shopping basket.

"Whatever is going on?" she asked. "We could hear raised voices all the way to Master Scutt's house."

Mother Anne, who was inclined to let Bridget have her way, now stepped in. "It will not do to have the entire neighborhood privy to our business. You will say no more, Bridget."

With a snarl, Bridget whirled around and stalked to the window that overlooked the street. From that vantage point she had a fine view of the back of the Cordwainers' Hall, but I doubted she saw it. All her thoughts were turned inward. A visible tremor made her entire body vibrate as she seethed with frustration.

"Master Petre," Mother Anne said in the firm voice she used to correct the servants and apprentices, "I believe a compromise is in order."

She drew him deeper into the room and settled him in the Glastonbury chair that was Father's favorite. Marking his flushed face and continued inability to string more than two words together at a time, she called for Ticey, another of the maids, and sent her to the kitchen for a soothing posset.

Slowly, Master Petre regained his composure. After he had drained the goblet Ticey brought him—steeped chamomile with a few other herbs mixed in—Mother Anne informed him that he would be teaching *all* the daughters of the house.

By that time, he had lost the will to argue.

When my tiring maid arrived later that same day, Bridget's wrath found a new target. Her name was Edith Barnard, a plump young woman who looked down her nose at the other servants in the household, especially Lucy.

"You will also serve me," Bridget informed her.

Edith regarded my sister through heavy-lidded eyes that were most effective at hiding her thoughts, but she made no effort to adjust her implacable attitude. "I am here to serve Mistress Audrey," she said, and thereafter ignored Bridget as if she had no more sub-stance than an annoying bug.

A quarter of an hour of such treatment and Bridget, fuming, went away. I heard her flounce down the stairs to the tailor shop. With any luck, flirting with the apprentices would put her in a bet-ter mood.

"Your bedchamber is passing small," Edith said when we were alone. She had already begun to reorganize my belongings, separat-ing them from my sisters' possessions.

Light on her feet, Edith moved with an efficiency and sense of purpose I could not help but admire. At the same time, I found her self-confidence daunting. I had never met a maidservant who put on such airs, and it was not as if she had obvious cause to think so well of herself. She was no more than twenty years old and was afflicted with a splotchy complexion.

"Lucy, poor thing, is slow-witted," I ventured as Edith inspected my shifts and folded each one neatly before tucking it into a drawer in the wardrobe chest. I sat atop another of the storage chests we used for clothing, with Pocket once again nestled on my lap. It soothed me to stroke his soft fur. "We are obliged to repeat orders two or three times before she understands what it is we want. It would be a great help if you could assist her in her duties. My sisters—"

"Indeed, I cannot, Mistress Audrey. I have been sent here to serve you and you alone."

That had a familiar ring to it, but Mother Anne had prevailed upon Master Petre to change his tune. I was certain I could reason with Edith.

"What if I order you to serve them?"

She shook her head, which was so thoroughly covered by a white coif that I could not tell what color her hair was, or even if she *had* any hair. She sent me a pitying look that said, plain as day, that she thought me slow-witted, too.

"If you are here to serve me," I said, trying again, "that means you *must* obey me."

"I must attend to your needs. And look out for you when you go to court. That is not the same thing."

My lessons had not extended to exercises in logic, but even at that young age I knew there was something peculiar about Edith's attitude. She behaved as if she were the equal of anyone in the household . . . and superior to most!

"Who did you serve before you came to me?" I asked.

For just a moment, her self-assured manner faltered. I gave her a hard look. She avoided meeting my eyes.

"Am I your first mistress?" I was astonished by the thought, but her reaction made me believe I was right. "It is true! You have no previous experience as a tiring maid."

Edith's chin went up. "I have been well instructed in all the skills necessary to care for a young woman's clothes and person."

"And I am fully capable of dressing myself, and of choosing what to wear. I have no need of my own tiring maid."

"But you do require someone to watch over you at court, and I am ideally suited for that task."

"Why?" She seemed a little less formidable now that I knew she was on the defensive. I patted the space next to me on the chest. "Come and sit down and tell me all."

For a moment I thought she would refuse. Then, with a sigh, she obliged me. Pocket nuzzled her hand. That seemed to soften her further.

"When she was younger, my mother served in the Earl of Oxford's household."

"Is he a very great lord?"

"Of middling importance. Dukes have more consequence. But Mother is devoted to the family, the de Veres. Her first post was as a nursemaid to the earl's daughter, Lady Frances de Vere. When Lady Frances went to court, Mother went with her, and she was allowed to bring me along."

"Is your mother still at court?"

Edith shook her head. "Not now. Not until King Henry marries again and we have a new queen. But Lady Frances went on to marry Henry Howard, the Earl of Surrey, becoming a countess. When she started having babies, she asked Mother to come to her to look after them. There are three children in her nursery now."

Having assuaged my curiosity, Edith began to question me. She did not seem to find my answers very satisfactory. From her gloomy expression, I concluded that she feared she'd come down in the world.

"I will go to court again soon," I assured her, "but in the meantime it might be wise to cater to Bridget's whims. She'll make your life a misery otherwise." I considered for a moment and then added, "You'd do well to befriend the other maidservants. They are wise to her tricks."

That evening, when all the women of the household gathered around the largest of our embroidery frames, Edith did her part, impressing everyone with the smallness of her stitches. She followed my advice, although I suspected that it pained her to do so.

When Bridget excused herself to visit the privy, I could not help but notice how long she was gone. The door to the external latrine opened out of the west gable wall in the room at the back of the house, so that we could not see it from where we sat in the hall. I feared my sister had taken some petty revenge on Edith for her earlier snub, but all seemed well when my new tiring maid retired for the night. It was only much later, when a faint but persistent sound awoke me, that I discovered Pocket had been locked in the wardrobe chest with my clothing. By then it was too late to salvage my best kirtle. The poor little dog had relieved himself all over the pale blue brocade.

9

Our first week of lessons with the dancing master had scarce concluded when the second of the tutors the king had promised me arrived at the house in Watling Street. I saw him first from an upper window. It extended out from the front of the house above the entrance to Father's shop and gave those within a clear view of passersby.

Watling Street is a very ancient highway, part of the old Roman road that runs from a spot near Dover all the way to Chester. Within London's walls, it is inconveniently narrow, with barely room for one cart to pass another without scraping, but it is lined with the houses of wealthy merchants. Our neighbors were all drapers and tailors. Fashionable ladies and gentlemen visited their shops daily, searching for the latest imported fabric or bespeaking a new suit of clothes.

At first I thought the young man in the king's livery was bent on some similar errand, or that he'd come to collect a fresh supply of garments like the ones he wore. In addition to making the fancy robes and doublets worn by the king and his noblemen, royal tailors also provide livery for the king's servants. But this individual stopped beneath my window, considered the house for a long moment, and then, as if he sensed me watching him, tilted his head back until our gazes locked.

Bright noonday sun revealed eyes of a deep, dark brown flecked with amber. The rest of his face was equally appealing—strongly defined features and a ready smile.

I recognized him then. When the king had first said the name John Harington, I'd known which of the gentleman choristers he meant, but I'd only seen Master Harington from a distance. His impact had been muted.

When I continued to stare at him, he doffed his feathered cap, revealing a full head of thick brown curls. Then he bowed in my direction.

Behind me, I heard the rustle of fabric. One of my sisters came up to stand beside me, but I did not look away from the young man below to see which one it was. He, however, took note of her, bowed again, and then passed out of sight beneath the overhang.

"What a toothsome young gentleman!" Bridget leaned far out the window, hoping for a glimpse of the back of him as he entered Father's shop. "And he wears the king's livery. Who is he?" She was already heading for the stairs.

Mother Anne's sharp command prevented her from descending. "Your father does not need your help with a customer, Bridget. Return to your mending, if you please."

Bridget looked mutinous and would surely have argued, had she not heard the sound of heavy footsteps coming our way. Father entered first but Master Harington was right behind him.

My throat went dry. Close at hand, he was even more pleasing to look at. Indeed, he was the most appealing man I had ever seen. Yes, I know I was not yet twelve years old, but he had barely reached his eighteenth year. To the mind of a girl on the verge of womanhood, even the king himself, with all his glittering jewels, could not surpass this young and handsome fellow for masculine beauty.

Bridget was no more immune to Master Harington's charms than I was. Her avid gaze devoured him. Had Mother Anne not caught hold of her arm, she'd have been across the room to his side in a flash.

Father cleared his throat. "Allow me to make known to you Master John Harington, gentleman of the Chapel Royal. He has been sent by the king to give Audrey music lessons."

Bridget's face fell. "Have we not already suffered enough? She is always humming some tune she heard in church or on the street."

Stung by her derisive tone, I defended myself. "Sometimes I sing the words."

"For the most part, you do not *know* the lyrics, if there even *are* any. You invent your own."

"An admirable skill," Master Harington interrupted, turning Bridget's taunt into a compliment. His eyes twinkled with delight. "With my teaching, Mistress Audrey will become even more proficient at singing and songwriting."

Father presented Mother Anne to Master Harington. As is the custom when greeting those who are truly welcome, she gave him a friendly kiss, making me think that he, unlike Master Petre the dancing master, must have desirable connections at the royal court.

Elizabeth was next to be introduced, then Bridget. Giggling, they followed Mother Anne's example. When it was my turn, I went up on my tiptoes to brush my lips against the smooth, soft, sweet-smelling skin of his cheek. The touch was brief but sufficient to send heat flooding into my face.

Master Harington cocked his head and studied me. His interest lingered longest on my hair, which I wore long and loose, as maidens are wont to do. He glanced back at me again as Father presented Muriel to him.

"A fine family," Master Harington said, accepting Muriel's shy kiss of greeting. He was already returning to me. "I have been sent to teach you to play the lute, Mistress Audrey, and any other instrument you care to learn. What will it be? The virginals? The harp? I am proficient with everything from the cittern to the sackbut."

There were too many choices. And he was standing too close to me. I was unable to form an answer.

"The instruction shall be as pleases you, Master Harington," Father cut in, "but it would please me greatly if you would extend your teaching to all my children."

Master Harington hesitated. Then his gaze roved to Bridget. She smiled and dimpled . . . and subtly shifted position to better display the rounded fullness of her breasts.

"It shall be as you wish, Master Malte." Turning to my sisters, he began to question them about what skills they already possessed. He seemed pleased at the prospect of tutoring them, especially Bridget.

I stood a little apart to watch her preen and flirt, and struggled with emotions I had never felt before. For the first time in my life, I understood why my sister reacted so violently when she saw me singled out to receive something *she* wanted.

10

*M*aster Eworth cleared his throat. "I have lost the light," he announced. "I can paint no more today."

Surprised by how much time had passed since she'd begun her tale, Audrey eased herself to her feet. Hester had already scrambled out of her chair and gone to look at the unfinished portrait on the easel.

"I have no face," she complained.

Although the artist had lovingly reproduced the embroidery on the child's dress, her features were as yet little more than a pale blur.

"After the next session you will have eyes and a nose," Audrey promised, touching a fingertip to the latter appendage and making Hester giggle.

Master Eworth made no promises. He finished packing away his supplies and departed, trailing a whiff of linseed oil in his wake and seeming as glad to be done with them for the day as they were to see him go.

"Was that the truth?" Hester asked when the door had closed

behind him. "Did you fall in love with my father the first time you saw him?"

Audrey laughed. "Near enough. He was . . . and is—as my sister said—a most toothsome fellow."

"And did he return your love?"

Holding her smile while she answered required considerable effort. "You must remember that I was only a little girl when we first met. But he was always considerate of my feelings. And he was an excellent teacher."

"Father is the most wonderful man in the whole world," Hester said.

The child idolized him, as she should. Audrey knew exactly how she felt. "Your father has a way with people."

Jack Harington had charmed everyone in the house on that long-ago day . . . everyone except Edith. Audrey's new maidservant had been dismissive, calling him "a puffed-up courtier."

"Will you tell me more on the morrow, when Master Eworth comes to paint me again?"

"Perhaps not then," Audrey temporized. "Parts of the story I have to tell you are for your ears alone."

"Then we must find another time, for I want to know *everything*!"

"The entire tale will take some time in the telling."

"Then you must continue it as soon as may be." Hester's eyes were bright with anticipation. "Tonight? After we sup?"

"I . . . yes. That will do very well."

Hester's enthusiasm had the girl capering in a circle before she left the room. Audrey watched her go with mixed emotions. How much, she wondered, *should* she tell her daughter? She would not lie, but there were incidents that could be omitted from the tale. Indeed, Hester's tender years argued in favor of an expurgated version of the past.

On the other hand, Hester was an intelligent child. Her lessons had begun when she was still on leading strings. Besides that, from an early age, she observed those around her and learned from what they did. It had been more than a year ago when she'd shocked her mother with an account of watching the milkmaid couple with one of the stable boys in an empty horse stall at Catherine's Court. She had pronounced the experience "interesting" and had seemed to grasp the power of the attraction between a man and a woman even though she was still far too young to experience it for herself.

Better to tell her all of it, Audrey decided, even the painful parts.

That evening, Audrey joined Hester in the child's bedchamber and sent the servants away. She tucked her daughter into bed with the pillows plumped behind her head and positioned herself at the foot, her legs folded under her. This was the way tailors often sat, their work in their laps. Audrey kept her fingers busy with a piece of embroidery but her mind was not on her stitches.

"Tell me more about you and Father," Hester demanded as soon as she was settled. "You promised you would tell me everything!"

Audrey smiled. "Some of it you have heard already. There is no secret about your father's background."

"Father came from an impoverished gentry family," Hester related, happy to show off her knowledge, "but he had a gift for composing songs and writing poetry. The king admired that talent and rewarded him. Is that what giving him the commission to teach you was? A reward?"

"I suppose it was. As a gentleman of the Chapel Royal he had an annuity of thirteen pounds, eight shillings, and nine pence and the king paid him another ten pounds a year to teach me. That does not seem a very great sum to him now that he is a wealthy man, but back then, Jack was grateful for every crumb."

"Were you good at your lessons?" Hester asked.

"I had a natural aptitude for the lute. I found other instruments more challenging, but none of them defeated me. In time, I mastered the virginals, the recorder, and the viol."

A wicked gleam came into Hester's eyes. "How did Aunt Bridget fare?"

Audrey's sister had never shown much interest in her niece, but they had met on several occasions. These days, Bridget and her husband and their son lived in Somersetshire, although she was not fond of life in the country. Her envy of Audrey was never more apparent than when she visited Catherine's Court.

"Bridget never learned to carry a tune or play well on any instrument. But, to be fair, she far surpassed me in her ability to perform the intricate steps of the pavane and the galliard. Her accomplishments on the dance floor eased her resentment of me and made her a trifle less likely to give me privy nips." Those sly pinches had hurt, and sometimes they had left ugly bruises.

"What other tricks did your sister play on you?" Hester asked. "Did she put frogs in your bed?"

"What a notion! No, for she slept there, too."

Hester's brow furrowed in concentration. "Did she pretend to trip and spill the contents of a chamber pot all over you?"

"Hester!"

"Well? Did she?"

"No, she did not. Although, if I must be honest, she might have if she could have reasoned out an excuse to be carrying such a thing. We had servants to empty the night soil." That task had most often fallen to poor, half-witted Lucy.

"Only pinches, then?" Hester tried to hide her yawn, but sleepiness overtook her. She watched her mother through half-closed eyes.

"Pinches and cutting remarks about my appearance, especially the sallow cast of my skin. Bridget's complexion was as pink and white as that of any great lady at court."

"Did you go back there?" Hester asked. "To court?"

"I did. And that sparked Bridget's envy all over again. In time, I learned to ignore both jabs and jibes because I enjoyed every moment of those visits. Your father had a great deal to do with my pleasure." She smiled, remembering. "I fondly believed that my presence had gone unnoticed by members of the Chapel Royal, but that was not the case. I had simply been ignored, tolerated because I made no attempt to talk to any of them. After Jack was ordered to give me instruction in music, I was formally introduced and invited to listen to their rehearsals. After one such session, the gentleman choristers declared I should be their mascot. I suppose they thought of me the way I thought of Pocket. That is not such a flattering comparison, now that I look back on it, but at the time I was thrilled to be permitted to linger on the fringes while they made their glorious music."

"Did you see the king again?" Hester murmured in a sleepy voice.

"Not for some time. My lessons began in December. In January, His Grace married Anne of Cleves and he was often . . . distracted. But learning from your father was a delight. He was endlessly patient with me, praising my musical ability while gently correcting and improving my efforts. After the first week, I grew easy in his presence, although an occasional blush did creep up on me when I least expected it."

A soft exhalation drew Audrey's gaze to her daughter.

There was no need to tell Hester any more of the story tonight. The little girl had fallen deeply asleep. Careful not to wake her, Audrey slid off the bed, stumbling a little as she landed on the rush-covered floor. The scent of strewing herbs wafted up to her, juniper and costmary, as she turned to draw the curtains closed against cold night drafts.

She stood there a moment longer, gripping the heavy cloth, waiting for her head to stop spinning. She hated this lingering weakness. She was accustomed to good health and a hardy constitution.

Tomorrow, there would be more questions. Audrey repressed a sigh. It was only natural for a child to want to know all about her parents.

Steady again, she crept out of her daughter's richly appointed bedchamber and into her own. The enormous bed yawned before her, far too big for one person, a potent reminder that Jack had not shared it with her for a long time.

Did Hester need to know that, too? Audrey pondered the question as she used her toothpick and tooth cloth and combed out her hair. She preferred to tend to these chores herself and not have the bother of servants.

The girl idolized her father and he was fond of her. Audrey thought she could reveal the rest of the story without tarnishing Jack's image. She would do her best, she resolved, to let Hester keep her illusions.

In the morning, after mother and daughter broke their fast, they went out into the garden. It had been planted to suit Audrey's fancy. Each flower had been chosen not only for color and scent but also for the values it was said to represent. Honeysuckle grew near the door, a symbol of undying devotion. The blossoms were long gone but the fruit, which had the appearance of little bunches of grapes, was red and ripe.

She'd sown gillyflowers to mark the start of the path—pink, crimson, and white and smelling like violets. They were said to represent faithful and undying love, especially when worn in a man's cap. "I must remember to plant more of these on St. Remy's Day," she murmured, speaking to herself as much as to Hester.

"When is that?" her daughter asked. Since King Henry's break with Rome, many of the old holy days had been forgotten.

"The twenty-eighth day of this month. The gillyflower is a most useful plant. Many grow it as a potherb throughout the winter, using it to flavor wine, for the taste is much the same as that of cloves. You know already that cloves are imported and are too expensive for everyday use. Gillyflowers can also be used in after-dinner syrups, sweet tarts, and preserves."

Hester showed not the least interest in her mother's impromptu lesson in herbal lore. She ran on ahead, along the length of a path notable in high summer for the bright colors on both sides. Audrey's favorite blooms were the vivid orange marigolds, symbolizing both death and hope. They began to flower in May, and in some years, like this one, continued to do so until the cold days of winter were upon them.

A stone bench held pride of place on a little knoll beneath a rose arbor. Pale red eglantine climbed over and around it. In summer those flowers filled the enclosure with their sweet scent.

"Do you remember what eglantine represents?" Audrey sank gratefully down onto the hard surface. Even such a short ramble tired her. The basket of mending on her arm felt as if it were filled with lead.

Obediently, Hester recited one of her lessons from the stillroom. There she, like every other young gentlewoman, spent many hours learning how to concoct home remedies to keep the household healthy and to turn the distilled essence of flowers into perfume. "It is a symbol of love, devotion, romance, and virtue. Does that mean this is a suitable place to continue your story?"

"It will do well enough." Audrey patted the bench beside her. "Shall I recount more tales from the court of King Henry, or is it your father of whom you wish to hear me speak?"

Hester grinned up at her. "Can you not tell me a story about them both?"

11

May 1540

Every year, King Henry celebrated May Day. His Grace was surpassing fond of pageantry, everything from tournaments to disguisings. In the spring after I began my lessons with Jack Harington—I still addressed him as Master Harington, although I already thought of him as Jack—there was a great tournament held in the tiltyard in Westminster. King Henry and Queen Anne watched the jousting from a newly built gatehouse at Whitehall. It was a grand spectacle, or so everyone said.

"All the young noblemen of the court participated and some of the gentlemen, too," Jack told me as, with Father's blessing and Edith in tow, he escorted me to the riverside stairs and hailed a two-oared wherry, "but only those who are the king's favorites." He sounded wistful.

"I am glad you were not one of them!" I exclaimed. "I'd not want you to be injured." This was a very forward thing to say and provoked a mutter of disapproval from Edith.

"No chance of that! A mere chorister has other duties. But I was able to watch most of the contests. Tom Culpeper, one of the gentlemen of the privy chamber, was unhorsed in a most undignified fashion." Jack's satisfied smile told me Master Culpeper, whoever he might be, was no friend to my music tutor.

The waterman, leaning on his oars, waited impatiently while we settled ourselves in his craft. "West or east?" he demanded, and spat into the murky waters of the Thames.

"Durham House, if you please," Jack told him, and handed over a coin.

"Your father thinks you are going to court," Edith said in a whisper as the little boat caught the tide and began to move swiftly westward. Gulls and seabirds wheeled overhead, filling the air with their raucous cries. "What business have you going to Durham House?"

Overhearing, Jack chuckled. "You need not be concerned for your charge's virtue, Edith. Today the whole court is at Durham House. That is where those bold knights who excelled in the lists are to be awarded their prizes—gifts of money and grants of houses. The king will be there, and the queen, and all the courtiers you could wish for."

Durham House sits in the middle of the curve of the Thames. Just beyond it, on the land side, the city of Westminster begins. I had noticed its gardens before, when passing by en route to the royal palace of Whitehall. They are planted in three descending terraces on the London side of the mansion. The house itself is built close to the river, allowing easy access by way of a water gate that is part of a two-storied galleried range that flanks the great hall. A screens passage leads into that high and stately chamber. That day we could have located the hall by the level of noise alone.

Jack veered off just short of the entrance to lead us up a narrow flight of stairs to the musicians' gallery. Only three of the musicians were playing. The trio produced exquisite sounds that could scarcely be heard over the hubbub below, but the other members of their company were a more appreciative audience.

"The Bassano brothers," Jack said. "Newly arrived from Italy. They make my poor skills seem little more than an amateur effort by an untalented child."

Taking the comparison as a criticism of my own ability, I shrank back, but Jack was the noticing sort. It took him only a moment to realize how I had misinterpreted his words.

"You are naturally gifted," he assured me. "You have inherent talent. Why else should I have brought you here today? I have a surprise for you."

Mollified, I demanded to know what it was.

"All in good time, Mistress Audrey. All in good time."

Jack showed me to a place by the rail and then left me to exchange greetings with some of the other royal musicians. They were not gentlemen of the Chapel Royal but rather the king's secular musicians. Some twenty-five of them, many foreign born, played for His Grace at masques and for dancing.

I peered at the crowd below, and was glad I was not down there among them to be jostled and buffeted. Spectators seemed to fill every inch of space, vying for the best position from which to see the king and his bride of barely five months. Anne of Cleves was a very plain woman but she had a kind smile. As I watched, Her Grace handed out arms and expensive robes and silver vessels to that day's champions.

Edith, having settled herself with much grumbling, suddenly gave a little cry of pleasure. "Only look, Mistress Audrey! There is the Countess of Surrey."

She indicated a young woman in her early twenties in close attendance on Queen Anne. Lady Surrey had wide-spaced eyes, a broad nose, and a strained expression on her pale face. She did not appear to be enjoying the festivities.

"Is your mother here, too?"

"Oh, no, Mistress Audrey. She will be at Surrey House in Norwich with the countess's children. They are too young yet to be brought to court. The fourth, another boy, was born less than three months past."

No wonder the countess lacked enthusiasm!

"Do you recognize anyone else among the ladies attending Her Grace?"

"That is the countess's sister-in-law." Edith pointed out a compactly made, richly dressed young woman who kept her eyes downcast, almost as if she was lost in her own thoughts. "She was born Lady Mary Howard, the Duke of Norfolk's only daughter, but she's Duchess of Richmond now. Poor creature. She was married to the king's bastard."

I must have given a little start of surprise because Edith looked at me and then away, as if she'd said too much. I poked her.

"Go on. Tell me all. I did not know the king had a son other than Prince Edward."

Curiously, in spite of the noise and laughter all around us, private conversation was possible. We were hidden from the view of those below and seated in a little well of relative quiet.

"Henry FitzRoy, he was called. Before Prince Edward was born, the king made him a duke. Some said His Grace meant the boy to be king after him, bastard or no, so it was a fine marriage for Lady Mary. But then the boy died and she was left a widow before she was ever truly a wife."

I made a sympathetic sound, but my thoughts had strayed. I did not often remember that I was a bastard myself. Even Bridget did not taunt me about it. But it had never before occurred to me that a child born on the wrong side of the blanket could rise so high. I supposed it made a difference when your father was the king.

"Oh, there is Mistress Catherine Howard." Edith gestured toward a pretty girl with golden hair. She did not look much older than I was. "She is a cousin to the Duchess of Richmond and the Earl of Surrey and serves as one of the queen's maids of honor."

Jack joined us then, putting an end to Edith's confidences. I was content to watch the spectacle at his side, observing in silence as the defenders and the challengers from the tournament were rewarded first with gifts and then with food.

A space had been left for tables, and dozens of platters overflowing with steaming dishes were carried in—roasted meats and sauces and sweets of all sorts. Each new course was announced with a thunderous fanfare provided by military drummers. Softer sounds filled the air at other times.

The only person Jack pointed out to me was the Earl of Surrey. "The earl was Queen Anne's 'Chief Defender' in the lists," he explained. "He led twenty-nine brave men and true into mock battle. He ran eight successful courses each of the first two days of the tournament without ever being unhorsed and was just as successful when they fought with swords instead of lances."

Boisterous and full of good cheer, Surrey slapped one of his fellows on the back and embraced another. I could make out little of his appearance from my perch, only a full head of auburn hair and a rather scraggly beard of the same color.

The official festivities ended when the king and queen departed. The rest of the company began to disperse as well. When Jack led me out of the musicians' gallery, I expected to return to the water gate, but the passageway he chose took us instead into an antechamber containing another narrow flight of stairs. Edith and I followed Jack up, and up, and up, until the steps ended in a little turret room. Its windows looked down into and out over the Thames.

"You should not be here with him," Edith hissed at me, alarmed by the remoteness and privacy of the chamber.

"I am in no danger," I whispered back. In truth, I wished there *were* some hope that Jack Harington might look upon me as a young woman he'd like to steal away and marry. I adored my music master, but he still looked upon me as a child. That I *was* a child—not quite twelve years old—was something I preferred to ignore.

"Put aside your foolish daydreams," Edith snapped. "That young gentleman is up to no good."

Jack was, in fact, arranging cushions on the floor and setting out beakers and cups.

Edith was still trying to push me toward the door when two very finely dressed courtiers entered through it.

"Jack!" the man exclaimed. "Well met! And this must be the lass they call 'Harington's pet.'" He looked straight at me when he said it, a friendly smile on his darkly tanned face.

"Tom! Mind your manners!" His female companion smacked his forearm with a closed fan, but she was laughing.

Edith bent to speak into my ear. "That fellow is Thomas Clere, squire to the Earl of Surrey."

Overhearing, the young man's head snapped around and he gave my maidservant a frosty stare. It faded as quickly as it had appeared. "Edith, by my spurs! We wondered where you had vanished to."

He might have said more, had not the Earl of Surrey himself arrived just then. The woman with him was not his wife. She was his sister, the Duchess of Richmond. Without standing on ceremony, they settled themselves on the cushions Jack had arranged. Master Clere and the other woman joined them.

I glanced at Jack, who remained standing, uncertain how to act.

Was this the "surprise" he had promised me? I could not imagine why he would think I'd wish to meet these people, but when he seized my hand and thrust me forward, I went. With a flourish, he presented me to the earl and the duchess first and then to the gentlewoman who had come with Thomas Clere, Mistress Mary Shelton, companion to the duchess.

Up close, I saw that the earl and his sister shared that auburn hair. Both had hazel eyes, but while her fair coloring was untouched by the sun, his skin had a weathered look. Both he and his squire, I surmised, spent many hours out of doors, hunting, hawking, and riding.

Mistress Shelton's face was not as full as the duchess's and her nose was longer and more tapering, but she shared that pale complexion. Along with Master Clere, they were all of an age, and it was nearly twice my years. I managed a curtsey and a mumbled greeting, but apart from that I found myself tongue-tied. This was very grand company indeed for a merchant tailor's daughter.

Several others soon joined us. I cannot now recall which members of the earl's circle they were. Surrey often held impromptu musical and literary gatherings. Some of those who attended never came again. Others were part of an intimate group always in attendance on the earl or on his sister.

At first the talk was all of the tournament.

"M'lord Surrey was magnificent." Mistress Shelton addressed this remark to me in a friendly fashion, attempting to draw me out. Edith had retreated to a corner, effacing herself as any good servant must when in the presence of her betters. "He rode onto the field behind an exquisite float depicting the Roman goddess of arms. His pennant and shield had a silver lion emblazoned upon them and other Howard emblems were embroidered all over his white velvet coat."

"My father may have made that coat," I ventured, trying to overcome my shyness around these glittering strangers. If Jack was comfortable with them, so should I be.

"Your father?" Confusion had her brow furrowing.

"Master Malte, the royal tailor." There was no apology in my voice. I was proud of Father's work.

She gave me a peculiar look, but if she thought I should go join Edith in the corner, she was kind enough not to say so.

By then, the general conversation had turned away from jousting onto poetry. An earnest young woman begged the Earl of Surrey to recite some of his verses.

He stood and declaimed:

> *Give place, you lovers here before,*
> *that spent your boasts and brags in vain:*
> *my lady's beauty passeth more the best of yours,*
> *I dare well sayn,*
> *than doth the sun, the candle light,*
> *or brightest day, the darkest night.*

"Mary is working on a new poem," Lady Richmond announced, nudging Mistress Shelton.

"It is not yet ready to be heard," Mary Shelton protested.

"Let us judge that." Thomas Clere slung a familiar arm around her shoulders and planted a smacking kiss on her cheek.

She pushed him away, and none too gently, but after a moment she closed her eyes and recited:

> *And thus be thus ye may assure yourself of me.*
> *No thing shall make me to deny that I have promised thee.*

"It needs work," Surrey said.

"It is the worst sort of doggerel," Mistress Shelton admitted in a rueful voice. "I am a better copyist than I am a poet."

Jack Harington cleared his throat. "I wish to present to this company a new poet."

I looked at him expectantly, and then in slowly dawning horror as I realized I was the one he meant. "Oh, I cannot. My verses have no more merit than an amateur artist's sketches."

Thanks to Jack's lessons, I had discovered talents I'd never dreamed I possessed. Not only had I shown an affinity for playing the lute and for singing, but I also had begun to develop the knack of setting words to music. Encouraged by my tutor, I'd tried my hand at composing my own verses, but they were poor, pitiful things.

"Come, Mistress Malte," Mary Shelton urged me. "Your attempt can be no worse than mine and we are all friends here, united in our poor efforts to emulate the great poets of antiquity."

"My efforts are worse than poor and were intended only to be set to music."

"There is nothing ignoble about writing lyrics," Lady Richmond said. "Why, the king himself wrote the words to 'Pastime with Good Company' and many of Sir Thomas Wyatt's verses have been set to music."

"Thomas Wyatt the Elder," Surrey clarified. I gathered from this that the poet had a son by the same name, but at the time I had never heard of either of them.

"Wyatt is greatly to be admired," Tom Clere said, "if only for keeping his head."

Nervous laughter greeted this remark.

"I do not understand," I whispered to Mary Shelton.

Mistress Shelton's shoulders tensed. Her lips flattened into a thin, tight line. I learned much later that she had once been courted by Sir Thomas Wyatt the Elder and that he'd written poems to her, even though he'd had both a wife and a mistress at the time. Still, she was, as I was to learn, the most blunt-spoken of that company and was nothing loath to fill in the gaps in my knowledge.

"Sir Thomas Wyatt, when a young man, was in love with Anne Boleyn . . . *before* she married the king. He might easily have gone to the block, accused of having been one of her lovers. Together with my sister, Margaret, one of the queen's maids of honor, I was at court to witness these events. I truly believe that it was one of Wyatt's poems that saved his life, for King Henry took it as proof that the poet never meddled with the queen."

"Whoso list to hunt, I put him out of doubt; As well as I may spend his time in vain!" the Earl of Surrey recited in a low voice. "And graven with diamonds in letters plain there is written her fair neck round about, *Noli me tangere*, for Caesar's I am, and wild for to hold, though I seem tame."

"*Noli me tangere?*" I was ignorant of foreign languages. "What does that mean?"

"Do not touch me," Mary Shelton translated. "And Caesar was meant to be the king. Now you, Audrey. Share something you have written."

I knew I did not approach within a mile of Sir Thomas Wyatt's poetic talent. I doubted I even reached the heights of Mary Shelton's "doggerel." But I was emboldened by her encouraging smile.

Because I was not accustomed to reciting verses in a normal speaking voice, I sang the words:

> *The linnet in the window sings despite her cage*
> *when other creatures would rail and rage.*

And I, beside that same window, do peruse my page
and wait for the one who'll free me when I come of age.

I faltered into silence. An unnerving pause followed.

"Clever," the Earl of Surrey conceded. "Although you would do better to follow Petrarch's model and write a sonnet."

As if the rest of the company had only been waiting for the approval of the highest-ranking person in the chamber, they all chimed in with words of praise and helpful hints for improving my verses. For the most part, the criticism was kindly meant. More remarkable still, in spite of my youth and my inferior station in life, they treated me as an equal.

I left Durham House that day with my heart overflowing with emotion and my mind full of new ideas. Jack Harington had introduced me to a world I'd never dreamed existed.

12

May–June 1540

In the weeks following my introduction to the Duchess of Richmond and her companion, Mary Shelton, I was invited on several occasions to Norfolk House in Lambeth. Father hesitated the first time but, after the Tudors, the Howards were the most powerful family in England. The Duke of Norfolk, father to the Earl of Surrey and the Duchess of Richmond, was an important and influential man. Courtiers flocked to Norfolk House, just across the Thames from Whitehall, much as they did to the royal court, seeking favor and presenting petitions.

"You must be careful not to presume upon their friendship," Father admonished me as Edith and I were about to set off for the river stairs, accompanied by one of his apprentices, a gangly lad named Peter. "At the same time, it would do no harm to make yourself useful to the duchess. It would be a great honor were you to be asked to enter her service."

"I am not a maidservant," I protested, "nor am I in need of employment." I knew full well how wealthy Father was.

"Young gentlewomen are customarily sent away from home to finish their education. They learn how to manage a household, against the day when they will marry, under the supervision of some great lady skilled in such matters."

"But I am not a gentlewoman, either. I am a merchant's daughter and proud of it."

"Master Malte," Edith interrupted in a timid voice. "If I may make an observation, it seems to me that the duchess favors Mistress Audrey because of her talent. The ability to create poetry and music is what matters in that circle. They pay no mind to whether someone is of merchant, noble, gentry, or even peasant stock."

Father hemmed and hawed and scratched his nose, but in the end he sent us off with his blessing. If nothing else, he was loath to offend.

Norfolk House was a huge, sprawling place. It was not as big as its Lambeth neighbor, the Archbishop of Canterbury's palace, but there was more than enough space for several separate households. The Duchess of Richmond occupied one section of the house. Her father, when he had business in London or Westminster, lived in another. And a third was the domain of the old dowager duchess, Agnes, the Duke of Norfolk's stepmother. A bevy of young relatives had been entrusted to her care—to finish their education, as Father had explained—and they were in residence, too.

"They live in a dormitory, country gentlewomen and the duchess's granddaughters all mixed together." Edith sounded as if she was not sure she approved of such an arrangement. Mother Anne preached the same philosophy, that overfamiliarity between mistress and servant inevitably led to trouble down the road.

"Did you live here for a time?" I asked as we approached the water stairs on that initial visit. "With your mother and the Earl and Countess of Surrey?"

"A brief period only, but I still have a few acquaintances among the servants."

I gave Edith leave to seek them out while I spent time with the duchess and her companion and this soon became the established pattern of our trips to Norfolk House.

The house was adjoined by substantial gardens, several paddocks, and a two-acre close. On a pleasantly warm day in June, we left the music room where we usually met and brought our instruments out of doors. Seated in a bower, surrounded by flowers and trees, a light breeze cooling our faces and stirring the lace on the duchess's sleeves, I picked out a new tune on my lute.

It was private there, just Lady Richmond and Mary, as Mistress Shelton insisted I call her now that we had become better acquainted. I had brought Pocket with me, for the duchess was fond of dogs. She kept several spaniels. Mary had a cat, a great striped beast with an uncertain temper, but it had gone off on business of its own.

"An appealing melody," the duchess said when I finished playing. "Have you set words to it?"

"Not yet, my lady. Perhaps you might compose something."

She suggested a verse and Mary contributed another and we were soon laughing together as we tried different variations on a theme. I felt at ease with them both, almost as if they were my sisters, although they were much more considerate of me than Bridget ever was. When we were engaged in the composition of poetry or the setting of verses to music, it was just as Edith had told Father. There were no boundaries. They treated me as their equal.

When we were satisfied with our song, Mary produced a small box full of sugared almonds. "A reward," she said, and passed it around.

Seated on a blanket on the grass, silent save for the sounds of our contented munching, we had no need to talk. I was so comfortable I was almost dozing. It came as a shock to hear a familiar laugh boom forth.

I sat up straight, eyes wide. "The king," I mouthed at Mary Shelton.

She held her finger to her lips, warning me not to speak aloud. Heavy footsteps were coming closer, but they were on the other side of a hedge. We were hidden from view and, so long as we made no sound, His Grace would pass by without ever knowing we were there.

King Henry went past the spot where I sat, holding my breath, but he stopped only a few steps beyond. He spoke, a low rumble of sound in which the words were indistinct.

A high-pitched giggle and a murmur answered him.

Lady Richmond and Mary exchanged a speaking glance. Lady Richmond's eyes narrowed. Mary's lips thinned into a hard, flat line. They knew the identity of the female in His Grace's company, but I did not. I was sorely tempted to peek through the shrubbery and see who she was, but I did not dare move a muscle. All I could do was stretch my ears and hope for a clue.

Silk whispered. Gravel crunched underfoot. Someone sighed. The leaves in the hedge shook as if someone had leaned against the other side. The woman laughed again, and this time when she spoke, what she said was clearly audible. "No, no, Harry. No more until we are wed."

I frowned. Perhaps it was not the king after all, for King Henry was already married. And what woman would dare to call him anything but Your Grace or Your Majesty?

After a moment, the lovers continued on. I looked at the duchess, and expected her to say something about the strange incident, but she held her tongue. In a little while, we returned to the house and soon after that I bade them farewell and collected Edith for the journey back to London. It was at the horse ferry, where we went to hail a wherry for the return trip, that I overheard two watermen talking.

"The king's come to dine with the old duchess, again," one said.

"I warrant 'tis not the duchess he's spending his time with," the other replied with a laugh that made my skin crawl.

"The king was with a woman in the garden," I whispered to Edith when we were out on the river. "Do you suppose he has a mistress here?"

She sniffed. For a moment I thought she would refuse to answer me, even though it was clear she knew who the giggling female was. Servants always know more than their masters. I waited, hoping she'd relent. After a few minutes, my patience was rewarded.

"Queen Anne has been packed off to Richmond Palace without the king. She does not know it yet, but she is about to be divorced. The king has found another lady he wishes to marry in her stead."

"Who?"

"One of her own maids of honor, Mistress Catherine Howard."

I blinked at Edith in surprise, recalling the vivacious blonde she had pointed out to me at Durham House. "But . . . but . . . she is—that is, His Grace is—"

Words failed me, which was perhaps just as well, when I could be overheard by the boatman. Catherine Howard was the same age as my sister Elizabeth. Although King Henry was a magnificent figure of a man, he was old enough to be her father. He was very nearly old enough to be her *grand*father. Of its own volition, my lip curled in distaste.

"Perhaps this rumor will prove untrue," I said. "Many do."

And surely the king would never allow himself to look ridiculous by trying to rid himself of yet another wife.

I was wrong about that. Queen Anne was persuaded to accept

an annulment. A bit more than a month after that day at Norfolk House, King Henry married Catherine Howard.

I was never presented to Queen Catherine, even though I was at court with Father during her tenure as queen. I doubt she even knew of my existence. I saw the king only occasionally and when I did he seemed distracted. Once, when he was with the queen, he walked right past me without a flicker of recognition in his eyes.

It was Anthony Denny, by then elevated to the post of chief gentleman of the privy chamber, who unfailingly stopped by Father's workroom when I came with him to court. He chatted with me in a friendly, avuncular way, inquiring after the progress of my studies. When I expressed an interest in learning to draw, tutors were sent to Watling Street to give me instruction in sketching and calligraphy. Master Denny never said so in so many words, but he led me to believe that he reported on our conversations to the king.

Lessons, friends, family, Pocket, poetry, and music filled my days. When I noticed the first sign of a developing bosom, I felt truly blessed. My first flowers came soon after—that was not so pleasant— but I knew that the arrival of my courses meant that I had entered womanhood and was, if barely, old enough to wed. This encouraged me to flirt outrageously with Master Harington. Sometimes he responded in kind, but he did not take me seriously.

He took a far greater interest in Bridget's more obvious charms. My breasts were saucepans. Hers were stew pots. She encouraged him, too, doubtless to spite me, for she had already set her sights on someone far wealthier than Jack Harington.

Self-absorbed as I was in private pleasures and frustrations, I was only dimly aware of a heightened tension affecting both the city and the court. It was an exceeding hot summer with no rain. There was drought. Men feared the return of the plague. Although that devastating sickness did not come upon us, at least not that year, there were outbreaks of another sort. Short tempers led to fights. Some became near riots. After the court went on progress during August, September, and October, thankfully without a full contingent from the Chapel Royal, rumors drifted back to London that the king was in failing health.

These proved unfounded, God be praised, but His Grace chose to remain at some distance from London until mid-December. Most of the courtiers who were not attached to the so-called riding household took themselves off to their country estates. The Duchess of Richmond left for Kenninghall in Norfolk, taking Mary Shelton with her. There was no mention of adding me to her household.

13

Norfolk House, January 1541

I waited until after Epiphany to pay a visit to Norfolk House, although the duchess had spent Yuletide there. I brought Pocket with me, since he was easy to carry and got along well with my Lady of Richmond's spaniels. All the dogs avoided Mary Shelton's cat.

The Earl of Surrey and some of his followers were in his sister's rooms when I arrived. Surrey looked at Pocket askance, not having seen him before.

"That is a glove beagle," he remarked, "not the usual sort of lap-dog."

"He was a gift, my lord." The slight sneer on Surrey's face prompted me to add, "From the king."

One auburn eyebrow lifted and he darted a questioning glance at the duchess. She ignored him. I tucked Pocket away, out of sight, uncomfortably aware of the earl's scrutiny and that of a member of his entourage, a fellow I had not noticed before.

He was the oldest person present, by at least a decade, and, by his dress, of lower birth and status than the earl. His mouth turned down while his nose stayed up in the air, as if to avoid smelling something unpleasant. He was clean-shaven, a poor choice since it revealed a weak chin.

"Have you heard about Anne of Cleves's visit to court over Yuletide?" Mary Shelton asked, glancing up from her needlework. With a gesture, she invited me to sit beside her and join in the task of hemming what appeared to be an altar cloth.

I was glad of the excuse to move farther away from the stranger, who was now whispering in a servant's ear. The lad scurried away as if he feared a beating if he did not make haste. I thought perhaps he had reason.

"I heard that the former queen was installed at Richmond Palace," I said to Mary. King Henry had given it to her in return for her agreement to annul their marriage.

"She's hardly a prisoner there! In any case, she arrived at the gates of Hampton Court on the third of January, two days after the traditional exchange of gifts on New Year's Day."

"You make it seem as if she was not expected." Surrey sounded disgusted by the subterfuge. "The entire production was carefully staged." He helped himself to a goblet of wine and drank deeply.

"No doubt it was." His sister kept her eyes on the intricate stitches she was using to attach a piece of black-work lace to a kirtle. "But it was a splendid spectacle all the same. You'd have enjoyed it, Audrey. Lady Anne of Cleves, who now must call herself the king's sister where once she was his wife, threw herself to her knees before Queen Catherine like the most common suitor. Then the king arrived on the scene—just in time to witness this touching tableau. He raised Lady Anne up and kissed her and embraced her and then they all sat down to sup like three old friends."

"Has Anne of Cleves finally learned enough English to converse properly?" I asked. Her difficulties with the language had been widely reported.

Lady Richmond laughed. "So it would seem. But the highlight of the evening came after the king retired to his own apartments. Catherine called for music and then the two ladies danced together, whiling away the rest of the evening in that manner."

"A display of perfect amity." Scorn laced Surrey's words.

"Why are you so wroth with Cousin Catherine?" the duchess asked. "It is to our benefit to have a kinswoman in the king's bed."

Seated beside Mary on her bench, I felt as well as saw her wince. "Is aught wrong?" I whispered.

Mary, blunt as ever, gave me a frank answer. "A momentary pang, I assure you. Having a kinswoman in the king's bed is not always comfortable for the rest of the family. You see, during Anne Boleyn's tenure as queen, she ordered her kinswoman, my sister Margaret, to allow the king to seduce her. The queen hoped to distract His Grace from lavishing his favors on another young gentlewoman at court."

She kept her voice low, but the same gentleman who had earlier been so rudely staring at me cocked his head in our direction, blatantly eavesdropping on our exchange. Tom Clere, who was also close enough to overhear, leaned past me to give Mary a quick peck on the cheek. As he did so, I caught a whiff of bay leaves.

"Here you have the only woman in England who would not think it an honor to be the king's mistress," he said with a chuckle.

Mary swatted at him, missing when he ducked and nearly striking me. "Terrible man!" She sent me an apologetic look and sighed. "The truth is that people often confuse me with my sister. It is most annoying."

"Better that than to be mistaken for your namesake the nun," Clere teased her.

"Former nun," Mary muttered through gritted teeth. There were neither nuns nor monks in England anymore, not since King Henry dissolved all the religious houses.

Clere, unrepentant, wandered off. I realized, with a sense of surprise, that the duchess and her brother were still talking about Lady Anne's visit to court. The exchange between Mary and Tom Clere had passed unnoticed by anyone but myself and the stranger.

"After dinner the next day," Lady Richmond said, "well pleased with his new bride, the king presented her with a ring and two lapdogs. The queen, to show favor to her guest, promptly offered all three to Lady Anne, who accepted them most graciously."

"Did the queen not fear to offend His Grace by giving his gifts away?" The question burst out of me before I could stop it. I stammered an attempt at an explanation: "I . . . I would never give Pocket to someone else."

Surrey laughed. "No, indeed. The king would not be pleased to hear of it if one of his glove beagles were to go to another. I am surprised he parted with that one. But these dogs were just ordinary spaniels, like that lazy beast." He sent a contemptuous look in the direction of one of his sister's lapdogs. Curled up close to the hearth, it was snoring gustily.

"I suspect they had arranged it all between them beforehand," the duchess said, "for the king was quick to make a gift of his own to his former wife—an annuity of a thousand ducats."

My eyes widened at the magnificence of this sum. King Henry must have been very grateful indeed to Anne of Cleves for allowing him to put her aside without protest.

"Lady Anne's gift to the king," Lady Richmond continued, "was also very fine—two splendid horses caparisoned in purple velvet."

I scarce heard her. That man was watching me again. He had an intense, disconcerting gaze. His heavy-lidded eyes shifted as I moved, leaving me with the uneasy feeling that he had some special reason for wanting to examine me so closely. Unable to imagine what it was, I fixed my attention on my stitches and attempted to ignore him, but I found no true relief until the earl and his gentlemen took their leave of us.

"Who was that older man?" I asked. "The one who stared at me so boldly."

"Sir Richard Southwell." Mary's lips pursed as she spoke his name, as if saying it left a bad taste in her mouth.

"He is one of my father's retainers," the Duchess of Richmond said.

I looked from one woman to the other, puzzled by their reticence. Only the strength of my own reaction to the man persuaded me to pursue the matter. "Neither of you cares for the fellow. What has he done to make you so dislike him?"

Mary's derisive snort spoke volumes, but did not clarify matters for me.

"What has he *not* done?" The Duchess of Richmond made a moue of distaste. "Some seven or eight years ago, he and several accomplices pursued a man into sanctuary at Westminster and slew him."

I gasped. Murder was a heinous crime, but to violate sanctuary made it a hundred times worse.

"There was no doubt of his guilt," Lady Richmond continued, "but my father the duke did not wish to do without his services. He persuaded the king to grant Sir Richard a pardon. The villain was fined a thousand pounds, but he kept his life, his property, and his freedom."

"And he did not even have to pay the entire fine," Mary put in. "He gave the king two of his manors in Essex to make up the difference, and after that it was as if nothing untoward had ever happened. He has been at court ever since, regularly collecting honors and new grants of land."

"Why was he so interested in me?" I asked.

"No doubt because you are new to our circle," the duchess said.

Mary snorted. "Say rather because she is young and innocent of the ways of men. And her looks are . . . pleasing."

I had the oddest sense that she'd meant to say something quite different, but I did not pursue that point. An alarming possibility had occurred to me. "Is he looking for a wife?"

Mary laughed. "Oh, he has one of those already, and one in waiting, too. A mistress," she clarified when I failed to comprehend her meaning. "But he's not the sort of man to be faithful."

She set aside her needlework to stare into the past.

"I was newly at court at the time of his pardon, young and foolish, though not so young as you are. My sister and I thought him fascinating—an outlaw like Robin Hood rather than the vicious killer he really was. Sir Richard can be courtly when he chooses. He was on his best behavior with us . . . in public. In private he took liberties he should not have."

She resumed embroidering with a vengeance, jabbing needle into cloth with unnecessary force.

"Then I found out about his wife . . . *and* his mistress. I accused him of deceiving me, and when he realized that I had thought he was courting me, intending marriage, he *laughed* at me."

This time when the needle struck, it drew blood. Mary raised her wounded finger to her mouth with a sound of annoyance.

"It is not such an unusual thing," the duchess remarked. "Married men often prey on innocent young women. The practice is not limited to the court, either."

"My sister Margaret had more than one married suitor," Mary said.

"So did you," the duchess murmured.

"Not Master Clere!" Horrified by my outburst, I started to apologize, but Mary cut me off.

"Not Tom. He's good and true. But Sir Thomas Wyatt the Elder, the poet, held in high regard by all of us for that talent, like Southwell has a wife and a mistress and still tried his luck with me."

"At least Wyatt is not a murderer." The duchess smiled at me. "It is well to be wary of the ways of men, Audrey. Your good Edith will protect you, but only if you stay within her sight. No slipping off on adventures of your own." She wagged a finger at me.

"How can the king condone such behavior in his courtiers?" I asked.

The duchess and Mary exchanged a look.

"Murder?" Mary asked. "Or licentiousness?"

"The king has been known to ignore both the law and common sense when they stand in the way of what he wants." I heard the bitterness in the Duchess of Richmond's voice. "His punishments can be as fickle as his forgiveness. In the manuscript Mary keeps of our poems you may read an exchange of love sonnets between the king's niece and my uncle. They married in secret, without King Henry's permission, and when he found out he imprisoned them both. Lord Thomas Howard died in the Tower."

She did not need to remind me that her cousin, Queen Anne Boleyn, had also lost her life in that grim fortress. Queen Anne had been a cousin to Mary Shelton, too, on the Boleyn side, and the king had rid himself of her for no better reason than that she'd given birth to a princess instead of a prince. No one had ever told me all the details but, even at that young age, I was astute enough to guess, from certain unguarded comments my friends had made, that the evidence of the queen's adultery had been fabricated in order to clear the way for the king to make a new marriage.

The saddest part of Anne Boleyn's disgrace and death was what it had done to her little daughter, Elizabeth. When the marriage was declared invalid, the child born during it became illegitimate. At barely three years old, Elizabeth Tudor went from being a pampered princess to a royal merry-begot.

14

Norfolk House, March 1541

"Sir Richard Southwell has been sent to Allington Castle
to confiscate all of Wyatt's possessions," Tom Clere
reported to the women gathered in the Duchess of Richmond's
rooms. He'd come alone to bring word of this development to those
anxiously awaiting news of the fate of Sir Thomas Wyatt the Elder.

Sir Thomas had been out of the country on a diplomatic mission to Spain when he'd inexplicably been taken into custody and
charged with making treasonable statements. He had been brought
back to England under guard and taken directly to the Tower of
London. Although I had never met him, I shared my friends' concern for their friend's safety. To be convicted of treason meant a terrible death. The condemned were hanged, drawn, and quartered and
their heads stuck on pikes on London Bridge.

"I pray that wildhead son of his will not try to keep Sir Richard
out," the duchess said. "Else young Sir Thomas will end up in the
Tower, too."

"The son is not the only one living at Allington who will object," Tom Clere said.

Mary turned to me. "He means Wyatt's longtime mistress, Elizabeth Darrell. She has borne him at least one child. And Thomas Wyatt the Younger has a wife and young family, too."

"But what of the elder Sir Thomas's wife?"

"Lady Wyatt lives with her brother, Lord Cobham. Wyatt set her aside many years ago, claiming she had taken a lover." Mary's lips twisted into a wry smile. "If she did, no one knows who he was, and she has always denied it. More likely husband and wife simply did not get along. That is the fate of many couples when their marriages are arranged by their parents."

"But how else *should* a marriage be made?" I had always expected that Father would find a husband for me, although not until I was at least fifteen. That was the age his stepdaughters had been when he began negotiations on their behalf. Elizabeth, the younger, was to wed later in the year.

"I myself am in favor of love matches," Tom declared, placing one hand on Mary's shoulder.

I expected her to remove his fingers and skewer him with a disdainful look. Instead, she laughed up at him. For the first time, it struck me that, for all their bickering, they had a deep and abiding affection for one another.

"Such marriages often end badly," Lady Richmond murmured, no doubt thinking of Lord Thomas Howard and the king's niece, "but it is far worse to be bound to someone you hate for all of your life." Seeing my confusion, she gave a rueful little laugh. "I speak of my parents, Audrey. The Duke and Duchess of Norfolk are notorious for their unhappy marriage. Ever since my father openly took Bess Holland as his mistress, my mother has shouted her anger to the world. Even locked away in a remote manor house, as she is now, she manages to make her wrath felt at court. She is a prodigious letter writer."

"It is the fate of wives to be unhappy," Mary said. "Better to refuse to marry at all. Look at that poor creature Sir Richard Southwell wed. She did nothing wrong except bear him a girl child instead of the heir he wanted and he treats her as badly as ever the ki—"

She broke off before she could say aloud what she truly thought of King Henry's behavior toward both Catherine of Aragon and Anne Boleyn. For failing to give him a son, he'd cast off both wives, annulling his marriages, making his daughters bastards. The king's third wife had given him the son and heir he wanted but she had died in the process. No doubt he hoped to get a second boy by wife number five.

"Be careful what you say, Mary," Tom Clere warned. "It was the word of an anonymous informant, repeating some careless remark that Wyatt made, that sent him to the Tower."

"I am among friends here. Surely friends can be trusted not to repeat what they hear."

"True friends can." Mary smiled at me. "No one in this room will ever betray us."

"But others might," said Tom Clere. "We do not know who spoke out against Sir Thomas Wyatt. It could have been someone he met at one of Surrey's gatherings."

"We come together to share music and poetry. Political machinations have no place in our circle."

We all turned to stare at her. Even I was not such an innocent as to believe that.

After a moment, the duchess sighed. "What a great pity it is that my brother is not always wise in his choice of friends."

Hesitantly, I posed a question. "Do you think Sir Richard Southwell could have been the one who informed against Sir Thomas?"

"He does appear to be the one most likely to benefit from Wyatt's downfall," Clere said.

The duchess's brow furrowed as she tried to remember what careless remarks might have been made in Sir Richard's presence.

Recalling his intense interest in me, I shuddered.

"It will all turn out to have been a mistake," Mary declared, determined to be optimistic. "I am certain of it. After all, in Wyatt's case, arresting him on a charge of treason is as foolish as charging him with writing bad poetry!"

15

*Y*ou are sad, Mother." Hester snuggled closer to Audrey on the garden bench. "Was Sir Thomas Wyatt executed for treason?"

"No. He was released on the condition that he give up his mistress and reconcile with his wife." Audrey's smile was rueful. "The royal court is a contradictory place. No one would ever have told King Henry the Eighth that he could not take a mistress, or that he could not set aside a wife if he chose to. He was not a faithful husband, but two of his six wives were executed because he accused them of taking lovers."

"Two?"

She nodded and returned to the mending basket the fine linen smock in which she'd just repaired a tear. She removed the next item, a shirt with an unraveling hem, and took up her needle once more.

"Not long after Sir Thomas was released from the Tower, the king discovered that his beautiful young queen was not the innocent he'd supposed when she first came to their marriage bed. She was raised by that same Dowager Duchess of Norfolk I have already mentioned, the duke's stepmother. Duchess Agnes had a number of young charges under her supervision at Norfolk House. She allowed them to run wild and Catherine Howard, as it turned out, was the wildest of them all. She took at least two lovers before she married the king and another afterward and for that deception the king had her put to death. To prevent such a travesty ever happening again, Parliament passed a law making it treason for an unchaste woman to marry the king."

"What of your friends? Did they suffer for their cousin's sins?"

How like Hester, Audrey thought, to think of how others might be affected.

"The old dowager spent some time in the Tower, and so did one of her sons, the duke's half brother, but neither the Earl of Surrey nor his sister was implicated in the scandal. Overall, the death of their cousin affected them very little. They mourned the family's temporary loss of influence at court more than they did the life of the young woman who was, ever so briefly, their queen."

"And Sir Thomas Wyatt? What of him? Did he reconcile with his wife?"

Audrey chuckled. "No one expected that he would. At the time of his release from the Tower of London, he and his wife had been estranged longer than I had been alive. Neither one of them wanted anything to do with the other. Wagering was heavy in the Earl of Surrey's circle. I won a gold crown by taking the position that Sir Thomas's loyalty to his mistress would outweigh his fear of royal reprisal."

Standing, she held a hand out to her daughter, inviting Hester to walk with her awhile. Although exercise of any sort tired Audrey, sitting too long in one position left her with joints as stiff and sore as those of an aged crone. They strolled down one graveled path past raised beds sweet with herbs and turned at a sundial, keeping their pace slow and measured.

"I must skip ahead a bit in my story," Audrey said, "else I will never finish my tale."

"Promise you will not leave out anything important."

"You have my word on it, but some events can be summarized without much detail." She thought for a moment, letting the sun warm her upturned face, before she continued. "That year, the one that ended with the arrest of Queen Catherine Howard, was an eventful one. I have told you of my doings, but there was also good fortune for John Malte. The king granted him the reversion and rent of the rectory of Uffington in Berkshire and the revenues from other properties in that area. Father was already a wealthy man. With that generous gift, he could lay claim to being a gentleman."

"Did you go to live in the country?"

Audrey shook her head. "Father preferred London. Besides, my sister Elizabeth was about to marry Tom Hilton. His father had been a royal tailor in his time. It was usual, you see, to look to other members of the merchant tailors' guild when it came time for the child of one to marry."

"But not for you."

Startled by her daughter's perception, Audrey hesitated. "I had not yet given much serious thought to my own future. I daydreamed about your father, but I was young yet. Both Bridget and Muriel were older. Their futures had to be settled before anyone considered a marriage for me."

"But you were already in love with my father." It was not a question.

They stopped at the edge of the garden, where a high hedge

marked the boundary of the property. Hester went up on tiptoe to see if she could glimpse the neighbor's yard, but the foliage was too thick.

"After the fiasco with Queen Catherine, the king lost no time beginning his search for another wife. Even before Catherine's execution, he was inviting eligible young women of the nobility and gentry to court, but none of them caught his fancy for long. Winter turned into spring and spring into another summer. My life went on much as it had before, with lessons and the occasional foray to court with Father. On some of those occasions I would make my curtsey to the king and he would speak a few words to me before moving on. At other times, I would see him only from a distance, though he did seem to be looking back."

"What about the duchess and Mary Shelton? Did you go back to Norfolk House after the queen's disgrace?"

"I did whenever the Duchess of Richmond was in residence there but I was never, as Father had hoped, offered a place in her household. Still, I did sometimes stay in Lambeth for a day or two at a time and I was often invited to take meals there. I must confess I preferred dining in Lambeth to eating meals at home. Even in Lent, there was meat. The Earl of Surrey had a special dispensation that extended to everyone at his table. It made me feel quite wicked to eat something other than fish."

Audrey fell silent, remembering that when word had come to Watling Street of the earl's arrest, her first foolish thought had been that it was for his defiance of church law. She had feared that she, too, might be taken off to prison.

That had not been the charge against him.

"In July, shortly after I attained the age of fourteen, the Earl of Surrey was sent to the Fleet for challenging a member of the royal household to a duel."

Hester's eyes went round with delight.

"Such things are forbidden," Audrey reminded her, her voice sharp with reproach. "His sister prudently withdrew to Kenninghall, the family estate in Norfolk. She took her household with her and, once again, I was left behind."

16

Watling Street, August 1542

The great poet Petrarch sang his words to the music of a lyre," Jack Harington lectured. "It was once the custom for long poems to be recited to the harp. Nowadays courtier-poets sing to the accompaniment of their lutes. Without one skill, the other is useless."

Bridget scowled at him. "I can strum a lute as well as Audrey can." This was a blatant lie, and even Bridget knew it.

"You lack her delicate touch and your voice . . ." With a sigh, he gave up his attempt to find words adequate to describe Bridget's singing. The raucous cawing of a crow is a sweeter sound.

We had no songbooks. Jack would perform a piece of music over and over again until we committed the sequence of notes to memory and could reproduce it accurately. Vocal music was easier to learn. Most songs were short and repetitious and often several different ones were set to the same melody. Had Bridget been able to carry a tune, she would have excelled at singing, for she memorized lyrics without difficulty.

Jack took the lute from her and handed her the cittern, a similar stringed instrument that was easier to master. "Play 'And I Was a Maiden,' if you please."

Well before that summer, Elizabeth had married and gone to live in her husband's house, and Muriel, having learned the rudiments, had asked to be excused from more lessons. She preferred to devote her time to perfecting skills more typical of the housewife she hoped to become. As the light in the hall was too poor for sewing that day—it had been raining since early morning—she was in the kitchen with Mother Anne and the maids, even Edith, making last year's quinces into marmalade before they could rot in their storage barrel.

Bridget had no interest in my other studies, but she insisted upon continuing her instruction in music. I winced as she plucked the wrong string. I enjoyed playing far more at Norfolk House, without my sister. There members of the duchess's intimate circle were wont to pass the time singing part-music. It was notated very straightforwardly, or so I had been told. I could not read the music for myself.

When the piece ended, I set my lute on the padded bench beside me and sent Jack an earnest look. "There is a bound ballad book at Norfolk House with all manner of strange marks in it. Mary Shelton says that even if a singer has never heard the song before, she can reproduce it just by looking at those notations."

Raindrops pattered against the window at my back, for a moment the only sound in the hall. Without sunshine, the chamber was steeped in shadow. I could not make out Jack's expression.

He cleared his throat. "Musical composition and theory are not fit subjects for amateur study. It is not necessary for you to read music."

"The Duchess of Richmond can."

"She is a noblewoman."

"*You* can."

"I am a *professional* musician."

"Are you well paid to sing?" Bridget was always interested in how much a man earned. She leaned forward with an eager expression on her face, forgetting all about the cittern. It fell to the floor, making a discordant sound as it landed on her feet.

Jack chuckled but there was a wry expression on his face as he answered her. "Not enough to buy land in the country or a house in the city, and to earn my stipend, I must teach you well."

"Teach us something new," I suggested, still thinking of musical notation.

"Improvising is a skill highly prized at court. Since you already know the tune to 'And I Was a Maiden,' you should be able to sing it in parts. It is all a matter of judging the length of the intervals."

In spite of Bridget's many deficiencies as a singer, we managed well enough and went on to sing "By the Bank as I Lay" as a round. Then Jack joined in to make a three-man song of "As I Walked the World So Wild."

By then the rain had stopped and the sky had cleared.

"Next time we will work on figuration," Jack promised, bringing the lesson to an end. "That is the ornamentation of a melody."

"I will walk out with you," I said. "Pocket needs to visit the yard."

We went down together to the small, walled-in space between the kitchen and Father's warehouse. Sensing that I wanted a few minutes alone with Jack to ask if he'd had any word from our mutual friends in Norfolk, Bridget insisted upon coming along. Shooting her a wary look, Jack sat gingerly on the edge of the well and watched Pocket splash through puddles and stick his nose into corners as he roamed.

"For a little fellow, he covers a great deal of territory."

"He thinks of himself as a mighty hunter."

Bridget made a sound of derision. "Dogs are not very clever.

They chase their own tails. And that one is more foolish than most."

"Only in his affection for you," I muttered.

Unaccountably, Pocket was fond of my sister. As if to prove it, he dashed across the yard, heading straight for her. Skidding to a stop, he rose up on his hind legs. His front paws landed squarely on the forepart of her kirtle. They were very dirty and left muddy prints on the light-colored, figured fabric.

Bridget squealed and backed away. "Bad dog!" she cried, kicking at him and at the same time trying to brush away the mud. Her efforts only succeeded in spreading the stain over a larger area.

"Good dog," I said under my breath. Bridget's foot had missed him. Tongue lolling, he trotted over to me and I patted him on the head.

When my sister flounced off, seeking a brush to remove the mud, Jack spoke quickly. "The Earl of Surrey has been set free."

"That is wonderful news!"

"Not entirely. The king has levied a fine against him of ten thousand marks."

That was an enormous sum, almost seven thousand pounds. A poor man like Jack would never have been able to raise it. Even a rich merchant like Father would have had difficulty. Worse, though, was that the Duchess of Richmond remained in Norfolk.

"All your new friends have abandoned you," Bridget taunted me a few days later, "and the only reason your tutors still come to Watling Street is because they are paid to do so."

I ignored her as best I could, telling myself her words were untrue, but a seed of doubt had been planted. *Was* that the only reason Jack Harington spent time with me?

As our lessons continued through that summer and into the autumn, Bridget elaborated upon this refrain. She made me wonder why Jack was so careful never to be alone with me for more than a few minutes. If Bridget was not with us, Edith was. Usually both of them were present.

For some inexplicable reason, Bridget grew even more hostile when Jack taught me to play the rebec, an instrument with three strings and a right-angled pegbox that was played at the shoulder with a bow. "It sounds as if you are strangling a cat," she remarked, holding her hands over her ears.

"Do you think you can do better?"

Jack, his face hidden from Bridget's view by the angle of his head, grinned at me and said, "It is true the pitch is high and has a shrill quality, but the sound is more usually compared to a woman's voice. Most men find it most pleasant to the ear."

Bridget glared at me.

"The rebec is best suited to duets with the harp, the lute, other rebecs, or the voice," Jack added. "Shall we try a tune together, Mistress Audrey?"

Left out of this duet, Bridget stomped away from the hall. Edith looked up from her sewing long enough to watch her go and roll her eyes.

And so that summer passed into autumn. In spite of Bridget's snide remarks and overt resentment, I eagerly anticipated each and every one of those twice-weekly music lessons.

17

Watling Street, October 1542

Wyatt's dead." One hand braced on the casement next to the window seat, Jack stared out at the rooftops beyond. Startled by the abrupt statement, I could think of nothing to say. I set the rebec on the small table beside the window and made room beside me for him to sit. He did not notice. His eyes closed, he rested his forehead against the back of his upraised hand.

"Who is Wyatt?" Bridget demanded.

We both ignored her. Edith intervened before my sister could say something even more intrusive, and took her aside to summarize, in a whisper, the life of the courtier-poet Sir Thomas Wyatt the Elder.

"Surrey is writing a sonnet in his memory," Jack said.

"He . . . he wasn't executed, was he?" I remembered all too well the concern Wyatt's friends had shown when the poet was imprisoned in the Tower of London. And their joy upon his release. And the wagering. Wyatt had never gone back to his estranged wife, king's command or no. Was that treason? I feared it might be.

Jack gave a short, humorless laugh. "No. He caught a fever while on an errand for the king. We'll not see his like again."

"There are other poets—"

"And how long will they survive?"

Without straightening, he ran his free hand through his hair, disordering the strands. My fingers itched to set them to rights. I frowned. Something I'd heard in his voice made me reconsider the words he'd just spoken and leap to an ominous conclusion. "Is the Earl of Surrey in danger of being arrested again?"

"Just at present, I suppose, he is in greater danger of dying in battle. The Duke of Norfolk is being sent to Scotland and his son will go with him."

"Is there to be a war?" I knew little about Scotland except that the Scots were England's traditional enemies, along with the French. Many bloody battles had been fought in the north, and good men had died on both sides.

"Word is that the king hopes to avoid it by attacking first. More than twenty thousand men march out with the duke. It is a formidable force, certain of victory." He glanced my way, the ghost of a smile flitting across his mouth. "I asked to go with them and was refused permission."

"To war? To be killed?" Of its own volition, my hand lifted to my throat.

"Being a woman, you cannot understand."

"Then explain it to me." I sounded annoyed, but deep in my heart I felt a little thrill of pleasure. He had called me a woman. He had finally stopped thinking of me as a girl.

Jack pushed away from the wall and began to pace. "I am a pawn. A puppet. As a gentleman chorister of the Chapel Royal, I have no freedom to make my own decisions. I am the king's to command and he does not wish to send his pet musicians into battle."

"Then seek new employment. Many great noblemen have musicians in their households."

"I . . . I do not want to be *only* a musician." The admission seemed to free something in him. He stopped pacing and looked at me. Our gazes locked. "Do you know what I really wish for?"

I shook my head.

"To serve a great man in some capacity that will allow me to advance. Messenger to secretary to steward. In that way I can come into my own, acquire wealth and property and a bride with a rich dowry."

"A bride?" I echoed. A nearly overwhelming surge of despair engulfed me.

Jack might have admitted to himself, finally, that I was an adult, but he still did not see me as a marriageable female. His confidences were such as he might share with a friend. I was flattered that he considered me worthy of that honor, but I longed for more. Much more.

For his sake, I tried to shove my wounded feelings to one side. He needed someone to listen to him and I could be that person. At least he was no longer talking about going to war.

"Mayhap you could ask the Earl of Surrey to take you into his household," I suggested. "You are already part of his circle. He would have no reason to say no."

A hint of wariness came into his eyes. He did not step back, but a chasm suddenly opened between us. It seemed I was expected to listen and not speak. How lowering!

"I should not burden you with my troubles, Mistress Audrey."

"Do not become all stiff and proper with me! Tell me why you do not wish to serve the earl."

He grinned. "You are too perceptive by half." But he did not answer my question.

"If Surrey will not do, then find some other master. I only want you to be happy, Jack."

Although I had long thought of Jack Harington by his Christian name alone, this was the first time I had used it. His eyes narrowed but he did not reprimand me.

"Are we to have a lesson today or not?" Bridget stood a few feet away from us, hands on her hips and glaring. "You can do nothing to bring back your dead poet, Master Harington. You may as well instruct us."

"Perhaps it would be better if you took yourself off to Norfolk House," I said. "We can manage without music for one day."

A moment's confusion showed on his face before he realized I meant he should go to the Earl of Surrey, not to offer his services but because the earl was surely gathering together others who had admired Sir Thomas Wyatt and collecting tributes to him.

"Surrey is not there," he said. "He has his own lodgings here in London, in St. Lawrence Lane."

"Then go to St. Lawrence Lane. Share this time of mourning, especially if the earl is to go into battle soon."

Jack might not wish to enter Surrey's service, but he was still part of the earl's literary and musical circle. I only wished I could go to the duchess and Mary to share their grief, but they were still at Kenninghall. Mary wrote to me now and again. They had no plans to return to Lambeth.

We did without a music lesson that day and when they resumed there was a subtle change in the way Jack treated me. I caught him watching me once or twice when he thought I wouldn't notice. He wore a most peculiar look on his face.

As for the Earl of Surrey, he did go north with his father. The English army spent only nine days in Scotland, but during that time they wreaked havoc on the Scots. There was a great battle at a place called Solway Moss, and the town of Kelso was burned to the ground. Then Surrey came south again, bringing with him all the noble Scottish prisoners who had been captured. They were made to swear fealty to King Henry.

The tales that came back from Scotland with the troops made Jack envious all over again. I did not even pretend to understand the attraction of fighting a war. It seems to me a dirty, deadly business, best avoided. The aftermath is not pretty, either. I do not mean for the side that has lost. I mean for the soldiers who return victorious and spend the next months, and sometimes years, celebrating their triumphs and attempting to recapture the excitement that accompanied them into battle.

18

January 21, 1543

On any given Sunday, once the eight o'clock bell of St. Mary-le-Bow rings to signal the evening curfew and the city gates are locked, all good Christian households bar their doors and remain indoors till morning. In the house in Watling Street we were at our evening prayers when, just after nine, a thunderous pounding disturbed our peace.

This was such an unusual occurrence that for a moment nobody knew quite what to do. At that hour, especially on the Sabbath, only the night watchmen were supposed to be out and about.

"Elizabeth." Mother Anne's thoughts went first to her daughter, wed a year and more by then and expecting a child. She stumbled to her feet and would have run downstairs to answer the door if Father had not caught her arm.

"Fetch a cudgel," he ordered one of his apprentices. "The rest of you stay where you are while I discover who is making such a racket." The pounding had resumed, louder and more frantic.

Why Father was so alarmed, I did not know, but his reaction infected the rest of us. Bridget and Muriel clung to each other. I stood alone, heart racing, scarce daring to breathe. When Pocket touched his cold nose to my hand I almost leapt out of my skin. Trembling, I cuddled him close against my bosom, but my eyes remained glued to the top of the stairwell down which Father had disappeared.

Voices reached us, faintly, from below. There were no shouts. No sounds to indicate the cudgel had been employed. After a moment, I heard the door close. The bar that secured it thudded into place. Then two sets of footsteps began to ascend the stairs. Expecting only Father and Peter the apprentice to emerge, I gasped when I recognized Jack Harington's familiar form. He wore a heavy cloak against the cold of the winter night and his face was flushed—as if he had been arguing or running . . . or both.

His gaze flew straight to me, but he addressed Mother Anne first, as was only proper, apologizing for intruding upon us at such a late hour.

"Explain yourself then, Master Harington. Why have you come?"

Edith bustled forward to relieve Jack of his cloak. Mother Anne sent Ticey to fetch a hot posset to ward off a chill. Jack scarce seemed to notice either kindness. "I came to warn you," he said. "You must shutter all your windows and keep indoors tonight."

"I have already given orders to my apprentices," Father interrupted. As if on cue, the outside shutters swung closed over the glass window that looked down on Watling Street. Father himself fastened the inside latches.

At last I found my voice. "What is happening? Are we in danger?"

"Sit, lad," Father said, steering Jack toward his own Glastonbury chair. "You owe us the whole story, at the least. And the reason why you chose to warn this household in particular," he added, although his quick glance in my direction suggested that he already knew the answer to that question.

"The Earl of Surrey and some of his friends are headed this way, high-flown with drink and looking to break windows and a few heads. They are armed with stonebows for that purpose."

"What is a stonebow?" Bridget wanted to know. She'd disentangled herself from Muriel to plant herself on a cushion just to the left of Jack's chair, forcing me to sit farther away from him. Mother Anne had already claimed the stool to his right.

"It is a crossbow that only shoots stones, far less deadly than one with arrows but capable of doing much damage all the same."

"What set them off?" Father asked. "Surrey is hotheaded, this I know. But what cause has he to rampage through the streets of London? And why should he target my house? I've done nothing to annoy him."

"I doubt he even knows where you live, but he's beyond caring who he hurts." Jack took a sip of the posset Ticey had brought, a soothing blend of chamomile and other herbs, and bowed his head. "I was one of his company at the start, drinking with them in the earl's lodgings in St. Lawrence Lane. He has rooms in Millicent Arundell's house and she and her husband keep him well supplied with food and drink."

Father frowned. "St. Lawrence Lane? Why, that is some distance from here."

"No place is far distant from any other in London," Jack countered, "especially at night when the streets are empty. Before I left them, they had already made their way from St. Lawrence Lane through the open passage known as Duke Street and into Milk Street, where they ran amok, breaking all of the windows in Sir Richard Gresham's house."

Even I knew that name. Sir Richard, a former Lord Mayor of London, was a very wealthy man, although not much loved.

"We have nothing to do with Sir Richard." The words burst out of me, so affronted was I that anyone should lump Father together with that avaricious moneylender.

"That this is the house of a merchant may be enough to make it a target. I . . . I did not wish to take any chances with those I . . . with those the king is fond of."

Jack avoided my eyes by drinking deeply of the posset, but I was not deceived. I was certain I was the reason he had come to warn us. He cared for me. I ducked my own head to hide my smile.

Father and Mother Anne peppered Jack with questions, which he answered as well as he could. I stopped listening when Pocket squirmed to get down and began to whine. I knew that sound. It meant that he needed to go outside.

Without ado, I slipped away from the company and hurried down the narrow back stairs that led, by way of the countinghouse and the kitchen, into our small, walled-in yard. I opened the door just a crack, enough to let the little dog through.

Chilly winter air seeped in, even with the door closed against it, and I wished I'd taken time to put on my fur-lined cloak. Hugging myself for warmth, I waited. Pocket would have to sniff every corner before he settled down to do his business.

When I judged he'd had long enough, I opened the door once again. "Pocket?" I called in a soft voice.

He did not appear, but I heard a faint scrabbling sound from the direction of the warehouse on the opposite side of the yard from the kitchen. My bold hunting dog was after a rat. I opened the door wider, trying to decide if I should go out after him or not. A full moon lit my way but there were ominous shadows everywhere and even though the night was quiet, I had not forgotten Jack's warning. I took a tentative step forward, again calling Pocket's name.

A cold gust of wind made my skirts flap and chilled my ankles right through my heavy wool stockings. Behind me, the door slammed shut.

I jumped at the sound, then laughed a little at myself for my foolish fears. But when I tugged on the latch, it would not budge. I tried again, and again nothing happened. Belatedly, I realized that the wind could not have blown the door closed. It opened inward. Someone had deliberately locked me out.

Bridget.

Furious, I flung myself at the thick wooden surface, beating on it with my fists. My fingers already felt half frozen.

With a cry of rage, I kicked the door. That accomplished nothing except to hurt my toes. Everyone was in the hall, even the apprentices and the maids. I could not make enough noise to be heard that far away.

Resting my forehead against the rough wood, I willed myself to be calm and think. I would have to go around to the front of the house and knock on that door, as Jack had done. I called to Pocket. This time he came at once. I gathered him up, taking comfort from his wriggling body and warm tongue.

In spite of the bright moonlight, the small, familiar yard seemed to be filled with obstacles. I knew it was not so very far to the gate in the wall, but I could not see where I was putting my feet. It was so cold that I could barely *feel* my feet. When hot tears sprang into my eyes and began to flow down my cheeks, I feared they would freeze into long, thin icicles.

I drew in a deep breath, steeling myself to take the first step. I went still as a statue instead. Sound carries well in clear, chill night air. I was certain what I heard was glass breaking. How close were the marauders? Could I count on being recognized as a friend by men high-flown with drink? Tom Clere would be with Surrey. I was sure of that. Perhaps there would be others I had met. But men, as Father had so often warned me when we visited the court, could not be trusted around unprotected females, especially when they were cupshotten.

I was afraid to venture out into Watling Street but, cold as it was, I had to wonder which would be worse—to risk being ravished or to freeze to death in my virgin state. My thoughts whirled, growing more fanciful with every passing moment. Pocket shocked me out of my inaction with that odd half barking and half baying of his. His howl was all the warning I had before the door to the kitchen swung open.

"She's here," Jack called. I could hear the relief in his voice, making me wonder how long I'd been standing there in the yard. A moment later, warm arms wrapped around me and he led me back inside.

Father pried me loose to enfold me in an embrace of his own. Then Mother Anne was making much of me, plying me with one of her hot possets, wrapping me in blankets, and finally hustling me off to bed.

To their demands to know how I came to be locked out, I pled ignorance. Let them think the door had blown shut—an accident. My teeth were chattering too badly in any case to explain that I suspected Bridget of deliberately locking me out. Besides, I knew my sister well. If I accused her and was believed and she was punished, she'd only find more devious ways to make my life a misery. I was safe, as was Pocket. And it appeared that Jack's feelings for me were as strong as mine for him. That was more than enough to make me content. I had no desire to take revenge.

Jack stayed the night, helping to guard our house. He and Father and the apprentices took shifts keeping watch. I saw him again when we broke our fast. Over bread and ale, he managed a smile for me, but his face was haggard and his usual cheerful disposition was nowhere to be found.

"You were right," I told him. "The Earl of Surrey would not be a suitable patron for you. Likely you'd end up in gaol if you entered his service!"

"I have been thinking of speaking to Sir Thomas Seymour about a post," he said.

I felt both my eyebrows rise at the name. I had never met Sir Thomas, younger brother of the late Queen Jane, but I knew that the Seymours and the Howards were rivals for power at court.

"Sir Thomas has recently returned to England from a mission abroad," Jack added, "but rumor has it that he's to be appointed ambassador to the regent of the Netherlands."

My heart sank at this news. I was not sure exactly where the Netherlands were, but I knew they were far away from Watling Street. What Jack was really saying was that he was not just planning to leave the Chapel Royal. He was planning to leave the country.

And me.

For days after the earl and his minions went on their rampage, that was all anyone in London talked about. Watling Street had not, after all, been in the path of the destruction. After attacking Sir Richard Gresham's house, the rioters had gone in the other direction, shooting their strongbows at apprentices in Cheapside, then moving on into the Poultry and through the Stocks Market. After that they'd headed east along Lombard Street into Fenchurch Street, stopping there long enough to break all the windows in an alderman's house. They damaged other merchants' property along the way, and even shattered the glass windows in some churches, before jumping into boats and crossing the Thames to Bankside to shoot stones at the whores there until nearly two in the morning.

Surrey was soon back in the Fleet thanks to this escapade, along with his squire, Tom Clere. Two of their fellow rioters, Thomas Wyatt the Younger and William Pickering, ended up in the Tower of London for their part in the vandalism.

Young men capable of fighting in the king's wars do not stay locked up for long. Surrey was free by mid-May and the others soon after. By then, Jack was in Brussels with Sir Thomas Seymour and my music lessons were a thing of the past.

"Poor Audrey," Bridget said, taunting me. "You have lost *all* your new friends!"

I feared she had the right of it. It had been a long time since I'd heard from Mary Shelton. I felt very sorry for myself.

I reached the age of fifteen in June of that year. As each of my sisters achieved that milestone, Father had begun negotiating marriages for them. I would be no different. By the time I was seventeen or eighteen, I would be wed, and not to Jack Harington. Father would look for a match where he always did, within the community of merchant tailors in London. That was why Bridget was about to become betrothed to our neighbor, John Scutt—a man old enough to be her grandfather.

She said she did not mind in the least. He was *very* wealthy.

19

The palace of Ashridge in Hertfordshire is a goodly complex complete with its own church and a cloister. It sits on high ground, surrounded by woods and hunting forests. Father was assigned to a double lodging—two rooms with a fireplace and a private privy—in the palace itself.

"This is a mark of the king's favor," he told me. "With so many royals and their attendants in residence, even some of the ladies and gentlemen in waiting had to be billeted in nearby villages and manor houses."

"No doubt King Henry wants you near at hand for fittings."

I sent Edith to see if a meal could be had. Peter stayed behind to put away Father's clothing and arrange his comb, brush, and toothpick on a table.

We had traveled to Ashridge on horseback. This had been a new experience for me, but not one I much enjoyed. Although the pillion attached to the back of Father's saddle was padded, it was still very hard, and I was obliged to sit in an awkward position in order to keep hold of his waist. I was fearful that if I let go, even for an instant, I would fall off the horse.

The journey had taken three days. It had seemed to me that we were traveling at a snail's pace, until Father told me that to make the same trip in comfort, carried in a litter, would require *five* interminable days on the road. Our speed had been set by the two wagons filled with fabrics and trimmings that accompanied us. Edith and Peter, and Pocket, had been obliged to ride stuffed into the corners in one of them.

The king sent a contingent of royal guards to escort our little convoy through the countryside, but that was more to protect our cargo than for our safety. At Ashridge, Father would turn the cloth in the wagons into garments for the king, his new queen, and his three children.

In mid-July, His Grace had married his sixth wife, a widowed gentlewoman named Kathryn Parr. Soon after, I had been invited to join the king's annual progress. Or rather, Father had been sent for and was instructed to bring me along.

It had been a strange experience for me to ride past all those open fields and to travel miles at a time without passing more than a handful of small, squat buildings. I was accustomed to London, where the town houses rose to three and even four stories and were crammed in so closely that only narrow alleyways could pass between them.

I'd had little opportunity to question Father as we traveled, since he would have had to crane his neck to speak to me. On each night on the road, I'd been so tired that my only thought had been to seek my bed. We'd stayed in courtiers' houses, but the courtiers had not been at home. Edith and I and Pocket had supped alone and retired early. Now, for the first time since leaving London, I took a good hard look at Father. His face was creased into a worried frown.

"What is it that troubles you, Father?" I asked. "Do you fear for Mother Anne and Bridget and Muriel and Elizabeth and the baby?" We'd left them all back in London, where this unusually wet summer had been punctuated by outbreaks of the plague. "Surely there is no greater danger there than there is in any other year."

"The plague is always with us," Father said. "It is God's will who lives and who dies."

I nodded. That is what we were taught and I did believe it. But I also knew that those who owned country houses regularly fled the city in the hope of avoiding contagion.

"Why was I singled out to come with you, and not the others?" I asked.

"It is not your place, nor mine, to guess at the king's reasons, Audrey. And you are not to trouble anyone with impertinent questions while you are part of the royal progress."

"Yes, Father." I agreed with suitable meekness, but my curiosity was far from quelled.

All three of the king's children were at Ashridge because the new queen sought to reunite them with their father and end the estrangement between His Grace and his two daughters, one by Catherine of Aragon and one by Anne Boleyn. Princess Mary, the eldest, was then twenty-seven years old, while Princess Elizabeth had nearly reached the tenth anniversary of her birth. Their brother, Prince Edward, nephew to Sir Thomas Seymour, was not yet six. He had been born in the month of October.

It was the young prince I encountered first. Father was ordered to go to his rooms to measure him for a new doublet. He took me along, although my presence garnered outraged looks from most of the all-male household. One or two of the gentlemen just looked amused.

"Speak to no one," Father cautioned me. "If you are very quiet, they will lose interest in you. The prince is allowed visits from other children, both boys and girls. Remember that and ignore rude stares."

I thought about reminding him that, at fifteen, I was no longer a child, but I decided against it. Who would not want the opportunity to meet a prince?

At first I did not find it difficult to heed Father's warning. The magnificence of my surroundings struck me dumb. I thought I had seen richly furnished chambers at Whitehall and Greenwich, but the prince's lodgings at Ashridge were more spectacular still. Every room was hung with Flemish tapestries depicting classical and biblical scenes. The prince's plate and cutlery, set out on sideboards, sparkled with precious stones. Even the cloths he used to wipe his fingers after meals were garnished with gold and silver.

In the prince's presence chamber it was a stack of books that caught my eye. The fact of them alone was impressive, for printed books were rare and expensive. These volumes could only belong to royalty. One had a cover of enameled gold. The clasp was a ruby. Others were decorated with crosses or fleurs-de-lis or roses made out of diamonds and other precious stones.

Prince Edward himself was a small, slight boy with fair skin and hair the color of ripe corn. At first glance, with his pink cheeks and pale complexion, he looked like an angel. Closer scrutiny revealed a pointed chin and tightly pursed lips. He did not like being told to stand on a stool and hold still while Father took his measurements. When Father turned away, the prince made a face at him.

This sign of disrespect angered me. I stepped closer, hands fisted on my hips, and glared upward, daring to meet his eyes. They were a very pale gray in color and widened at my boldness. Had he not been up on that stool, I would have towered over him.

"If you do not wish to have new clothes, you have only to say so,"

I hissed at him. When Father cast an appalled look my way, I hastily added, "Your Grace."

To my surprise, Prince Edward did not take offense. Perhaps having to obey his tutors had taught him to accept criticism. Or he had been fond of his nurse—he'd only recently been removed from the care of women. Whatever the cause, when he hopped off the stool he was smiling.

"I like new clothes," he said in a high, piping voice, "but I would rather be outside with the dogs."

"I have a dog. The king your father gave him to me."

"Where is he?"

I could not suppress a grin. "Here," I said, and opened the pouch secured around my waist by a sturdy, fabric-covered leather strap.

Sleepy-eyed, Pocket poked his head out. Prince Edward's mouth dropped open with a little "oh" of delight.

"He is so little!"

"Pocket is a glove beagle. They do not grow any larger than this."

The prince held out his arms. I hesitated before handing Pocket to him. "He is my most precious possession."

"My most prized possession is my dagger."

He cuddled Pocket, telling him what a pretty little pup he was until one of his gentlemen, who had been holding up the doublet he'd removed so that Father could take His Grace's measurements, cleared his throat. Reluctantly, Prince Edward relinquished the dog and allowed himself to be dressed. A boy only a few years older than the prince handed him a sheath garnished with diamonds, rubies, and emeralds.

Most daggers are worn suspended from a belt. This one hung on a rope of pearls and went around Prince Edward's neck. He withdrew it to show it to me and I saw that it had been cast of gold. A large speckled green stone was embedded in the hilt.

"It is a thing of great beauty," I assured him, but I doubted it would be much use in a fight. Gold is a very soft metal, and no match for steel.

Later, back in Father's workshop, I studied the fabric he meant to use for the prince's doublet. The cloth of gold had already been embroidered with roses and grapevines in metallic silver thread.

"When this garment is complete," Father said, "it will be decorated with pearls, diamonds, emeralds, and rubies." He shook his head at the extravagant taste of royalty. "Even the buttons will be made of solid gold."

The following day, Father permitted me to venture out of doors—with Edith to guard my virtue and Pocket to sound the alarm if we ran into trouble. The king and most of his gentlemen had ridden out at dawn, bent on bringing back enough venison to feed an army. I fancied I could hear the huntsmen's horns as I stood looking out over an expanse of woodland that seemed to stretch all the way to the horizon.

When I shifted to my right, all I could see were open fields. To my surprise, a small party of women was walking there, accompanied by a half-dozen greyhounds. The women were too far away to identify. "Do you suppose that is Princess Mary?" I asked Edith. I had heard that the king's eldest daughter made a practice of walking a mile each morning for her health.

The voice that answered did not belong to my tiring maid. It was higher and sweeter. "Much good it will do her. Mary has always been sickly."

She came up beside me before I could turn, a tall, slim, girl with red-gold hair, parted in the middle, beneath an elaborately decorated French hood—Princess Elizabeth. She spared me a sideways glance from beneath reddish lashes, revealing eyes as dark as my own. Momentarily, our gazes locked. Then she blinked and a crease appeared in her high, wide brow.

"Who are you?"

I bobbed a belated curtsey. "My name is Audrey Malte, Your Grace. John Malte, the king's tailor, is my father."

She kept staring at my hair. I could not blame her. I was fascinated by what I could see of hers. It was the exact same shade of reddish gold. The color was by no means unique, but it was more commonly found in combination with a very fair complexion. The princess's skin had a faint olive cast . . . just as mine did. The resemblance between us verged on the uncanny.

She lifted one hand, the long, tapered fingers liberally adorned with rings, as if she meant to touch my face. She thought better of it at the last moment and curled her fingers into a fist. For a child of nine, she was remarkably self-possessed. It did not surprise me at all that the servants who had accompanied her into the gardens kept a respectful distance, allowing the princess as much privacy as was ever possible at court. She contemplated me for a moment longer in silence.

It was Pocket who distracted her. Unlike her brother, she took no delight in him. Rather she gave my little dog a long, hard look. Then, without another word, she continued on her way.

The encounter left me feeling strangely vulnerable.

20

The next two days passed without incident. On the third afternoon, Father insisted that I remain in our lodgings, which also served as his workroom, while he went to the king's apartments to display an assortment of fabrics to His Grace. Edith stayed with me. It was hot and stuffy indoors, in spite of the thick stone walls, and we were both miserable.

"Pocket needs to go out," I announced, abandoning the sleeve I'd been halfheartedly embroidering.

"Your father said—"

"Would you have Pocket piddle on the floor? Or worse?" The rushes were fresh and strewn with meadowsweet, but their scent would not be so pleasing if they were littered with dog turds.

Edith gave in and went with me to the nearest door to the outside. It gave onto a small paved courtyard surrounded on three sides by palace walls and open of the fourth. It was conveniently deserted.

I would have stopped there, but Pocket had ideas of his own. The moment I set him down, he streaked toward freedom. Too late,

I heard the joyful baying of a pack of hounds and realized that my little dog had gone in search of friends.

Calling Pocket's name did no good. I sent Edith an apologetic look and followed my ears. The kennels were not difficult to find and it should have been a simple matter to retrieve my little dog. How could I know I would find my father and the king there before me? I never did learn how they came to be in the kennels instead of in the king's bedchamber, but by the time I recognized His Grace, it was too late to retreat.

"Can this be little Audrey?" King Henry asked in his booming voice. "By St. George, she is a woman grown and a beauty, too."

I felt heat rush into my face at his words and was glad of the necessity to make my obeisance. By the time I rose, I dared hope that some of the color had subsided. I might not be as fair-skinned as Bridget, but a blush still reddened my cheeks, turning my sallow skin an ugly orange that clashed most horribly with my hair.

Pocket came running up to me, distracting His Grace and giving me a few moments more to compose myself. I was grateful. The king's presence was as overwhelming as ever . . . and he seemed even larger than I remembered him.

It had been some time since I'd last seen His Grace. I could not help but notice that his girth had increased to enormous proportions. Folds of flesh spilled over his collar and his jowls sagged. His eyes looked smaller somehow, surrounded as they were by a pale, bloated face. His wonderful red-gold hair and beard were liberally streaked with gray. It was a shock to realize that the king was no longer the robust and healthy man he once had been.

When he bent to lift Pocket up, I heard an odd creaking sound. Only later did I learn that His Grace had taken to wearing wooden stays to contain some of his bulk. His fingers—so fat that they resembled sausages and heavy with jeweled rings—were gentle as they stroked behind the little dog's ears.

We spoke of animals—dogs, cats, the birds in cages in every window of the royal apartments, and even the ape His Grace had been given as a gift. "The queen," he added, "keeps a parrot, and she is very fond of greyhounds."

I was about to remark that Princess Mary also seemed fond of that breed when a royal page came rushing up to his master with a message. The king read it and frowned, but he was all smiles again when he turned back to me.

"You are a delight, Audrey," King Henry said as he bade me farewell. "We must think of ways to show our appreciation."

"What did he mean, Father?" I asked as we watched His Grace walk away. He carried a staff and limped a little, favoring the foot on which he wore a slipper instead of a shoe.

"I imagine," Father said, "that we will find out in good time."

Two days later, Queen Kathryn sent word to Father that he was no longer to hide me away. Henceforth, I was to pass my days in her apartments in the company of the female attendants who had accompanied Her Grace on the progress.

"This is an extraordinary honor," Father reminded me as I was about to set off for my first meeting with Queen Kathryn, "and we have already been shown far more favor than is our due. You must show yourself to be humble and grateful. Keep your head bowed and speak only when spoken to."

"Yes, Father." I was anxious to go, eager to experience more of life at court.

With a sigh, he sent me on my way, accompanied only by Edith.

Ashridge had been renovated after it came into the king's possession, although Father said not a great deal of alteration had been necessary. The principal rooms followed the usual pattern of palaces and other great houses. A great hall occupied the ground floor, serving as the main dining room for everyone in residence except the royals. In a slight departure from the usual arrangement, the great chamber was also on the ground floor. This was the principal reception room, where gentlemen and yeomen serving as an honor guard awaited orders from the king. On the floor above, the king and queen had separate suites of rooms, each with a presence chamber, a privy chamber, and a bedchamber.

The queen's rooms were so much grander than Prince Edward's that I could not begin to imagine what the king's apartments must be like. Sumptuous tapestries showed scenes of hunting and hawking and even the less expensive verdure tapestries used as window-pieces were worked with allover patterns of foliage. Gold and silver threads made them sparkle. There were more Turkey carpets than I'd ever seen in one place before, on cupboards and sideboards and even on the floors. The queen's chair was upholstered in cloth of gold and red velvet with gilt pommels and roundels of the royal arms. There were plump cushions for everyone else to sit upon, when the queen permitted. These were arranged on window seats, chests, benches, and stools.

The queen fit in well with such grandeur. Jewels adorned both her clothing and her person, especially diamonds. She was a surprisingly tiny woman, even smaller than the king's last wife. I was several inches taller and I had not yet reached my full height.

Queen Kathryn seemed as curious about me as I was about her and watched me closely as I approached. Although Her Grace had been twice widowed before she married King Henry, she was not yet thirty. Even at a distance, I could see that her skin was as smooth as that of a much younger woman. I learned later that she made a practice of bathing in milk.

One of the queen's carefully plucked eyebrows lifted perceptibly when I reached her chair. Her hazel eyes narrowed.

I dropped into a curtsey, bowing my head to hide my own expression. I did not want her to see how nervous I was, and how insecure about my appearance. I was very plainly dressed, although as Father's daughter the fabric and cut of my clothing were excellent. I wore no jewelry and my hair was severely confined in a net that dulled its too-bright color.

After what felt like an eternity, the queen bade me rise and come closer. When I was near enough to smell the rosewater scent she favored, she reached out with one beringed hand to touch the small portion of my hair that the net did not cover.

"An uncommon shade," the queen remarked. "Does it run in your family?"

"I do not know, Your Grace. But surely it is not all that rare." Queen Kathryn also had red-gold hair, although it was darker than mine.

She smiled. "And yet, I think you do not much resemble Master Malte."

I had always known that I did not look like Father or Bridget or Muriel. "My mother had dark brown eyes and my coloring," I murmured.

"And the red hair? It is very like a shade I have seen . . . elsewhere."

I wondered if she meant the princess or the king, but the full significance of what she was hinting at took longer than it should have to occur to me.

"I hope you will enjoy your stay in my household, young Audrey," the queen said, dismissing me. "If there is aught that you need, you have only to ask one of my ladies."

I backed away from her, as court protocol demands. It was only when I had retreated far enough to turn around that I realized how many people had observed our exchange.

The presence chamber was a large room used to receive important visitors as well as the ordinary ones like myself. The ladies, gentlewomen, and maids of honor who traveled with the queen on progress were all assembled there. There were men present, too—both members of the queen's household and some of the king's courtiers paying their respects. Dozens of pairs of eyes, their expressions ranging from curious to speculative to hostile, and none of them overtly friendly, bored into me. The queen's reaction to my appearance and this intense interest from members of her household confused me. Then it made me think.

The color of my eyes and my skin tone came from my mother, but the red-gold hair—the shade that was so distinctively *Tudor* red—had no explanation unless I believed . . .

No! The idea was too preposterous!

But it would not go away. And it would explain so much, explain why I had been singled out to receive gifts and be given lessons.

I was a merry-begot. No one had ever made any secret of that. But Father said I was *his* child.

Could he have lied to me all these years?

There did not seem to be any other answer.

It was not impossible that King Henry should have fathered me. I knew he'd had at least one bastard, Henry FitzRoy, the boy he'd created Duke of Richmond and married to the Earl of Surrey's sister. Richmond had died when he was only seventeen.

But if I was the king's child, why not claim me? His Grace had *given* me to John Malte. Hidden me away.

Although I longed for solitude to gather my thoughts, I was obliged to remain in the queen's presence chamber all the rest of that endless day. I did not even have Edith to offer solace. She'd been allowed to accompany me only as far as the outer chamber of the queen's apartments. A few people spoke to me. I suppose I answered sensibly. Only one of them was anyone I knew by name.

Sir Richard Southwell came upon me as I stood in a window embrasure a little apart from the crowd of courtiers. He positioned himself in such a way that I could not move past him and escape.

"You will recall we met at Norfolk House, Mistress Audrey." His voice matched his manner—obsequious and sly.

"I remember you, Sir Richard." I had to fight the urge to cringe, for I also recollected the story Mary Shelton had told me. He had murdered a man. In sanctuary. It had amazed me at the time that such a one could remain so high in King Henry's favor.

A traverse screened off part of that side of the room. I had sought greater privacy and now regretted my impulse. I was not afraid that Sir Richard would harm me physically, but just being so close to him made my skin crawl.

"The queen is not the first to . . . admire the color of your hair," he said. "I noticed it the first time I saw you."

I felt sick. He thought I was a royal bastard. And if he had seen the resemblance, perhaps others had, too. In my innocence, had I misunderstood the reason I'd been offered friendship by the Earl of Surrey's circle? Had they cultivated me only because they thought I was connected to the king? Was that why Jack had taken me to Durham House in the first place?

Or was that why Jack had gone away? Had he feared to become entangled with me? More than one person with only a trace of royal blood had ended up in the Tower accused of treason. Any children born to them carried that same taint.

My head spun with possibilities, none of them palatable. How many courtiers, I wondered, had known of the king's otherwise inexplicable fondness for his tailor's illegitimate daughter? How long had they been speculating about my origins? Some would readily believe I was the king's. Others would doubt. I desperately wanted to remain among the doubters.

"You must excuse me, Sir Richard," I blurted, putting my hand to my mouth as if I were about to retch. "I am feeling ill."

He backed up with alacrity and let me pass. I bolted from the presence chamber and did not stop running until I reached Father's lodgings.

Father? Was he? I wanted to ask and did not dare. I did not want my growing suspicion confirmed. I pled a raging headache and took to my bed, but the next day I had to return to the queen's apartments. One did not disobey a royal command.

At least Sir Richard did not reappear.

Soon after, the progress moved on, leaving Ashridge for Ampthill. I continued to spend my days loosely attached to the queen's entourage, although she was often off hunting with the king. They were both mad for the sport.

I did not speak to Princess Elizabeth again, although I sometimes saw her from a distance. She saw me, too, although she never acknowledged me. I tried not to think about how much alike we looked.

Desperate for answers, I asked Edith bluntly why she'd been sent to me. She seemed surprised by the question.

"It was the king's wish."

"But why favor me? I am naught but a merchant's daughter. You were trained to serve the nobility."

It amazed me that I had never before considered this odd. I'd simply accepted Edith, as I'd accepted the tutors and the gift of a little dog—one of the king's *own* dogs!

Edith frowned. "No one ever said."

"But you must have speculated."

My pleading look weakened her resolve. "A guess only. That perhaps you were . . . kin to someone important. I never heard who your mother was."

"A laundress. That's all. A servant far lower than you are yourself."

"Then if not your mother . . ." Her voice trailed off and her eyes widened. Suddenly, she was afraid. "It is not for me to say more. Ask Master Malte if you have questions."

"Does my father pay your wages?"

She would not meet my eyes. "I have a stipend from the Crown," she whispered.

I quailed at confronting Father with my suspicions. I needed to know the truth, but to ask if the king had fathered me would be to accuse John Malte of lying. I was loath to do such a thing. I told myself that my resemblance to the princess was pure chance. And we'd most certainly had different mothers. Why, then, should I suppose that our father was the same man?

We were still at Ampthill when, unexpectedly, Princess Elizabeth was sent back to Ashridge, where Prince Edward had remained when the court moved on. No one seemed to know why, but the king was said to be furious with his youngest daughter.

"I expect she asked an impertinent question," Father said when I asked him about Her Grace's sudden departure. "Childish curiosity is natural, but sometimes it has unforeseen consequences."

"A question about what?" I persisted, fearing his answer but feeling driven to ask.

Father glanced over his shoulder to make certain we would not be overheard. "About her mother, I expect. The king does not permit anyone to speak of either Anne Boleyn or Catherine Howard in his presence. The first was the child's mother, the other her cousin and, briefly, her stepmother. It is only natural that she should mention one or the other of them to her father, never anticipating how violent the king's reaction would be."

"Is there not a third possibility?" I avoided meeting Father's eyes as I asked my question. "Perhaps the princess asked her father about me. We look alike, Father. You cannot have failed to notice. Everyone else seems to have remarked upon the resemblance."

The snip of scissors ceased, leaving the workroom in silence. I could feel his gaze on me, but I did not dare look up.

"No one makes such observations in my hearing, Audrey. Or in the king's. Whatever you have heard foolish people say, you are *my* daughter."

"I told myself I was imagining things!" I flung my arms around him and burst into tears. Of course John Malte was my father! Any other conclusion was absurd.

"There, there, child." He produced a clean square of linen and mopped my cheeks. Then he kissed me on the forehead. "No more crying. You should know better than to believe half the things you hear at court. And if anyone is brash enough to repeat such foolish ideas to your face, you must tell them flatly that they are wrong. You are Audrey Malte, the royal tailor's daughter."

I gave one last sniff and blew my nose. "Even if it is the queen who says—"

"Even if it is the queen, but in Her Grace's case, you must say so most politely."

That made me smile, and I hugged him again.

With a newfound self-confidence, I returned to the queen's apartments the next day. I had been in the habit of bringing Pocket with me, since several of the other ladies had lapdogs. This time I also carried my lute and asked Queen Kathryn if I might play for her a tune of my own composing.

After that, things changed for the better. The queen's household grew accustomed to my presence. The maids of honor, who were the closest to me in age, began to include me in their pastimes. No one made any further references to my appearance.

The progress continued, stopping at Grafton and then moving on to Woodstock. There the court remained until mid-October, before returning to London by way of Hertfordshire.

I enjoyed much of my time on progress, but I was exceeding glad to go home.

21

Stepney, October 1556

Did they truly think you were the king's daughter?" Hester seemed more amazed than impressed by the idea. "You are no princess."

"No, I am not, but indeed they did. And I . . . wondered. But when Father told me it was a foolish notion, I believed him. I *wanted* to believe him. John Malte was the best father any girl could wish for."

"My father is all that is wondrous." Hester's certainty made her sound both older and younger than her years.

Audrey shifted uneasily, wondering how to proceed with her story. She and Hester sat the edge of the brick wall that marked one side of a garden within the garden. The knotted beds were outlined in low, close-growing plants—hyssop and germander and thyme. The open spaces in the simple pattern—elaborate knots forming coats of arms were not to Audrey's taste—were filled with primroses, but this late in the year they were no longer blooming.

After a little silence, Hester asked another question. "What did the queen believe?"

Audrey applauded her daughter's acumen. Courtiers, like sheep, followed the lead of those in charge. "In the hearing of many of her ladies, Queen Kathryn took pains to remark that there were a great many redheads about. And it was true. When I looked more carefully around me, I saw every shade from carrot to auburn peeking out from beneath women's French hoods and men's bonnets."

She smiled to herself, remembering the queen's many kindnesses to her during that long-ago progress. Kathryn Parr, for all that she had been raised up to such a high position by her marriage to the king, remained a country-bred gentlewoman. She was considerate of the members of her household. She saw herself as a peacemaker and strove to bring together those who were at odds with one another. And she loved to give presents almost as much as she loved to receive them. She had presented Audrey with a book of prayers and a new collar for Pocket when the progress ended.

"Although I was happy to return to London," Audrey said aloud, "there were some things about being part of the court that I missed. Having so many people about was sometimes overwhelming, but at the same time there was always someone to talk to, or challenge to a game of cards. There was always music. The Bassano brothers, the same Italian musicians who played at Durham House when Jack took me there to meet the Earl of Surrey and his sister, went along on progress that summer as part of the queen's entourage."

Hester turned toward her mother as a sudden thought struck her. "Was everyone in good health when you returned?" she asked. "Did they escape falling ill of the plague?"

"Everyone was well, although Bridget was much put out that I had spent nearly three months with the royal court while she'd sweltered in the London heat. I tried to tell her that it was just as uncomfortably warm in the country but she did not believe me."

"That is because it is not true," Hester said with a giggle.

"I did not want her to feel any more put upon than she already did."

"Why didn't your father send the rest of the family to Berkshire? I thought the king granted him property there."

"Father was granted the rents on property in Berkshire, but the lands and houses themselves already had tenants. Besides, I do not think Mother Anne would have gone, or Bridget, either, for all her complaining. Even more than I was, they were city bred." She gestured toward a decorative pool that had been dug nearby. "They were accustomed to rats and mice, and flies breed everywhere, but they'd have found the sight of frogs repulsive and I cannot imagine how they would have reacted to being wakened by loud birdsong and a cock crowing to announce the dawn."

"There are roosters in London."

"But other sounds, to which city dwellers become accustomed, drown out their raucous early morning greeting."

Audrey sat a little longer, still enjoying the feel of the sun on her face, but the afternoon was already fading and the air was chillier than it had been. She realized, of a sudden, that she had worn herself out with talking.

"It is time to go in. We will continue this on the morrow."

"Oh, no! Not yet. First you must tell me where Father was all the time you were with the court."

"He was in Calais by then, with Sir Thomas Seymour."

"But he came back to England. He must have. You and Father married and I was born."

"That was much later." Audrey sighed. So much of her story remained untold, but she was committed now to finishing it. "I must rest for a little, Hester. Tomorrow will be time enough to continue my tale."

"During my session with Master Eworth?"

"After, I think." The portrait painter had heard more than he should have already.

But on the morrow, there was no opportunity for private speech. Jack Harington returned that evening from his latest visit to Hatfield, the Hertfordshire manor house some twenty miles north of London where Princess Elizabeth and her recently reorganized household resided.

"We leave for Catherine's Court by the end of the week," he announced.

Hester was ecstatic. She loved their home in Somersetshire and was delighted at the prospect of spending time with her father. Audrey was less sanguine about this sudden change in plans. Jack's original intention had been to remain in Stepney through the coming winter.

"What have you done?" she demanded of her husband the moment they were alone together in their bedchamber.

"Naught that concerns you, my dear. Have you given orders for the maids to pack your belongings and Hester's?"

"I have, as you requested, but what are we to tell Master Eworth? Hester's portrait is not yet complete."

"Eworth will have to finish it from memory. We cannot delay our departure."

Worse and worse, Audrey thought. There was something amiss and his refusal to speak of it with her meant that it was deadly serious. Once she'd have thought he was protecting her. Now she suspected he simply did not trust her to obey him if she knew the whole truth.

Crossing the room, she placed one hand on his arm, frowning when she saw how bony her fingers looked against the dark fabric of his doublet. Jack shook her off and refused to meet her eyes.

He had done something foolish, she thought. Something that could imperil them all.

Throwing tact aside—it had rarely proven useful to her in the past—she moved in front of him, forcing him to look at her.

"Haven't you learned your lesson yet?" she demanded. "You've been a prisoner in the Tower twice already for meddling in the succession. If you are suspected of treason a third time, Queen Mary will order your execution without a second thought."

In these troubled days, when Queen Mary and her Spanish husband could clap a man—or a woman—into gaol for a careless word, it was sheer folly to tempt fate by plotting against them. Every attempt to replace King Henry's eldest daughter as queen had failed. First, supporters of the Lady Jane Grey had attempted to usurp the throne. Then there had been an ill-conceived rebellion led by Sir Thomas Wyatt the Younger. Arrests and executions had resulted from both. Following Wyatt's disastrous uprising, and as a direct result of it, Jack had found himself in the Tower.

She could not fault her husband's loyalty to Princess Elizabeth, or to the religious faith in which they'd both been reared, but so long as Mary sat on the throne, either allegiance might have deadly consequences. The fires of Smithfield burned bright to consume so-called heretics. A dank, cold cell in the Tower awaited those judged to be traitors, followed by the most terrible and ignominious death imaginable—to be hanged, drawn, and quartered, the severed parts afterward displayed to strike fear into all who saw them.

A shudder racked Audrey's thin frame. Only a few months earlier, the so-called Dudley Conspiracy had come to light. Jack had sworn he was not involved with the conspirators and she'd believed him, but he was plotting something now. She was certain of it.

"You cannot help the Lady Elizabeth if you are in prison, or if you are dead."

"Would you have me run away? Go into exile in France or the German states?"

"Others have, there to wait for the queen to die. Mary has borne no child and likely will not, given her age. In time, Elizabeth will succeed her half sister."

"How much time? We have already waited three long years."

"As long as it takes! Think of your daughter, Jack, if not of me! If you are condemned, your estate is forfeit. She will be left destitute."

"You have kin who will take you in." His cold voice held no hint of the laughing young man Audrey had once known.

"I'd rather beg in the street than throw myself on Bridget's mercy."

"You—"

"There is no one else, Jack. No one. Father, Mother Anne, and Muriel have all gone to their reward. My family consists of you and Hester and I will fight for what is best for our child."

He drew in a deep breath and ran the fingers of one hand through his thick, dark hair. He'd grown a beard since she first knew him, a luxuriant thing with a mustache above. He tugged on it, as if debating with himself how much to tell her.

"Have I ever betrayed you?" she asked.

He sighed again. "No. But the less you know, the better. All this may come to nothing."

"They why do we flee London? For that is what you are doing, Jack. Running away."

"Running to," he corrected her. "To safety." The rueful sound he made was not quite a chuckle. "I should think you'd be pleased about that."

"So you have done nothing yet to incriminate yourself?"

"Naught but listen."

That meant it was Princess Elizabeth who was planning something dangerous, Audrey thought. "Has she asked you to assist her?"

"No, she has not."

Audrey thought some more. It was no secret that Queen Mary wanted her half sister to wed the Duke of Savoy. Once married, King Henry's troublesome younger daughter, Mary's heir so long as she bore no child of her own, would fall under the control of a husband who was not only Mary's ally and a good Catholic, but a foreigner. He could take the princess out of England and keep her away.

"I pray every night for a return to the Church of England and an end to Spain's influence," she said in a hoarse whisper, "but treason is a fool's game."

"Do you not think I've learned that? I've seen far too many men I admired go to their deaths because they acted against those in power. My one desire is to keep Elizabeth safe from harm. She has only to survive to one day succeed her sister, peacefully and without civil war. There has been enough blood spilt."

So passionate was this declaration that Audrey found herself unable to argue with it. She slid her arms around her husband's waist and simply held him for a long moment. Then she pulled away and announced in a brusque and businesslike voice that she would have the household ready to leave Stepney within two days.

Two hectic weeks later, they were settled in at Catherine's Court. During that time, there had been no opportunity for Audrey to share further confidences with her daughter. She had warned Hester not to speak of what she had already learned. She felt strangely reluctant to have Jack find out what she had begun. She did not think he would approve.

Audrey was still in her bedchamber, breaking her fast with bread and cheese and ale, when Hester burst into the room. "Father has gone off with his steward to tour the estate!" she announced. "He will not be back for hours and hours."

Her daughter's excess of energy made Audrey feel tired just looking at her, but what the child wanted was abundantly clear. And she was correct. This was the perfect time to resume her narrative.

22

April 1544

nother war with both France and Scotland seemed imminent in the days just before my sister Bridget married John Scutt. Like Father, he was a royal tailor. A few years earlier, he had been master of the Merchant Taylors' Company.

He had been courting Bridget for the best part of two years, giving her all the traditional gifts a young lover sends to his future bride. But he was not a young lover. He was nearly fifty to Bridget's seventeen and had been married twice before. He had a daughter, Margaret, who was eight years old. But he was very wealthy.

Bridget greedily accepted everything he offered—coins, rings, gloves, purses, ribbons, laces, slippers, kerchiefs, hats, shoes, aprons, hose, whistles, crosses, lockets, brooches, gilt knives, silk smocks, a pincase, garters fringed with gold, and even a gown with satin sleeves. As we had all been encouraged to since earliest childhood, she'd stitched linens against the day she'd marry. She had accumulated a goodly supply and Father was prepared to provide anything else that was necessary for her to set up housekeeping.

"But will you be happy with Master Scutt?" Muriel asked her as we dressed her for the ceremony in a new russet wool gown with a kirtle of fine worsted. It was a lovely spring morning. Even London's air seemed fresher than usual. Our bedchamber was filled with the mingled scents of rosemary, to strengthen memory, and roses, to prevent strife.

Bridget laughed and tossed her long yellow hair, worn loose down her back like a veil on the occasion of her wedding. "He is besotted with me and I mean to keep him so."

"But he is so old," her sister persisted.

"If he cannot keep me satisfied," Bridget confided in a whisper, "I know how to find those who can."

"Really, Bridget," Mother Anne chided her, "you should not say such things, not even in jest."

"Are you certain I am jesting?"

"You had better be. You may not have experienced it yet, but Master Scutt has an evil temper when he feels he has been wronged. You would be wise never to provoke it."

Bridget only laughed some more. I was the one who worried. Although it rarely deterred any female from marrying, it was common knowledge that after the exchange of vows a husband took control of every facet of his wife's life. He owned everything that had once belonged to her. She was beholden to him for the clothes on her back and the food on their table. Worse, he could beat her if he chose, and no one would intervene. Once they were one in the eyes of God, he acquired ownership of all her possessions and also of her person. She was as much his chattel as a sheep or a cow.

Muriel and I had spent the last several days before the wedding knotting yards of floral rope. This now hung on every wall of the house. As Bridget's attendants, we had one more duty. We set to work stitching ribbon favors to her bodice, sleeves, and skirt.

"Baste loosely," Mother Anne warned us. After the ceremony, these favors would be tugged free by the wedding guests.

When she was ready, Bridget smirked at herself in the looking glass. She did look very fine, even though she wore only two pieces of jewelry. The "brooch of innocence" was prominently displayed on her breast. A gold betrothal ring glinted on one finger. Muriel handed her a garland made of rosemary, myrtle leaves, and gilded wheat ears to carry to the church. That done, we three set out to walk the short distance west along Watling Street from Father's house to St. Augustine's church.

The entire way was strewn with rushes and roses and our neighbors had turned out in force with makeshift instruments, everything from saucepan lids and tin kettles with pebbles inside to drums made of hollow bones. It was an old, old tradition—the noise was supposed to keep evil influences away.

The ceremony was one I'd witnessed many times before. I scarce listened to the droning words but the scene itself affected me strongly. In my mind's eye, I did not see Master Scutt. Jack Harington stood there, plighting his troth, far more toothsome, and with more teeth left, too. In Bridget's place, I imagined myself, face radiant, heart slamming against my ribs in anticipation of spending the rest of my life with the man I loved.

"Love, honor, and obey," I whispered along with my sister, "till death us do part."

I snapped back to reality when the wedding sermon began. It dealt with the duties of wedlock. The groom was urged to be tolerant, the bride faithful. I wondered if Bridget had any intention of keeping that vow. Most assuredly, she would never stop flirting with any man who appealed to her.

But for the present, the new husband and wife were in harmony. They passed the bride cup around to all the guests. Sops—small pieces of bread—floated in the wine. Before each person drank, he or she dipped a sprig of rosemary into the contents of the cup.

Afterward, everyone returned to Father's house. A great feast had been prepared, but first Muriel and I had another tradition to uphold, that of breaking a cake over the bride's head and reading her future in its pieces. It is possible that I enjoyed this act a bit more than I should have, and left a great many more crumbs than necessary ground into Bridget's long yellow hair, but the chunks that fell to the floor foretold much that was desirable—a son and heir and great wealth. Pleased, Bridget contented herself with finding occasion to pinch me—twice—during the festivities.

It was difficult not to be in a convivial mood. Food and drink were plentiful. Gifts were generous, both from the guests to the newly wed couple and from the bride to those who'd come to see her wed. I did not know all of them. Some were friends of John Scutt and others kin to Bridget's late mother. I was about to slip away to help Muriel and Mother Anne prepare for the last event of the day when Father beckoned to me.

"This is Audrey, Richard," he said to the young man standing beside him, a gangly, dark-haired youth who was a stranger to me. I judged him to be a year or two younger than I was. "Audrey, this is Master Richard Darcy. He is about to begin his studies at Cambridge."

I attempted to make polite conversation by asking him what he would study there. The expression on Darcy's face put me in mind of a rabbit Pocket had flushed out of the bushes at Ashridge. Did he think I would bite?

He managed to stutter out a reply but it made little sense. I thought he might be rattling off the names of Greek and Latin authors. None was familiar to me.

My effort to talk to him about the wedding was even less

successful, but it gave me an excuse to escape. "I must go and help my sister now," I told him. "It is time for the bedding."

"Oh, er, yes," he mumbled, and the rims of his ears turned bright red.

I could not resist. "We'll put her to bed stark naked," I said, "and when Master Scutt is brought in, he'll have been stripped of his clothing, too. They have to consummate their marriage, you know, or it will not be legal."

He looked everywhere but at me. Then he made a choking sound and fled.

I was smiling as I hastened to the bridal chamber. It was the room where Father and Mother Anne were accustomed to sleep, the best in the house.

Once the bride and groom were tucked under the covers together, Bridget's blue garters were presented to Master Scutt's groomsmen and all the pins she'd worn during the day were thrown away. Then Muriel threw one of Bridget's stockings over her shoulder. She laughed with delight when young John Horner caught it. He'd be next to marry, or so tradition said, and we all knew that his father had been talking to ours about betrothing him to Muriel.

Once Bridget and her new husband drank their posset, we left them alone. I yawned, ready to seek my own bed as soon as all the guests had left the house, but Father waylaid me, drawing me into the window embrasure where we could speak in private. He looked as tired as I felt.

"What did you think of young Darcy?" he asked.

I made a face.

He laughed. "It is early days yet, but consider that he might be a suitable match for you."

"I do not like him!"

"You have scarce had a chance to get to know him. What is wrong with him?"

He was not Jack Harington, but I could not say that to Father. "I do much dislike his chin," I said instead. It was the sort that sloped backward toward his neck. I frowned, trying to remember where else I had seen a face with such a feature.

Father sighed. "If you continue to find him distasteful when you get to know him better, I will not force the issue, but will you promise me to give him a fair chance? He's young yet, and timid in the presence of a pretty girl. He will doubtless improve on further acquaintance."

At least, I thought, Darcy was not as old as John Scutt. Nor, I supposed, was he as wealthy. "How can a mere stripling like that one provide for me?" I asked.

"It is my duty to make certain that you want for nothing. If you marry, his father will make a settlement of land on the two of you and I will do the same. Indeed, whatever man you wed, you will have a respectable dowry, Audrey, as befits your father's wealth and position."

Unspoken was the supposition that any prospective husband, or his family, would match or surpass Father's contribution to the marriage. That meant that Father would never consider Jack, even though he liked him. Jack had no land of his own and no wealthy father to grant him any. He was no better than a servant in the household of Sir Thomas Seymour, who was himself a younger son.

I knew it was foolish to pine for what could never be. And if I was honest with myself, I had to admit that Jack had never expressed an interest in courting me. We'd been friends. He'd opened up new worlds for me. But more than a year had passed since I'd last seen him. For all I knew, he had forgotten my very existence.

"I know you want only the best for me, Father," I said, resigned. "I will try to be fair-minded when it comes to Master Darcy."

23

Soon after Bridget's wedding, Father purchased leases for lands and manors in Somerset valued at nearly two thousand pounds. He had some idea of spending summers in the country, where there was less danger from the plague. Mother Anne would not hear of it.

"I was born in London and I'll die in London," she told him.

"What would we do with ourselves, locked away in some remote manor house?" Muriel wanted to know. Away from her newly acquired betrothed, she meant.

I was wholeheartedly in agreement with them. Only years later did I come to appreciate the joys of country life. That summer, the one during which I celebrated the sixteenth anniversary of my birth, I fed on the energy created by the sheer number of people living inside the old London wall. The wards and parishes throbbed with it.

Even on those days when all we women did was sit by the window, our needles busy on a piece of embroidery or a hem, all manner of things happened just beyond the panes. London is never quiet, never still. Bells toll the hour. Hawkers shout to sell their wares. Riders swear, attempting to make their way through a crush of pedestrians. Carts clatter past, filled with wares from every part of England. All that summer, finely dressed ladies and gentlemen sauntered by Father's shop, surveying the goods on display.

When we ventured out of the house, I found city life even more stimulating. Blue-coated apprentices mingled with black-clad clergymen, serving maids with staid dowagers. There was bustle and confusion and excitement. We had to be on our guard because pickpockets went everywhere to ply their trade, but that was part of the thrill. A retreat into peace and quiet and safety held little appeal.

In that year, the plague was not the threat people feared most. Invasion by French troops appeared to pose a far greater danger to life and property. We were at war again with our ancient enemy. In mid-July, the king himself left England to lead his troops into battle. His Grace named Queen Kathryn as regent during his absence.

The queen took up residence at Hampton Court, where Prince Edward already had his household, and sent for the two princesses to join them. I was not summoned. I had not expected to be. Nor did Father go to court. With the king gone, there was no employment there for the king's tailor.

John Scutt, Bridget's new husband, was royal tailor to the queen. He traveled back and forth by boat throughout the last half of July and all of August. When he was at home in London, he shared the latest court news with his young wife. Sometimes Bridget repeated what he told her. At others she hugged it close to her chest, delighting in knowing something Muriel and I did not.

On one late August evening when the air held the threat of rain, Bridget slipped through the yard and into our house by way of the kitchen. I'd seen Master Scutt return from Hampton Court less than half an hour earlier. Add to that the cat-swallowed-the-linnet expression on Bridget's face as she burst into the hall and it took no astrologer's horoscope to predict that she had a secret she was eager to share. I exchanged a speaking glance with Muriel, who knew our sister's ways as well as I did.

Father and Mother Anne had gone to a supper at the Merchant Taylors' Hall. So, I presumed, had Master Scutt. The merchant tailors often held meetings and social gatherings there. I do not remember what the occasion was for this one, but in consequence Bridget, Muriel, and I found ourselves alone save for Pocket, and he was sound asleep on a cushion. Edith and the other maidservants remained belowstairs, leaving us to serve ourselves comfits and wine and fresh fruit.

"You will never guess what I just heard." Bridget's smirk made me want to strike her.

"That is very true. Perhaps you should simply tell us." I had been composing a new tune for the lute when she arrived. Now I set that instrument aside and folded my hands in my lap. That seemed the safest place for them if I was to resist the urge to slap my sister's face.

Bridget wandered with apparent aimlessness from chair to table to window. She ran her hand over every surface, every piece of plate and glass beaker—as if she was trying to evaluate their cost. She had always been acquisitive. Since her marriage she seemed inclined to put a price on everything . . . even information. "What is it worth to you?"

I started to say "nothing" but Muriel spoke first.

"A penny."

"Not enough."

"Sixpence, then." When I looked at her askance, she spread her hands wide to indicate how helpless she was to resist. "Look at her, Audrey. She's bubbling over like a pot on the boil."

"And sooner or later she'll tell all without the necessity of payment. She will not be able to stop herself."

"Oh." Crestfallen, Muriel sent Bridget a resentful look. "I suppose you still want the sixpence?"

Bridget held out one hand, palm up, and waited until Muriel paid her. Her fingers curled tight over the silver coin, as if she feared her sister would try to snatch it back. Only after she'd tucked it securely into the purse she wore attached to her belt did she speak.

"The queen means to go on progress next month through Surrey and Kent."

"There is a royal progress every year," I said impatiently. "That is not news worth sixpence. I'd value it at less than a farthing."

"She will take the royal children with her."

"A penny's worth. No more." And not enough to account for Bridget's barely suppressed glee.

"Master Scutt has seen the itinerary."

I said nothing to this. A list of stops proposed for the progress did not interest me and I had vowed never to ask why, months after their wedding, Bridget did not yet call her husband by his Christian name. I did not want to be privy to the intimate details of their marriage.

"The queen will stay at Mortlake, Byfleet, Guildford, and Beddington," Bridget continued, "and at other great houses, too. Her Grace will honor friends at Allington Castle and Merewood with brief visits."

I pantomimed a yawn. Bridget's answering scowl pleased me very much.

"Do not tease her, Audrey, I beg you." Muriel looked truly distressed. "Bridget may decide not to tell us anything exciting, after all."

"She cannot have a very important secret. If it had to do with the king or the queen, the gossips of London would already have caught wind of it." Nothing spread faster in the city than a rumor.

Two bright spots of color appeared on Bridget's cheeks. "At Merewood the queen's host will be Sir Richard Southwell," she blurted.

I paused with a comfit halfway to my mouth. My appetite for the sweet abruptly vanished. "Sir Richard Southwell is nothing to me."

"Is he not? He made a great impression on you the first time you saw him. Do you remember, Muriel? Audrey came home from visiting her fine friends at Norfolk House all aghast at having been in such proximity to a man who had gotten away with murder."

Muriel shivered. "I remember. You did not like him, Audrey. And you did not like that he had been pardoned."

"Be that as it may, Sir Richard Southwell has naught to do with me." I might not have been able to recall telling my sisters about that initial encounter with him, but I was certain I had never mentioned meeting him again at Ashridge. I had tried very hard to forget it had ever happened. Just thinking about the fellow left a bad taste in my mouth.

"Master Scutt," Bridget announced, "says that Sir Richard will be coming to London soon to talk to Father."

"Does he need a new suit of clothes?" I threw out the question with what I hoped was a careless air, but my heart was starting to beat a little faster. Bridget was leading up to something and, knowing Bridget as I did, it was not news that would please me.

"He needs a wife for one of his bastard sons."

"Too late. Muriel is betrothed to young Master Horner and Father has already picked out a likely prospect for me. A Cambridge scholar, no less."

Bridget laughed. "Is his name Richard Darcy?"

I nodded. Never mind that I'd not cared for him the one time we'd met. I'd take him, gangly arms and legs, tongue-tied mumblings, and all before I'd consent to marry the merry-begot of a murderer.

Bridget's eyes glittered with a malice she did not trouble to conceal. "Richard Darcy, sister dear, *is* Sir Richard Southwell's bastard son."

24

I told Father I would never wed Richard Darcy. I even told him why.

He assured me that, given time enough, I might well change my mind. "Get to know the lad," he urged me, as he had after Bridget's wedding. "Marriage to a gentleman, Audrey, is not to be scoffed at."

"He is no gentleman. Sir Richard got him on a mistress. And he cannot be the heir so long as there are legitimate children."

"The late Lady Southwell bore Sir Richard only a daughter," Father said, "and so young Richard is his eldest son. He will come into a goodly patrimony. Besides that, his father has often said that he will marry the boy's mother when he can and make her the new Lady Southwell."

"If he is already a widower, why has he not done so ere now?"

Father looked uncomfortable. "She has a husband yet living."

"I am surprised Sir Richard does not simply murder him."

"A man should be forgiven one mistake," Father chided me. "The king himself pardoned Sir Richard."

"Perhaps the *king* made a mistake!"

Father's eyes went wide. Then he looked uneasily around to make certain no one had overheard my outburst. We were in the shop, but the apprentices had all been sent out on various errands and there were no customers. Father kept his voice low regardless. "You must never say such a thing again. The king is always right."

Shaken by how tense he had become, I hastened to apologize. "I beg your pardon, Father. I misspoke."

He pretended to believe me. And he ignored the rest of what I'd said. Negotiations for the match with Richard Darcy went forward. I reminded myself, having witnessed the process with my older sisters, that it could take as much as two years to work out all the details of a marriage contract. I had plenty of time to talk Father out of marrying me to Sir Richard Southwell's son.

King Henry returned to England at the end of September.

In October, quite by accident, I saw Jack Harington again. He was standing in front of the Sign of the Green Cap, a bookseller's shop, absorbed in a book of Latin poetry. More than a year and a half had passed since I had last set eyes on him. He was much changed in appearance but I recognized him at once.

I had time to take his measure before he noticed me. He was better dressed than he had been in the old days, but he had lost weight. His face, in spite of a newly acquired beard, had a pinched look. His eyes, when he sensed the intensity of my gaze and glanced up, had the sunken appearance that came from too many nights without sufficient sleep.

My first thought was that he had been out carousing but I was quickly disabused of that notion. Dissipation has a different look. I'd seen it in the Earl of Surrey and some of his friends but it was utterly lacking in Jack Harington. Whatever had left Jack with that bleak expression, it had not been wine and women.

"Mistress Audrey." He returned the volume to the bookseller's stock, displayed on a wooden pentice. At night, the books were removed and the pentice used to cover the open front of the shop.

The act of doffing a cap and bowing meant nothing of itself, but what I saw in his expression warmed me. He was genuinely glad to see me.

"Master Harington. I did not know you were back in England."

"Only just. Have you come to make a selection?" He gestured toward the offerings; everything from broadsides to Bibles vied for space with Greek plays—in Greek—and printed copies of sermons.

"Only if there are songbooks."

"I've not seen any."

"How disappointing, but I am not surprised. At the two other booksellers I've visited this morning, I found naught but liturgical service-books containing plainsong with Latin words."

"I am pleased to hear that you have continued with your music."

"How could I not, when I had such an enthusiastic tutor? But I suspect that my life since last we met has been very dull compared to yours. Will you tell me of your travels?"

Belatedly slapping the hat back onto his head, he said, quite firmly, "I will."

Then he made so bold as to take my arm and lead me a little apart from the noise and confusion of the street. Edith kept pace with us, disapproval writ large on her countenance. I ignored her. Jack's manner thrilled me and his touch sent tingles of pleasure throughout my body.

There were no convenient benches to sit upon so we kept walking, wending our way through quiet alleys and lanes to avoid the main thoroughfares. I did not care where we went. I was happy just to be in Jack's company.

"I have found some measure of success in Sir Thomas Seymour's service," he confided as we walked. "As Sir Thomas prospers, so will

I. He keeps me close and employs me as a messenger when he has important communications to send. I deliver his letters and return with the replies. Princes, generals, margraves—I have met them all."

"Where did you go first?" I asked. "You were bound for the Low Countries when you left England."

"To Brussels, to the court of Mary of Hungary, Regent of the Netherlands. She is a most remarkable woman."

"I know nothing of foreign princes," I admitted. "Who is she?"

"You will recall that King Henry's first wife was Catherine of Aragon, a Spanish princess. This Mary is her niece, and the sister of Emperor Charles V. It was Mary's brother who appointed her to rule over the Low Countries upon the death of another aunt, Margaret of Austria."

"Are the regents always women?" I was remembering that, until he'd returned a few weeks earlier to reclaim the reins of government, King Henry had entrusted Queen Kathryn to rule England in his absence.

"It is somewhat unusual, but then Mary of Hungary is an unusual woman. She is always flinging herself upon horseback and riding off to one place or another. Her courtiers can barely keep up with the pace she sets. Why, once she made the seventeen-day ride from Augsburg to Brussels in just thirteen days!"

I made an appreciative sound but, in truth, I had no notion what this accomplishment entailed. My journeys, save for that one year when I'd been summoned to join the royal progress, had all been short ones. When I traveled, it was most often by water. In all my sixteen years, I had never ridden a horse by myself, but only on a pillion behind a man's saddle.

"Sir Thomas enjoyed Brussels, as did I, but he was ordered back to Calais after only a few months. That he was appointed marshal of the army made up for any disappointment. The invasion of France should have taken place then, but first King Henry had to deal with the Scots."

"I am glad you were spared battle," I said in a fervent voice.

He stopped walking to stare at me. "But I was not. I will not say it was the glorious experience the poets write of, but I survived and Sir Thomas prospered. We saw a good deal of action during the ensuing four-month period. More to the point, Sir Thomas's activities so impressed His Grace that King Henry made him master of ordnance when English troops finally did launch their assault on France."

"More fighting?" I thought I understood the changes in him now. How terrible it must have been to see men die . . . and to kill.

His face took on a shuttered look. "More fighting. But Sir Thomas is now made vice admiral. We are based in Dover but will be much at sea these next few months, keeping the coastline safe."

"Is the war nearly over?"

"So they say, but peace has to be negotiated and reparations made. Many brave men were lost and more were most grievously wounded, among them Tom Clere and the Earl of Surrey. Clere saved the earl's life by flinging himself in front of him during the attempt to storm Montreuil."

"But Clere still lives?"

Jack nodded. "He's been brought back to England, but he suffered serious injuries. He may never fully recover."

Poor Mary Shelton, I thought. She and Tom had hoped to wed one day. Although it had been a long time since I had heard from her, even longer than it had been since I'd last seen Jack, I still held her in my heart with great fondness. She had always been kind to me.

"Enough talk of death and illness," Jack said. "Tell me—do you still write songs?"

I prattled on about my few accomplishments, but even in the

midst of frivolous conversation, Jack had a gravity about him that had not been present when he was a gentleman of the Chapel Royal.

"What about you?" I asked. "Have you written any new poems?"

"A few."

"And do you find time to sing and play music?"

"Very little of it." The regret in his voice was palpable, but he shook off impending melancholy to ask me if I'd ever heard of an instrument called a kettledrum. "It is something like a naker, but larger and tuned by making the drumhead tight. Sir Thomas arranged for several of them to be shipped back to England from Nuremberg as a gift for the king. His Grace likes nothing better than a new musical toy."

We had come, by chance or design, to the Eleanor Cross in Cheapside. Circling it were wide steps leading up to the monument itself. While heavy traffic flowed around us, here was a quiet central pool where weary shoppers could rest for a moment before moving on. Jack spread his cloak on the middle step for me to sit upon and stood next to me, using his body to shield me from the impertinent stares of passersby. Edith plunked herself down a few feet away, a disgruntled look on her face.

"You have grown up since I last saw you." Jack sounded so tentative that it made me bold.

"I was of an age to marry even before you left."

He looked away, lips tightly compressed. Did he regret going? Because of me? I knew it was foolish to keep hope alive, but I'd dreamed too many times of seeing Jack again. In my imaginings I always found a way to win his heart.

"I have a suitor," I blurted out. I suppose I was trying to make him jealous.

Instead, his voice took on a teasing note. "Only one? The young men of London must be blind."

"Only one, and I'd gladly do without him."

Suddenly Jack's attitude changed. He was not just concerned. He was ready to do battle to defend my honor. His hand was already on the pommel of his sword. "What has he done?"

I hesitated only a moment. "It is his father I cannot abide. You know him. Sir Richard Southwell."

A forbidding frown appeared on Jack's expressive face at the mention of that name. "Tell me." He moved to sit beside me and took my gloved hand in his.

I tried to explain. As had been the case when I talked to Father, I could see that Jack did not entirely understand my aversion to Sir Richard.

"A feeling?" he asked.

"He makes my skin crawl. I do not trust him. And I do not like him. And besides, he only wants me for his son because he thinks—" I broke off, appalled.

"He thinks what?"

We were in a public place. Even if we were private, I knew I'd hesitate to answer. If Jack had not already speculated about my father's identity, I did not want to give him a reason to do so now.

"It is not important. He is wrong."

"It is not Sir Richard you'd be marrying but his son," Jack said.

"And children tend to grow to resemble their parents." I felt myself flush and started again, this time more careful to avoid dangerous waters. "Marriage is for life, Jack. Any woman takes a great risk when she gives herself to a man."

"Marriage is a business arrangement best left to parents to negotiate."

"So all young people are taught. That does not make it true. If it is, then why are second marriages, when the choice is made by the couple themselves, so much more successful?" I was thinking of

Father and Mother Anne. I did not know if they'd married for love, but at least no one had arranged the match for them.

"You can always say no," Jack said. "I do not believe your father would force you into marriage."

I took a deep breath and kept my eyes on my clasped hands. "He might be more inclined to refuse Sir Richard if someone else offered for me. Someone I'd *want* to marry."

Slowly, Jack released his grip on my fingers and I could feel him withdrawing in other ways. He did not want me.

The pain of that realization brought tears to my eyes, but it also made me angry. "Would it be so very bad to be wed to me?"

"You will make some man a wonderful wife." So earnest was Jack's tone of voice that I could not help but believe him. That only intensified the hurt. "Some man" was not Jack Harington.

"Have you *never* thought of me that way?" Even though I knew the answer would add to my suffering, I could not seem to stop myself from asking.

"We have been friends, Audrey. That means more to me than you can possibly know."

I sprang to my feet. "I warrant you never gave me a passing thought all the while you were gone. I am nothing to you!"

"I thought of you. Far too often for my own good." He came after me as I descended the steps and plunged into the crowd. Edith, caught off guard, stumbled after us. She had the presence of mind to scoop up Jack's cloak as she went.

I had turned down a side street before Jack caught my arm and pulled me to a halt. His face was only inches from mine. "I have nothing to offer a wife—no house, no land, no fortune."

"I have a very fine dowry. Father said so."

"There is no question but that you do, and that only proves my point. Marriages are made for practical reasons and have little to do with feelings." Sorrow and regret were plain to read in his expression but he forced a smile. "You are not being asked to marry Sir Richard, only his son. Consider that you may find you manage very well together."

"I want to do more than *manage*!"

My vehemence attracted unwanted attention and I felt heat rise into my face as a shopkeeper and his customer stuck their heads out of his door to gawk. I lowered my gaze to stare at the cobbles. There was so much I wanted to say to Jack. I was certain that if he'd just listen to my arguments, I could convince him that he and I should wed. We had a love of music and poetry in common and—

And, to my dismay, I could think of nothing else we shared. Worse, since it had been so long since we'd seen each other, I had to admit that I had no real notion of what his life was like. Oh, he'd told me a little of his travels abroad with Sir Thomas, and it was clear he despised the wastefulness of war, but he had not really said anything about what he had experienced. Nor had he admitted to tender feelings for me.

"It is time to go home, Mistress Audrey." Edith was out of breath, but her voice was firm.

I felt Jack's grip shift to my elbow. I went where he steered me, lost in my own misery. A bleak future stretched before me, one without Jack Harington in it.

Far too quickly, we reached Watling Street. Jack stopped just outside the door of Father's shop. Edith, for once showing a trace of sympathy for my feelings, continued on, leaving us together.

"I doubt that I will see you again. As vice admiral, Sir Thomas will be much at sea and I will go with him. I return to Dover on the morrow."

"I give you leave to forget all about me," I whispered.

At the faint rumble of a laugh, I looked up and met his eyes. "You have a permanent place in my memory, Audrey. Never doubt it."

They were pretty words, but I wanted more. Perhaps I had learned something from Bridget after all. Without giving myself time to think about what I was going to do, I acted. I went up on my toes, seized Jack by the collar of the cloak he'd donned again after Edith returned it to him, and planted my mouth firmly over his.

I had kissed men before, but only in friendly greeting. I had no idea what to expect from an embrace fueled by passion.

For a moment, Jack's lips were cold and hard beneath mine. He held himself stiff and still. And then, in an instant, everything changed. His lips softened. They moved over my mouth, onto my cheeks, my forehead, even the tip of my nose before coming back to where they'd started. At the same time, he pulled me against him so that our bodies meshed from chest to toe. His arms wrapped themselves tight around me. His hands caressed everywhere they touched. When I heard a low moan of pleasure, I could not tell which of us had made the sound.

There was no doubt about the source of the shout that had us springing apart, faces flushed and eyes wide. Father's roar must have been heard as far away as St. Paul's. He emerged from his shop red-faced and glaring. I had never seen him so furious.

"Father, I—"

"Go upstairs at once," he bellowed at me.

"You are not to hurt him!" I shouted back, seeing that his hands were raised to throttle Jack. "The kiss was my doing."

"To your chamber, Audrey. Now."

This time I obeyed, but I stole one last glance at Jack as I went. The expression on his face warmed my heart. It was not the look one friend gave another. In spite of the imminent threat that Father might thrash him, he wore a silly grin. My kiss had finally forced him to accept that he had feelings for me.

25

1545

I did not see Jack again for many months, or hear from him, either. In the interim, Muriel wed John Horner. Father temporarily abandoned negotiations for my marriage to Richard Darcy, but only because he had other matters to concern him. Richard Egleston, who had been Father's apprentice and was married to Mary, Father's first wife's daughter by her first marriage, had begun a campaign to replace Father as the king's tailor. He claimed Father was too old to perform his duties. This was arrant nonsense, but Egleston had made powerful friends among the other artisans at court, some of whom had long been envious of Father's favor with the king, and they supported his suit.

In April, Bridget gave birth to a son she named Anthony. Anthony Denny, who had been knighted by the king and was now Sir Anthony, was one of the boy's godfathers. Bridget often brought the baby with her when she came to visit Mother Anne. On these occasions she regaled us with all the news her husband, John Scutt, had lately brought home from court. Most were tidbits Father had been too preoccupied to mention.

"It is all the talk at court, or so Master Scutt tells me." Bridget handed little Anthony to Mother Anne to make much of and fixed her bright-eyed stare on me. "The Earl of Surrey's squire left all he had to Mary Shelton. She was his mistress, they say, for it is certain they never married."

"They planned to wed."

The news that Tom Clere had succumbed to his wounds saddened me. I had never known him well, but I had seen him with Mary and knew they loved each other deeply. I had hoped he'd recover from the injuries he received in France. He'd lingered nearly seven months.

How terrible his suffering must have been. Had he known all along that he was slowly dying, or had there still been some hope for his recovery? Either way, how devastating his death must have been for poor Mary.

Bridget felt no such stirrings of sympathy. "She should have married him long since, then, old as she is! And since Clere did come home from the war, why not wed on his deathbed? Then she'd have inherited as his wife and have avoided all this furor."

I had no answer to give her. Mary was more than ten years my senior. What was more surprising was that her father had not arranged a marriage for her. I wondered if he was still living. I had no idea. I had never asked.

Having failed to pick a quarrel with me, Bridget moved on to other scandals. I soothed myself by stroking Pocket, who lay curled in my lap. He licked my hand. He was no longer young. I'd had him more than seven years. He'd gotten fat and lazy and spent most of his time sleeping in front of the fire.

Father, upon being questioned, recalled that Tom Clere had been buried at Lambeth only a few days previously. The Earl of Surrey had written his elegy.

Thoughts of Mary Shelton and her lost love haunted me all the rest of that day and half the night. The next morning I sent a message of sympathy to Norfolk House. An invitation to visit arrived later the same day.

Little seemed to have changed at Norfolk House in four years, except that everyone was older and I was much more finely dressed than I ever had been as a girl. The exception was Mary Shelton. Black-clad, her face showed the ravages of long sleepless nights of weeping.

"Come, Mary," the Duchess of Richmond said in a bracing voice. "Greet our guest."

Lady Richmond, at least, was just as I remembered her, right down to the spaniel on her lap. I did not suppose it was the same one, but it might have been.

Mary required a moment to recognize me. "Audrey?" Her pale blue eyes narrowed. "How long has it been? You are a woman grown, and the resemblance is even more remarkable."

Taken aback, I blinked at her. "I beg your pardon?"

"She is rambling again," the duchess cut in. "Come and see Father's new garden."

We went outside, with Edith and several other waiting women trailing behind, but while Lady Richmond sang the praises of the Duke of Norfolk's head gardener, who had coaxed violets, periwinkle, and bluebells into flowering, I stole sideways glances at Mary. She showed no interest at all in the early variety of rose the duchess was showing me. After a moment, she withdrew a piece of paper from the pocket concealed in her black damask skirt. She did not unfold it. Merely looking at it made her cry. As tears streamed down her cheeks, a tiny sob escaped her.

The duchess whirled around with a sound of disgust, dropping the rose. "Give that to me!"

When she would have snatched the paper out of her companion's hand, Mary clutched it to her bosom and backed away. "It is precious to me." She sent a pleading look in my direction, over Lady Richmond's shoulder. "Do not let her take it, Audrey. It is a copy of the elegy my lord of Surrey wrote to honor Tom."

"And you know it by heart," the duchess snapped. "As do I!"

"It is a beautiful poem!" Again Mary looked to me for help.

I wanted desperately to do something to ease her despair. "I have not heard this poem. Will you recite it for me?"

Smiling through her tears, she did so:

> *Norfolk sprung thee, Lambeth holds thee dead;*
> *Clere, of the Count of Cleremont, thou hight.*
> *Within the womb of Ormond's race thou bred,*
> *And saw'st thy cousin crowned in thy sight.*
> *Shelton for love, Surrey for lord thou chose;*
> *(Aye me! whilst life did last that league was tender).*
> *Tracing whose steps thou sawest Kelsal blaze,*
> *Landrecy burnt, and batter'd Boulogne render.*
> *At Montreuil gates, hopeless of all recure,*
> *Thine Earl, half dead, gave in thy hand his will;*
> *Which cause did thee this pining death procure,*
> *Ere summers four times seven thou couldst fulfill.*
> *Ah! Clere! if love had booted, care, or cost*
> *Heaven had not won, nor earth so timely lost.*

"It is a fine tribute," I said, although I had not understood most of the references.

"Better than any of the three poems his lordship wrote when Sir Thomas Wyatt died."

The duchess rolled her eyes. "Well, then. You have recited the elegy. Put the paper away and come and sit in the shade of the rose arbor. We will talk of happier things. It is what Clere would have wanted," she added when Mary began to protest. "He much disliked excessive mourning and well you know it."

Mary's grief and unhappiness could not so easily be set aside, but when she entered the duchess's service she had sworn to obey her mistress. With at least the appearance of meekness, she did as she had been told.

The garden was lovely, colorful, and soothing to look at. Delicate scents filled the air. The faint buzz of insects and the distant shouts of watermen on the Thames were the only sounds to intrude on the peaceful quiet.

"Do you still write poetry?" the duchess asked me, breaking the silence.

"I have not done so lately, Your Grace."

"But you still sing, I warrant." She sent one of her maids indoors to fetch a lute. "Will you play something cheerful? One of your own compositions, perhaps?"

I did so, and after that one of the king's songs. Then the duchess persuaded Mary to sing with us a piece written to be performed in three parts. By the time we had achieved some semblance of harmony, the faintest of smiles played upon Mary's lips.

I returned to Norfolk House the following day, at the duchess's invitation. To my astonishment, she had also invited Jack Harington.

"Come and tell us of your exploits." She patted the cushion beside her on the window seat. A steady rain fell beyond the panes, discouraging us from venturing outside.

"There is not much to tell, my lady. On a ship, a great deal of boredom broken only by short periods of sheer panic. In truth, I prefer to fight on land."

"That anyone should wish to fight at all is madness," Mary said with something of her old blunt outspokenness.

Jack sent a sympathetic look her way. The duchess ignored her.

"Will our troubles with France ever be over?" I asked. "I thought the war ended months ago when the king came home."

"King Henry returned, but not his troops," Jack said. "The French do not give up easily. Their fleet continues to harry our coast."

"There's talk at court of a curfew in London," the duchess remarked.

"And perhaps a special watch of citizens from nine at night until four in the morning," Jack agreed. "Everyone needs to be on the lookout for French agents. They are more than capable of planting explosives that could set the entire city on fire."

The very thought terrified me. Wooden buildings and thatched roofs burn quickly. It would not take much to start a conflagration that would spread from house to house, street to street until there was nothing left of London but ashes.

Seeing the color drain from my face, Jack leapt to his feet and took my hands in his, murmuring comforting words. Mary's eyebrows lifted but she made no comment.

We both stayed to dine and later that day, after the rain stopped, Jack escorted me home. He did not speak of the kiss we'd shared when last we'd been together. Nor did he give any indication that he intended to see me again. He left me at the gate to the yard—out of sight of father's shop—without lingering. His parting words were a reminder that he was the vice admiral's man and therefore was expected to remain close to Sir Thomas in Dover. They would be there for some time to come. Sir Thomas had been named acting warden of the Cinque Ports.

"How far away is Dover?" I asked Edith after Jack had left us.

She gave me her usual disapproving look and answered in a taut voice. "It is a journey of two or three days. Not one to be undertaken on a whim or without proper escort."

I knew already that I could follow Watling Street, which had started life as one of the old Roman roads, nearly all the way there, but for the nonce I was forced to accept that it would be some time before I saw Jack Harington again. This did nothing to lessen my determination to be reunited with him at some point in the future.

As usual, I remained in London throughout the summer.

In July, a ship called the *Hedgehog* blew up on the Thames at Westminster. The explosion could be heard everywhere in the city. We were fortunate indeed that the fire did not spread to any houses.

The very next day, in Portsmouth, where the king and the Earl of Surrey and the English navy had been gathering to repel the expected invasion by a French armada, a much more important ship, the king's own *Mary Rose*, sank in the Solent. King Henry, it was said, watched helplessly from the ramparts of Southsea Castle as almost all aboard were lost. In an entire summer, the French fleet did less damage to morale.

Shortly thereafter, the Duchess of Richmond returned to Kenninghall. She took Mary Shelton with her.

In all, it was difficult year, filled with bad weather and bad luck. A great tempest struck Derbyshire, Lancashire, and Cheshire. A dearth of corn and victuals affected every county. There was famine, and the sailors manning those ships at Portsmouth suffered from an epidemic of the bloody flux followed by an outbreak of the plague. The only good news was that the French fleet turned tail and sailed back to France.

I prayed nightly that Jack would remain safe in Dover with Sir Thomas Seymour, but in September Sir Thomas was relieved as acting warden and took up new duties with the fleet in Portsmouth.

Jack stopped at the house in Watling Street on his way through London, but only long enough to pay his respects. Father and Mother Anne were present throughout his visit and he said nothing to indicate he had any interest in asking for my hand in marriage.

Father saw him on his way. By the time he returned to the hall, Mother Anne and I had resumed work on a large piece of embroidery held in a wooden frame.

"Sir Richard Southwell has settled Horsham St. Faith and other properties in Norfolk on his son," Father announced.

"A gentleman's portion." Mother Anne looked approving. "And young Richard will be entering the Inns of Court ere long. The law is a respectable profession, and lucrative, too."

I feigned a yawn. Country gentleman, courtier, or solicitor, it made no difference to me. I did not intend to marry the offspring of a murderer.

Determined upon resistance, I ignored every effort to change my mind. Lectures from Mother Anne did not move me. Father tried logical arguments, stressing the advantages of marriage to a comfortably well-off husband. I affected deafness.

It would not be so very bad, I thought, to continue just as I was and never marry. I filled my days with music and reading, sewing and works of charity in the parish. I had Father and Mother Anne close at hand and sisters nearby. I had Pocket, who loved me unreservedly. I told myself I was both happy and content.

I lied.

26

December 1545

King Henry spent the last part of the year in Surrey, moving between Nonsuch, Petworth, Guildford Castle, and Woking, but when he came to London for the opening of Parliament, he sent for me. It was the first time I'd seen him since that long-ago progress, more than two years earlier, when I had met Prince Edward and Princess Elizabeth.

Once again we met at Whitehall, this time in the privy gallery that overlooked the gardens. The king, even more obese than when we'd last met, sat in a wheeled chair. He had no reason to rise when I entered and made my curtsey, but I had to wonder if he could. All that had once been muscle had turned to fat. His Grace had always had small eyes, but now they were nearly swallowed up by the abundant fleshiness of his face. A faint, unpleasant odor clung to him, in spite of the strong sweet perfume he wore.

"How is that little dog we gave you, eh?" the king asked.

Father had prudently retreated. The king's attendants also moved out of earshot.

"Pocket is well, Your Grace." I did not think I should mention that my dog, like my king, showed the effects of overindulgence in rich food. Early on, Pocket had learned to beg table scraps from me and my sisters. Even Bridget had tossed him choice bits of meat and bread.

For several minutes, the king spoke of trivial matters. I was considering how to broach the subject of Father's post as royal tailor, in the hope of preventing its loss to Richard Egleston, when King Henry placed one bloated hand on my arm. His words, although gently spoken, had the force of a command.

"It is our wish that you wed young Richard Darcy."

I bit back my first response, well aware of the folly of outright refusal. "I am too young yet to wed," I temporized.

The king chuckled. "Many girls your age are not only married but mothers twice over."

Greatly daring, I answered him. "And many wait until they are five and twenty, with a good dowry saved up and a chest full of linens ready for their new home."

Maidservants like my Edith, if they wed at all, did not do so until they were able to afford to leave service entirely. Some never reached that point. Or they failed to find anyone to marry them.

"You may wait awhile if it is your wish, Audrey," the king said. "It is true that you should come to the marriage with a proper dowry. It is a father's duty to provide one. We will talk with Malte about that, never fear. But marry young Darcy you must. I have promised his father."

I could not bring myself to agree, but I dropped into a subservient curtsey in the hope that the king would not ask for more. His Grace seemed satisfied. When I rose, he waved me away. Father was waiting to lead me back outside.

"His Grace is not well," I said as we made our way to the water stairs.

"No, he is not. He must use what he calls 'trams' to get around inside the palace and there is a winching device in use to hoist him up flights of stairs."

"His Grace should lose some weight."

Father stumbled on the uneven walkway and I had to catch his elbow to keep him upright. "Pray do not tell him so. I should hate to see you sent to the Tower."

"His Grace does not hesitate to tell me how I should proceed."

"That is his prerogative. He is your liege lord. You owe him obedience."

"I will not marry Richard Darcy." I grew tired of repeating this, but no one ever listened.

"If you think to wed young Harington instead, abandon that idea at once. He is no fit match for you." Father signaled for a boatman to bring his watercraft closer and offered a hand to help me climb in.

I ignored it and managed by myself, muttering under my breath that if that were the case then I would not marry at all. I'd said that before, too, and had not been believed. Every woman was supposed to want a husband and children.

We made the journey back to London in stilted silence. I did not want to talk anymore about marriage or betrothals or dowries. I recognized Father's right to make such arrangements for my future, but what business was it of the king's who I wed or when? That Sir Richard Southwell had somehow influenced King Henry made everything worse.

Home again, I said as much to Edith as she helped me out of the elaborate clothing I had put on for my visit to the court: "Why should His Grace *care* who I marry?"

"The king has known you since you were a little girl," Edith said. "He is fond of you and wants what is best for your future."

"He should let me decide that."

"Choosing a girl's husband is her father's responsibility. A daughter has a duty to obey her father and we must all obey our king. In this case, your obligation is one and the same. You must marry Richard Darcy."

One and the same.

Those words stuck in my mind, taunting me during the long, sleepless night that followed, forcing me to remember the suspicions I had chosen to forget. On the day I'd seen my own features reflected in those of Princess Elizabeth I'd wondered if I'd been told the truth about my parentage. Young as I was, I'd been aware of the speculative glances, the knowing looks. I'd shoved my suspicions aside when Father insisted that I was his child, but what if he had only meant I was his by adoption? He called Mother Anne's Elizabeth and his first wife's daughter, Mary, his children, too.

I had no doubt but that he loved me and thought of me as his daughter, as he did Mary, Elizabeth, Bridget, and Muriel. And yet two, perhaps three, of us were not his kin at all.

Was King Henry my real father? Was that why he had rescued me from the man my mother married? Was that why he had taken an interest in my upbringing all these years, giving me Pocket to care for, sending tutors to me, inviting me along on one of his progresses when the danger of plague in London was higher than usual? Was that why he sought to force my marriage to the son of his old friend, Sir Richard Southwell?

There was no one to answer my questions. Father would simply repeat that I was his daughter. I wished I had thought to ask the king, but I knew full well that even if I *had* thought of doing so, I'd never have dared. To blurt out such an impertinent question, whether or not I had royal blood running through my veins, might well send me to the Tower.

If King Henry had wished to acknowledge me as his bastard, he would already have done so. He had not hesitated to claim Henry FitzRoy and had gone on to create him Duke of Richmond and marry him to the Duke of Norfolk's daughter.

Rolling over, I punched my pillow into a more comfortable shape. What did I expect? Sons, even those who were illegitimate, were valued. A bastard girl-child had no worth. If the king *was* my father, I should consider myself fortunate that he'd done as much for me as he had.

Who knew? I wondered. Some might *think* they knew. Sir Richard Southwell certainly did, else he'd not have been interested in an alliance between me and his son. On the surface, I was only a merchant tailor's daughter. Father was wealthy, but not excessively so. A match with a country gentleman's heiress would have been far more appropriate for young Master Darcy.

And Jack? Did he suspect? Was that why he thought he wasn't worthy to court me?

Then an even more insidious thought crossed my mind. What if Jack did guess and because of that was tempted to change his mind? How would I ever know if he truly loved me or was just interested in me because of my supposed connection to the king?

27

Catherine's Court, November 1556

*Y*ou were confused, Mother," Hester said.

"I was indeed," Audrey said with a faint smile.

They were still in her bedchamber, where they had spent almost the entire day. Jack would return soon.

"Father loves you for yourself," the girl said with such confidence that Audrey almost believed her.

"I am tired now, Hester. I would rest awhile."

"How can you be tired? We've done nothing but talk."

"Reliving my memories is exhausting, I assure you." She felt passing frail and sapped of strength, as if a good wind could blow her away.

Reluctantly, Hester departed.

Audrey slept.

Somewhat restored, she supped with her husband that evening, feigning an interest in his talk of land and tenants.

"How long do you mean to remain here?" she asked when the last course had been set before them. The cheese and fruit were fresh and flavorful but she had little appetite.

"As long as is necessary."

"What does the princess mean to do? What is it you want no part of?" Although she applauded his common sense in avoiding trouble, she feared he might already be implicated in whatever scheme was afoot.

"She talks of leaving England for the greater safety of France."

Stunned, Audrey simply stared at him. France? Their ancient enemy? The place where Tom Clere had been mortally wounded and so many brave English lads had died?

Jack had no difficulty reading her thoughts. "The enemy of my enemy is my friend. Spain wants to invade France. The French king will gladly take in an English princess. The question is whether they will treat her as an honored guest or as a prisoner once they have her."

"And if she stays in England?"

"She is in constant danger from her sister the queen. You know already that King Philip wants to marry her to his kinsman, the Duke of Savoy. The princess knows what great folly it would be to agree, but her continued refusal may send her back to the Tower."

Audrey shuddered. "Are you truly safe here, Jack? Will they come after you if they turn on the princess? They must know how much time you have spent of late at Hatfield House."

"They . . . they will accept another reason for that. If it comes to it, I'll give it to them."

Audrey closed her eyes and prayed for strength. It was not as if she had not known about Isabella Markham for some time now. The princess's maid of honor might not have been Jack's mistress, but he was most certainly in love with her. Audrey had seen the poems he'd written to the other woman.

"Good," she said, and excused herself, pleading a headache and saying she would go straight to bed.

She let Edith give her a posset to help her sleep. To her surprise, when she awoke the next day she felt strong enough to agree when Hester suggested they spend the morning on horseback. It would provide another opportunity to continue her tale. It would also be an excellent way for Audrey to avoid speaking to her husband.

Hester was an avid horsewoman. Her father had presented her with a gentle mare as a New Year's gift the previous January. Since they did not keep their own horses at Stepney, Hester and Fleetfoot, as she had named the mare, had been separated for several months. To make up for her absence, Hester brought several apples to feed to the animal under the watchful eyes of one of the grooms.

"Mustn't give her too many now, Mistress Hester," he warned, an avuncular smile on his weathered face. Hester had always been able to charm the servants.

"Saddle her, Parks," Audrey instructed him, "and saddle Plodder for me."

The ambling gait of the aging palfrey was all Audrey could manage, even riding astride as they did in the country. She had never learned to be comfortable on horseback, but she could think of no better way to secure the privacy she needed to confide in her daughter. Parks would have to come along for propriety's sake, but he could ride well behind them, out of earshot.

When they reached the hill that overlooked the house and outbuildings, Audrey resumed her story.

28

June 1546

During the following year I did not see Jack at all, nor was I invited to court by the king. Talks between Sir Richard Southwell and my father continued, although neither seemed in any hurry to formalize the betrothal. The boy they intended for my husband was still at Cambridge.

I, too, continued my studies. I taught myself to read and write musical notation. I had been composing songs to amuse myself for some time but now I had a way to record my music for posterity.

In June, quite unexpectedly, I encountered Mary Shelton again. There was a gathering at the Merchant Taylors' Hall, which is situated near Bishopsgate Street. I had been suffering from a wretched headache all that day. The noisy crowd inside the hall made it worse and I begged to be excused from the festivities. With Edith accompanying me, I left through a side door. What chance took me in that direction, I do not know, but as I emerged onto the street, I recognized Mary just passing by with her own maid and a groom.

She had been shopping, for the maid was juggling a half-dozen parcels and the groom carried a large bolt of cloth. Instead of mourning, she wore bright colors, and on one finger was what was unmistakably a wedding ring.

When we had exchanged delighted greetings, she invited me to accompany her back to her brother's house, where she was staying while in London. The ache in my head having miraculously vanished, I accepted with enthusiasm.

We did not have far to go. Sir Jerome Shelton lived within the close of what had once been the priory of St. Helen's, Bishopsgate.

"Is this where your namesake was a nun?" I asked when we had settled into a luxuriously appointed chamber with cakes and ale and dismissed the servants.

Mary laughed. "It was. Poor old thing. These days she is obliged to live out in the world, and on a paltry pension of four pounds per annum, too."

"She could marry, I suppose."

But Mary shook her head. "It is forbidden for the former religious to wed. A foolish ruling, if you ask me. But no one did." She sipped thoughtfully, then put her goblet aside. "You are doubtless wondering how I could wed another with Tom so recently dead. I will save you the trouble of finding a tactful way to ask. I wanted children. I have for a long time, and it is problematic to conceive one without a husband. Having near to hand an older cousin, a widower of whom I am very fond, I married him."

"But, Mary," I blurted out, "if you longed for children, why did you never marry Tom Clere?"

She fiddled with the ribbons she'd just removed from one of her parcels, avoiding my eyes. But after a moment, impertinent though my question had been, she answered it.

"I could not. After the debacle at court with Southwell, I foolishly agreed to a match my father arranged for me with a Norfolk gentleman. Because I hadn't the sense to refuse that legal entanglement, our pre-contract prevented me from marrying anyone else while he lived. He's dead now," she added, "but he did not have the courtesy to leave this world until my Tom was no longer in it, either."

I had always appreciated her candor and tried to answer it in kind. "Children will bring you the happiness you deserve."

"So I do hope. And I am content with my choice of a husband."

"Is he here with you?"

"He remains at Ketteringham, his country estate, while I, and his heir"—she patted her still flat belly—"spend the summer in London, badgering the courts to confirm the grant of lands in Hockham Magna that Tom Clere left to me in his will."

I thought better of pointing out that her new husband could fight her legal battles for her. "In truth," I said instead, meaning every word, "I envy you. I would like to have children someday, but I do not care for the father my father proposes for them."

"Somehow I thought you and Jack Harington would marry one day."

"That was my hope, too, but he . . . that is, I do not even know where he is." I sighed deeply. "He could be dead for all I know."

"He is not dead. He's in Calais, which may amount to the same thing," she added with a grin. "This endless war with the French takes all the best men away. Always excepting gentleman farmers like my new husband. Even the king is melancholy."

"You have been to court?"

"To visit friends only. I would not live there again for all the world. Do you know that there are now rumors that His Grace tires of Queen Kathryn and would rid himself of her to marry another."

"A *seventh* wife!" I clapped my hands over my mouth and felt my eyes widen above my fingers. The words had slipped out unbidden, but that did not make them any less dangerous. It is never wise to criticize a king.

"Have no fear," Mary assured me. "I'll not betray you." Although we were alone, she nevertheless leaned closer and lowered her voice to continue confiding what she'd heard at court. "It is said the king has tired of the queen's endless lectures on the subject of religion. Her Grace is a confirmed evangelical, advocating all manner of reforms in the church beyond those King Henry has already enacted. He has caused to be issued a new proclamation prohibiting possession of heretical books—the same books known to circulate within Queen Kathryn's chambers. What happened in Anne Boleyn's day is happening all over again!"

"But surely Queen Kathryn has not been unfaithful to His Grace!" I thought of that sweet-natured, kindly woman and could not fathom it.

"I meant that Anne was an advocate of Lutheranism and encouraged her ladies to read forbidden tracts smuggled into England by her silkwoman and other friends of reform."

I was confused, and said so. "The king himself reformed the church. That is why he is now head of the Church of England."

"There are reforms and then there are reforms. Just as there are many rival factions at court, each party has its own agenda. Did you know that after Queen Jane died, the king briefly fixed on me as a replacement?"

"You might have been queen?"

"You need not sound so astonished."

"Did you *want* to be queen?"

"No. Nor did I wish to become a pawn in some political game of chess." She reached for her goblet, her expression suddenly hard. "If our old friend, Sir Richard Southwell, had had his way, I'd have seduced King Henry into marriage and returned power to the Howards and their clients. He has never forgiven me for failing to cooperate."

The square of cake I'd just picked up crumbled in my hand. "He is a very bad man."

She nodded. "And although he claims always to put the Duke of Norfolk's interests at the forefront, his only true loyalty is to himself. You must never allow yourself to fall under his control, Audrey, else he'll find a way to use you for his own ends."

I did not see how he could benefit from an alliance with my family, other than by securing the use of my dowry, but I had every intention of following her advice. "I want nothing to do with him," I assured her.

We talked of more pleasant matters for a time—fashion and food for the most part. When she asked if I had been to court of late, I admitted that I had not.

"Then come with me on the morrow. I mean to pay a visit to the duchess. She's had lodgings at Whitehall these last few months, while she's been attending on Queen Kathryn. She will be happy to see you again."

I accepted with pleasure.

29

We found the Duchess of Richmond in an antechamber in the queen's apartments, a comfortable little room set aside for quiet pastimes. Several other ladies-in-waiting sat on stools around a low table playing a game of cards. The duchess had been reading. She hastily put her book aside when Mary and I came in, and rose to embrace us warmly, each in turn.

We had scarce begun to exchange news when the Earl of Surrey appeared in the doorway. A ferocious scowl contorted his otherwise pleasant features.

Ignoring everyone else, he stalked toward his sister. Mary and I quickly rose from our places on either side of the duchess and backed away as the earl loomed over her. He did not seem to notice.

"Did you know of this?" His face turned a mottled red as he bellowed the question.

"Know of what, Brother?"

"Father's grand plan for an alliance with the Earl of Hertford."

Mary and I exchanged puzzled looks. The Earl of Hertford was Edward Seymour, oldest brother of the late Queen Jane and of Sir

Thomas Seymour, Vice Admiral of England. The Duke of Norfolk had not been notably friendly toward any of the Seymours since Jane supplanted Anne Boleyn, Norfolk's niece, as queen.

Despite her brother's anger, the duchess remained calm. "Father does not confide in me, Harry. What is he plotting now?" A deep furrow marred the smoothness of her high forehead.

Surrey continued to glare at her. "He means to have you wed Sir Thomas Seymour."

I gasped. So did two of the ladies playing cards. The duchess's already fair skin turned whiter still. Beside me, I could feel Mary's tension as if it were my own.

"There's more. He proposes that my two sons marry two of Hertford's daughters." Vibrating with outrage, his voice rose to a shout. "Who are these Seymours but upstart country gentlemen! Father must be mad to treat with them."

"They are the brothers of a queen and the uncles of our future king," the duchess reminded him.

"We have as much royal blood in our veins as Prince Edward!" Surrey raged. "Better you should become the king's mistress and play the part in England that the Duchess d'Étampes does in France than be married to a Seymour."

This time the gasps were louder and there were more of them. The earl was oblivious to his audience as he continued to berate his sister. I did not follow most of his rant. I am not certain anyone could have. The shifting allegiances of the court were near impossible to track, even by those close to the center of power. That the duchess had the misfortune to be part of her father's newest scheme to gain influence at court appeared to be sufficient to bring Surrey's wrath down on her head. Clearly overwrought, his words were ruled by emotion rather than logic.

"Who is the Duchess d'Étampes?" I whispered to Mary.

"The chief mistress of King Francis of France," she whispered back.

We retreated farther from the fray but others moved closer, reluctant to miss a word of the earl's tirade. His ill-considered outburst was the talk of the entire court within an hour. Wagering was heavy that his rash words would have dire consequences the moment they were repeated to the king, but those who thought the earl would be clapped in gaol lost their money. Nothing happened as a result of the incident—no marriages, no alliances, and no arrests.

Or so it appeared at the time.

30

*M*ary Shelton had been correct about the risk Queen Kathryn had run by preaching to the king. The story was all over London in early August. King Henry had gone so far as to issue an order for the queen's arrest. Then he had changed his mind. When one of his ministers appeared at court, warrant in hand, King Henry berated him loudly and with as much profanity as he ever allowed himself for daring to suggest that Queen Kathryn was aught but a loving and loyal spouse. To make up for the insult, His Grace showered the queen with gifts. She, having learned her lesson, stopped trying to influence the decisions he made as head of the Church of England.

A few weeks later, on the eve of St. Bartholomew's Day, a delegation sent by the French king traveled by water to Hampton Court to sign the peace treaty between our two countries. The war was finally over. There were to be ten days of banquets and masques and hunting trips to celebrate.

King Henry sent for his royal tailor. Once again, Father was ordered to bring me along to court.

Tents of cloth of gold and velvet had been set up in the palace gardens at Hampton Court to house some two hundred French gentlemen. Two new banqueting houses had also been erected and were hung with rich tapestries. Awed by all these trappings, I wondered if I would have the courage to carry out the plan I had conceived the moment Father told me that the king wanted to see me.

I meant to demand the truth. His Grace owed me that much, did he not? If the speculation was untrue, then he should be glad to deny it. And if I *was* his daughter . . . my imagination stopped there. I did not expect anything from him beyond confirmation or denial, but would King Henry believe that? Daily, he was petitioned by hundreds of subjects, all of whom wanted something—lands, money, pardons. I sought knowledge, a far more dangerous thing.

When the king did not send for me, the news that he was to appear at an open-air reception seemed to present me with an opportunity to remind His Grace of my presence. I dressed with great care and left the palace—Father had been assigned both double lodgings and a workroom—to make my way through the grounds.

I stopped some little distance away from the marquee beneath which King Henry stood. His Grace had lost some of his girth since our last meeting. That should have made him appear healthier. Instead he just looked frail.

His clothing was as magnificent as ever, his jewels as plentiful and as sparkling, but he leaned heavily on the shoulder of Archbishop Cranmer, who stood beside him. From time to time, he even allowed the High Admiral of France, the French nobleman who had come to England to sign the peace treaty on behalf of the French king, to support him.

Both the Earl of Hertford and Vice Admiral Sir Thomas Seymour were in close attendance on His Grace. As soon as I recognized the latter, I looked around for Jack Harington. I did not see him at once, but only because of the size of the crowd. I found another familiar face first—that of Sir Richard Southwell.

He had not yet noticed me. Coward that I was, I considered creeping away before he did. Although our encounters had been few and far between, each one had left me with a bad taste in my mouth. I did not relish enduring another conversation with him.

I did not move quickly enough. The young man at his side turned his head my way. With a start, I saw that he was Richard Darcy, the boy Father intended me to marry. Darcy tugged on his father's sleeve. A moment later, two coldly analytical stares pinned me where I stood.

"This way," said a familiar voice behind me, and my heart began to race as fast as a cinquepace.

Jack Harington tugged on my arm, drawing me into the concealment of a very large yeoman of the guard. As swiftly as we could, given the crush of people, we fled toward the safety of the palace. I did not look back. If Southwell and his son were following us, I did not want to know it.

"Father's workroom," I hissed when we'd slipped through the nearest entrance. "No one will disturb us there."

"Nor will we be private," Jack whispered back.

When my steps faltered, he pulled me onward. He said no more but steered me away from the place where Father and two of his apprentices worked and into a deserted passageway. We paused by a window that overlooked the expanse of garden we'd just left. Sir Richard Southwell was still there. He had not pursued me.

Breathing a sigh of relief, I waited for Jack to speak. For the longest time, he did not. He simply stared at me, as if he were trying to memorize my appearance. All the while he looked deeply troubled.

Finally, I grew impatient. "What ails you, Jack?"

"I have begun to think I was wrong." He reached out to finger a lock of my hair. It had come loose during our precipitous flight. With great care, he tucked it back into place. Everywhere he touched, I felt a line of fire.

"Wrong about what?" I spoke in a breathy whisper. Was he going to declare himself at last?

"About how beautiful you are."

I frowned. I did not want praise. I wanted love. "I am eighteen years old and not yet betrothed," I said bluntly.

"You soon will be. They will wear you down."

I stepped back from him, a spurt of anger burning through my besotted state. "I cannot be forced to wed someone I do not like."

"You can be coerced. As can I."

"You are to marry?"

He must have heard the stunned surprise in my voice because a faint smile began to play around his lips. "No, Audrey. I mean that I have been warned to stay away from you."

"By Sir Richard Southwell?"

"By Sir Thomas Seymour."

I frowned. "But . . . Sir Richard is Surrey's man, not Seymour's."

"Is he? There are forces at work at court that you know nothing about, Audrey. A struggle for power that will affect us all. You must have a care for yourself. Hold out too long, and there could be terrible consequences for all those you hold dear. For John Malte, mayhap. Or for your sisters." He gave a short, bitter laugh. "And yes, mayhap for me. No one is safe from the king's whim, not even the highest peer in the land."

I blinked at him in confusion. The highest peer in the land was the Duke of Norfolk. Surely Jack did not mean to say that the duke was in danger. "Say what you mean in plain English, Jack."

"If you anger Sir Richard sufficiently, he will turn vindictive, and he has King Henry's ear. He has never hesitated to destroy those who stood in the way of something he wanted."

"Perhaps I, too, have the king's ear."

Jack went very still. "Is it true, then?"

I looked away. So, he *had* wondered if I was a royal merry-begot. "I . . . I do not know. No one will tell me."

We stood that way, unmoving, staring into each other's eyes, until the sound of rapidly approaching footsteps broke the spell. A liveried page, scurrying past on some errand, barely spared us a glance, but his appearance was enough to remind us that to be seen together by anyone at this juncture would be most unwise.

"Know this," Jack said before he left me. "If I were in a position to marry any woman I wished to, it would be you, Audrey."

Then he was gone.

He hadn't said he loved me.

Neither had he said that he did not.

Two days later, in Father's company, I had my long-awaited audience with the king. There was no opportunity to speak with His Grace in private. He called us to him only to inform us that he intended to grant us, jointly, the lordship and manor of Kelston, the lordship and manor of Easton, the capital messuage of Catherine's Court, and four hundred ewes. The properties were located in Somersetshire. They'd been monastic lands once, forfeited by the nunnery of Shaftesbury when it was dissolved. They were valued at slightly over thirteen hundred pounds.

"It is an exceeding generous gift," I said to Father after we'd backed out of the presence chamber and returned to our lodgings.

"I am being pensioned off, Audrey," Father said. "I am to leave my post at court before the end of the year."

As a young child, I might have believed that was all there was to it, but I knew better now. The king's largesse was too great. Royal retainers rarely received annuities amounting to more than one hundred pounds.

"How much of this grant is to be included in my dowry?" I asked.

"You will be a considerable heiress," Father allowed.

"And so this is all part of the king's plan to push me into marriage with Richard Darcy."

"I do not understand why you are so opposed to the young man." For once, Father let his annoyance show. "He has no flaws that I can see."

"And if he turns out like his father? Unfaithful to me? Begetting bastards right and left? Murdering men in sanctuary?"

"Sir Richard Southwell has his faults, but he is not without good qualities. He has served the king long and well and continues to do so."

Father's words lacked conviction, but the stubborn tilt of his jaw warned me that there was no profit in further argument.

31

The next day, Richard Darcy sought me out, sent by his father. He seemed as reluctant as I was to spend any time together. We passed a quarter of an hour in stilted conversation, most of it concerning his studies at Cambridge and his desire to make something of himself when he entered one of the Inns of Court.

"Do you like music?" I asked him.

"I am not particularly musical. When I have time for amusements, I prefer to hunt. I am a good shot with a crossbow."

"Have you ever written poetry?"

He looked at me as if I had gone mad. "Whatever for? It is difficult enough to copy out what others have written and I only do that when my tutors insist upon it."

"Master Darcy," I said. "I bear you no ill will, but I will never tie myself to you with the bonds of matrimony."

"I do not much care for you, either," he said.

"Oh. Well . . . that is good."

His quick smile almost made me like him.

Father and I remained at court until the king left on a hunting progress on the fourth day of September. I did not see His Grace again, but I was thrust repeatedly into Richard Darcy's company. Every time, as I had on that first occasion, I told him bluntly that I would never be his wife.

"You will, you know," he said on the last day. "Father will not give up. He says you are too rare a catch."

"I cannot think why. My father is naught but a simple merchant tailor."

If I had not been watching for his reaction, I might have missed it. As it was, I saw the slight widening of his eyes and heard the quick, indrawn breath.

"That is not what your father thinks, is it?"

"I do not know what you mean."

"You need to spend more time at court, Master Darcy. You would learn to be more convincing when you tell a lie."

He looked over his shoulder toward the door of the workroom. We'd been left alone there except for Edith. She sat in a distant corner and appeared to be absorbed in her mending. I had no doubt but that she could overhear what we said to each other, but I did not care.

"Father believes you are the king's child," Darcy admitted.

Although the idea was scarcely new to me, this was the first time anyone had said the words aloud. I started to utter a denial but before I could say a word, Darcy spoke again.

"It is the color of your hair. Father says he knows of only two other people who share it. One is Princess Elizabeth. The other is King Henry. And then there are your eyes. Was Anne Boleyn your mother, too?"

Taken aback, for this was an idea that had never once crossed my mind, I blurted out the raw truth. "My mother was a laundress at

Windsor Castle who gave birth to me out of wedlock." I drew in a steadying breath and then added, with slightly more dignity, "I am a bastard, Master Darcy. A merry-begot."

"So am I." He said it as though it did not matter, but I suspected that it did. "Still, I am Father's heir. And I am not Richard Darcy any longer. Father says I'm to call myself Richard Southwell the Younger."

"I liked you better with your original surname," I muttered.

"The Darcys of Essex are my mother's family." He elaborated on that subject, but I had stopped listening.

I'd been struck by an intriguing notion. I wondered that I had never thought of it before. The one person who must know who had fathered her child was that child's mother. To learn the truth about myself, all I had to do was find Joanna Dobson, née Dingley, and ask her.

There was a difficulty, however. I had no idea what had happened to my mother. I did not even know if she was still alive. I had not seen her for fully fourteen years, not since the day the king placed me in John Malte's care.

32

September 1546

I was still trying to think of a subtle way to ask Father for information about the woman who had given birth to me when an odd incident occurred. A foundling was left at our gate. Some poor woman abandoned her child where it was certain to be found by the maidservant who went out to empty the chamber pots.

Such events were not unheard-of. The hope was that the rich merchant who lived within the gate would take pity on the abandoned infant and give it a home. In this case, the baby was a little girl only a few weeks old. She had pale skin and blue eyes and was still bald. She was also covered in flea bites and stank most abominably. Mother Anne ordered Lucy to bathe her.

"Well, my dear," Father said to Mother Anne. "What shall we do with her?"

I was not included in their discussion. I was not even supposed to be privy to it. But I had been about to enter the hall when Father spoke. I paused at the top of the stair, just out of their sight. Simple curiosity compelled me to remain where I was.

"I suppose you want to adopt her," Mother Anne said. "You have always been a great one for taking in strays."

At first I thought she meant the occasional dog or cat who came our way and was put to work catching rats in Father's warehouse. Then a more personal interpretation of her words occurred to me. I felt myself blanch. Was *that* why Father had accepted responsibility for me fourteen years earlier? Because he saw a little girl who needed a loving home? Because he felt *sorry* for me?

I told myself I must be mistaken. I had no doubt of Father's affection for me. Or Mother Anne's. But shaking off doubt was not an easy process. With an effort, I kept my focus on the conversation in the hall.

"I am too old to take on the care of another young child," Mother Anne said.

Had I imagined the slight emphasis on the word *another*?

Father did not answer. He could not. One of his ever more frequent fits of coughing rendered him incapable of speech.

"You are not fit now, either, John," she added. "You know this to be true."

"It is nothing," he whispered. "This catarrh will pass."

A little silence fell.

"Let us send the child to Muriel," Mother Anne suggested after a time. "She has taken to motherhood far better than Bridget did. She has room in her heart for a second baby, and milk enough to feed it, too."

This proved to be an excellent solution, although Father continued to take an interest in the infant who'd been abandoned on his doorstep. He worried about her. He worried, it seemed to me, about everyone and everything in his life, the more so since he no longer went to court.

Day by day, his catarrh worsened. The bouts of coughing weakened him and made him dizzy, forcing him to take to his bed. One morning, soon after that overheard conversation, he called me to him, along with Mother Anne and the apprentices. He'd already sent for John Horner and John Scutt. When they arrived, we all gathered around his bed.

"I have spent the night writing out my will," Father announced.

At his words, silent tears began to flow down my cheeks. Mother Anne moaned aloud.

"This is to protect you, my dears. A precaution only."

I watched him sign it and saw Master Horner and Master Scutt add their signatures to his as witnesses.

A great sense of calm seemed to come over Father. When the others left, Mother Anne and I remained. We sat one on each side of the bed, clasping Father's icy hands. The expression on Mother Anne's face told me that she feared Father's death was imminent.

Of a sudden, his hand went limp in mine. His eyes were closed. I could see no movement of his chest beneath the coverlet. In a panic, I leapt up, upsetting my stool.

"Father!" I cried.

The anguish in my voice roused him. His eyes opened. He even managed a weak smile. "I am not dead yet, child, only resting."

"You gave me such a scare!"

Pocket, who had tumbled off my lap when I sprang to my feet, barked in agreement.

"Put the little dog on the bed. He comforts me."

With Pocket lying next to him, licking his hand and being petted, Father did seem better, until another spasm of coughing gave the lie to appearances. It took him a long time to recover his breath. I stayed with him while Mother Anne went off to fetch more barley water and a soothing lozenge.

"There are things I must tell you," he whispered as soon as she left us.

Not now, I thought. If I am not John Malte's daughter, I do not want him to tell me so.

This man, who had given me nothing but love, who had acted in my best interests even when I did not agree with him as to what those were, was my true father, no matter who had coupled with the black-eyed laundress who had given birth to me.

I berated myself for failing to notice how frail Father had become during the last few months. No wonder he had stopped fighting to keep his post at court. Since our return to Watling Street from court, since he'd fallen ill, he seemed to have aged a decade. The hand I once more took in mine trembled. Veins bulged in the paper-white, paper-thin skin.

"I may yet live for many years, Audrey," Father said, "but a wise man makes provision for his family. That is why I made my will. Everything that the king intends to grant us jointly will go to you when I am gone, as will my manor of Nyland in Somerset. I have left property to your sisters as well, and to their sons. John Scutt and Bridget will serve as executors."

He went on to enumerate several smaller bequests. He was generous. He even left five pounds to the foundling so recently abandoned at our gate. That made me smile, but my expression changed to one of shock when he added that he'd made a bequest to my natural mother of twenty pounds.

"I . . . I had wondered if she was still living," I murmured. "Where is she, Father? Where is Joanna Dobson?"

His hand tightened painfully on mine. "There is no need for you to know that, Audrey. She is no longer part of your life."

"And yet you would include her in your will."

"She gave me you."

"Did she? Or was it the king who gave me to you? Is—?"

"Stop badgering your father!" From the door, Mother Anne's voice snapped like a whip, making me cringe and shrink away from her.

"Anne, I—" That was all Father managed to say before yet another fit of coughing overtook him. Pocket fled.

"He will recover," Mother Anne said in a fierce voice. "If he stays in bed and drinks strengthening broths, all will be well. But he is far from well yet. Go away and let him mend."

Banished from the bedchamber, I took comfort in my lute and in playing with my little dog. Father and Mother Anne were my parents, I told myself, no matter whose blood flowed in my veins. But the need to know the truth about myself continued to gnaw at me. Now that I was certain that my mother was still living, I knew I must find her.

Fourteen years earlier, she and her husband had lived and worked in Windsor Castle. That was a long time ago, but I was sure someone there would remember where they'd gone.

All I had to do was find a way to get to Windsor.

33

Although Father continued to suffer from a nagging cough, his recovery was swifter than anyone expected. He was up and about a few days after he made his will and, just a week after calling us all in to witness the signing, he announced that he intended to pay a visit to the local barber-surgeon to ensure that he remained in good health.

"This is the seventeenth of September," he informed us, "the traditional day to be bled as a preventive against dropsy."

"You do not *have* dropsy." Mother Anne glanced up from the beaker of ale with which she'd broken her fast. "You do not even suffer from tympany."

"Nor do I wish to become afflicted with either ailment." And with that, taking only a bit of bread and cheese to sustain him, he left the house.

"What is tympany?" I asked when he'd gone. I had already finished eating and was tempted to follow Father to make sure he returned home safely. Being bled always made me dizzy. I worried that it would affect Father the same way, especially as he'd been so weak during his recent illness.

"Tympany is wind colic." Mother Anne pushed aside her trencher with more force than necessary. "If your father wishes to avoid wind after meals and excessive gas in the abdomen, then I will make him a draft to drink an hour before eating. There is no need for him to be bled."

As she left the room, I could hear her muttering to herself. The list of ingredients—coriander, conserve of roses, galanza root, aniseed, sugar, even cinnamon—sounded more like a receipt for cookery than physic.

Father returned an hour later, unsteady on his feet and white as parchment. "The humors have been restored to their natural balance," he assured me as I assisted him to climb the stairs. "Dropsy is caused by superfluous cold and moist humors. That is why it was necessary that I be bled."

I make no pretense of understanding the theory of humors. To me it sounds as mad as predicting the future by the stars. All I cared about was that Father not fall ill again. Our household might have escaped, summer after summer, from the ravages of the plague, and been spared other dread diseases, too, but I knew full well that life, like a candle, could be snuffed out in an instant.

Father's dizziness abated but he began to pass water an immoderate number of times a day. Mother Anne was worried enough to consult a physician about that condition. This doctor charged an angel for just one visit. He examined Father's urine, prepared an astrological chart, and gave him a purge. Then he made him drink cold water until he vomited. To complete the cure, Father was supposed to eat four eggs prepared with powdered red nettle and sugar every morning. This he refused to do. For a time, his health improved.

In October, the royal grant we had been promised was duly issued, more than doubling Father's wealth.

We were not cut off from news of the court, even though neither Father nor I went there anymore. John Scutt was still the queen's tailor and Bridget still took pleasure in repeating every juicy tidbit he shared with her. In this way, I learned that King Henry had been ill.

"The king and queen are at Windsor now," Bridget announced in mid-October, "but the king is not hunting, as is his wont. It is said he's not well enough to stand the exertion." She rolled her eyes. "I do not see that His Grace ever exerts himself overmuch. Master Scutt told me once that King Henry is accustomed to shoot at deer from a fixed standing. And even when he did ride down game on horseback, armed with darts and spears, he used a purpose-built ramp to mount his horse."

"You must not be disrespectful of the king," Mother Anne warned her.

"Is it disrespectful to speak the truth?"

"It can be," I murmured.

Bridget, who had never been to court herself, paid no attention to our warnings. She prattled on, repeating the latest rumors. I assumed that what her husband told her had some basis in fact. The stories she picked up in the marketplace were less reliable, but she repeated those, too. Unable to tell the wheat from the chaff, Bridget was always certain they were all true.

It was from Bridget that I first heard that Sir Thomas Seymour was in residence at Seymour Place, a house in the parish of St. Clement Danes. The king had given it to him, so Bridget said, for his good service to the Crown.

I knew where Seymour Place was located. It was situated on the Strand, just beyond Temple Bar on the way to Westminster.

Although this was outside the city gates, I reckoned that it would not be a very great journey from Father's house. It was, in fact, nearer to Watling Street than Norfolk House and even easier to reach by wherry.

On the pretext of a shopping expedition to buy new shoes, I set out with Edith at an early hour. I walked rapidly to Paul's Wharf, where I hailed the first boat I saw. Edith had been sworn to secrecy but she was a reluctant accomplice and was already out of sorts because she'd had to trot to keep up with me.

"I hope you know what you're doing," she muttered as the small rowing boat took us smoothly past Baynard's Castle, Puddle Wharf, and the former monastery of Blackfriars. The old city wall ended there, but Temple Bar marked the true city limit, the point where, on land, Fleet Street became the Strand.

By water, the riverside façades of Bridewell, Whitefriars, the Inner Temple, and the Middle Temple led up to Temple Bar. Beyond that there were many great houses. The one the king had granted to Sir Thomas Seymour had once belonged to the Bishop of Bath. It had already been a very grand place, complete with orchards and gardens and tenements, when Sir Thomas began making improvements. The rebuilding had been ongoing ever since.

I told the boatman to deposit me at the private water stairs between Milford Lane—a narrow way across from the church of St. Clement Dane—and Strand Bridge Lane.

"Are you sure, mistress?" He pointed to two men who appeared to be on guard there. "They are wearing the king's livery. They may not let you disembark."

"Do as I say!" I snapped at him because, in truth, I was not at all certain I would be able to talk my way onto the property.

A challenge came the moment the rowing boat put in at the foot of the privy stairs.

I had just room enough to step out of the boat and did so, hauling Edith after me. "I am here to see Master John Harington, the vice admiral's man, on urgent business." I did not give my name.

One of the henchmen sneered, but the other, peering more closely into my face and having served at court for some time, saw more than his companion. He escorted me, with Edith dogging my heels, into the main building. Instructing a servant in Seymour's livery to make sure neither of us wandered off, he left us in an antechamber.

"Has Sir Thomas been in residence long?" I asked when the silence began to fray my nerves.

"Since the King's Majesty went to Windsor, mistress."

As the fellow did not seem to mind answering questions, I asked another. "Is this a large household? Aside from the builders, I mean."

"Comfortably so, mistress. There are twenty-four liveried servants like myself in daily attendance on Sir Thomas."

"A goodly number."

"He is Prince Edward's uncle."

Before I could ask anything else, Jack Harington entered the room and dismissed the talkative servant. He waited until his footsteps faded away before he spoke.

"What in God's name do you think you are doing, Audrey? You could ruin your reputation by coming here."

"Seymour Place is scarce a bawdy house! And I would not have come if I were not so desperate for your help."

At once his hard features softened. "What has happened? Is it Malte? I heard he was ill."

"No. No, Father is much better. It . . . it is something else." Now that the moment had come, I found it harder than I had expected to confide in him.

"Let us walk in the gardens," he suggested. "It is as private there as here, but with less potential for scandal."

I gathered my courage in the time it took us to leave the house. As we strolled arm in arm along the carefully laid-out alleys, across decorative bridges, and through banks of flowers, Edith trailing a discreet distance behind, I began at the beginning, with the day King Henry rescued me from my mother and that man Dobson. I recounted each incident that had led me to believe John Malte was not my father, ending with the king's extremely generous grant of land.

"It was not just a pension for Father, Jack. His Grace named us jointly. How can I interpret that in any other way? The king wished to provide for me because I am his daughter, not John Malte's."

Jack said nothing.

"You've suspected the same thing. You had only to look at the color of my hair."

Still nothing.

"Sir Richard Southwell believes it. Why do you think he is so anxious to marry me to his son."

Jack caught my arm and pulled me down, rather more roughly than was necessary, to sit beside him on a convenient bench. Once I was seated, he released me at once. He was always careful not to touch me more than was necessary. It was as if he feared that close contact would weaken his self-control. For my part, I tried to behave as he wanted me to, although I wished with all my heart that I could be the sort of woman to tempt him out of his reticence.

"What if Southwell learns you were here with me?" he asked. "Have you thought of that? He's not a man to be trifled with, Audrey."

"Are you afraid of him?"

"In a word—yes. You should be, too."

"And that is precisely why I am not going to marry his son."

"You could do worse."

"You?"

Frustrated, he pulled off his bonnet and used it to thwack a nearby shrub. Then he ran his fingers through his hair, leaving it standing on end. I had to fight the urge to reach up and smooth it down again.

"Yes, me. I'd marry you in a minute, Audrey, if I had the means to support you. But I have no land, no money, and no great prospects. All was going well. Sir Thomas uses me as a messenger and seems to trust me. But it appears that, after all, he is in no position to advance himself, let alone his servants."

His declaration warmed me, even as his determination not to marry me for my dowry made me want to slap him. Abruptly, I changed the subject.

"I had a reason for coming here, Jack. I need your help to get to Windsor."

His astonished expression was almost comical. "To Windsor? Why? You cannot imagine you will be allowed to speak to the king!"

"His Grace might see me. He has favored me before. But that is not my reason for going there. I hope to find my mother. My real mother. Don't you see, Jack? She is the only one who can tell me for certain who my father is."

"Is she still at Windsor? It has been years, Audrey. Is she even alive after all this time?"

"I am certain she is. Father made a will when he was ill. He left her twenty pounds."

Jack stared out across the Thames. There were a few scattered houses on the other side. Beyond, in the direction of Westminster, I could just glimpse the highest towers of the archbishop's palace at Lambeth, hard by Norfolk House.

"Sooner or later, I will doubtless be sent to Windsor with messages. Let me ask your questions for you."

But I shook my head. "I need to go myself. I need to see her face when she answers me."

"*If* she answers you." He sat with his head bowed, his elbows on his knees and his arms dangling between them. His strong hands crushed and mangled the bonnet they held. "Let me find her for you first."

"No, Jack. I must—"

"It will be difficult enough for you to devise a excuse to be gone from home long enough to travel from London to Windsor and back again. I can save you the addition of days of searching."

I had not thought through that part of things. I could not simply go haring off on my own. I would have to invent some story Father and Mother Anne would believe. "Very well. As to the other, I could say that the Duchess of Richmond has invited me to stay with her at Norfolk House. Father will not question that. I've spent a night or two there in the past."

"The duchess is at Kenninghall, as is the Earl of Surrey." His frown deepened. "No. Your plan is unwise."

"If Father finds me out, I will face the consequences, but I must talk to my mother."

Jack hesitated. "It is not that. Or, rather, not only that. The truth is, just now is not a time when you want to have anything to do with the Howard faction."

"But I will not. Not in truth. My stay at Norfolk House will be a lie."

"A lie that could come back to haunt you." He placed both hands on my shoulders, holding me so that I was obliged to meet his eyes. "I cannot explain, Audrey, but you must trust me on this. Find some other excuse that will allow you to go to Windsor when the time comes. Leave the duchess and her brother and their father out of it."

What choice did I have but to agree? His refusal to explain why he was so insistent on this point troubled me, but I have never pretended to understand the power struggles that are so much a part of the life of the court. I recalled that the Seymour faction and the Howard faction had been at odds ever since Jane Seymour replaced Anne Boleyn as King Henry's queen, but Jack had remained, or so I thought, on friendly terms with both Sir Thomas Seymour and Henry Howard, Earl of Surrey.

We took leave of each other at the privy stairs. When I turned to wave one last time, from the middle of the river, Jack had already disappeared from view. With a sigh, I shifted my attention to the route ahead. I saw that it would not take us long to make the journey back to Paul's Wharf because the tide had turned in our favor. Those boatmen rowing upriver now had to work harder. I gazed with sympathy at several small watercraft going the other way. Then my focus sharpened. I recognized the passenger aboard one of them. It was Sir Richard Southwell.

He was not looking my way, for which I was grateful. I planned to keep my face averted, but I could not resist another peek in his direction to see where he was bound. It was with a sinking sensation in the pit of my stomach that I saw his boat make for shore just beyond Temple Bar. As I had myself only a short time earlier, he disembarked at the privy stairs of Seymour Place.

This could not be a casual visit. Southwell, although he served the king, as we all did, was supposed to be the Duke of Norfolk's man, a loyal advocate for the Howard faction at court. He'd never been a particular friend to any of the Seymours, not to the Earl of Hertford nor to Hertford's younger brother, Sir Thomas. When I added Southwell's presence at Seymour Place to Jack's enigmatic warning, his words seemed doubly ominous. I returned to the house in Watling Street in a most agitated frame of mind.

34

Windsor, early December 1546

*S*een from the river, Windsor Castle rises ominously against the paleness of the southern sky. It loomed over the tilt boat that had brought us all the way from London for ten shillings apiece. The steersman and four oarsmen made the trip every few days, taking passengers back and forth on a river that was tidal as far as Teddington. It was slow going against the tide and faster with. By this water route, travelers could reach Windsor in a little more than ten hours, but at this time of year there was not that much light in a day. We had stopped for the night at Shepperton and covered the last fourteen miles the next morning.

The opposite shore of the river was heavily wooded, making it seem almost as forbidding as the castle. I felt certain there were dangerous animals hidden in the trees, everything from wild boar to wolves. That winter was almost upon us made the landscape seem even more bleak. The swans, usually so much in evidence, were ominously absent.

"There are no wolves in England," Jack assured me when I shared my concerns with him, "although there may once have been. Nor are there lions, bears, tigers, or leopards, except in the royal menagerie. Even there, these days, only four lions and two leopards remain, safely confined behind wooden railings. The worst you will find here in the wild are foxes and badgers and the occasional boar. Far more dangerous are the animals that live indoors, wearing fine clothing and smiling."

I tugged my warm, fur-lined cloak more closely around me, glad of its warmth and the protection of its hood. The chill from the water had turned my booted feet to ice and the stiff breeze blowing toward us from the shore pierced straight through all my layers of clothing.

As he'd promised, Jack had gone ahead to Windsor to make inquiries. He'd had no difficulty finding my mother. She lived in one of the small houses built right up against the castle walls. We would not have to venture inside them and risk being recognized.

In the time it had taken to make the remaining arrangements, the danger of meeting anyone we knew had decreased. The king was no longer in residence at Windsor Castle. His Grace had left for Oatlands in mid-November with what was called his "riding household," a much reduced number of attendants. The rest of the courtiers had thus been freed from their duties and could go where they would.

If everything went as Jack planned, we would talk to my mother and be on our way back to London again in a matter of hours. By sunset, another tilt boat would have carried us a goodly distance downriver. After one more night in an inn, we'd continue on to the city. I had spent two nights away from home before without arousing suspicion. What I had never previously done was lie to Father about where I would be. I'd told him that I was going to stay with Lady Heveningham—Mary Shelton—at her brother's house in the parish of St. Helen's Bishopsgate.

With Edith close beside me, I followed Jack toward the ramshackle dwelling where my mother lived. It was set a little apart from the others, nearer to the river than most.

I smelled it before I saw it. My mother still earned her living as a laundress. A wooden bleaching tub sat beside the privy for the collection of urine. Not far away, in a larger tub, discolored sheets and table linen soaked in a thick green mixture of water and summer sheep's dung.

I stopped.

"Audrey?" Jack sounded concerned. I knew that if I changed my mind, he would escort me back to London without demur.

"It has been many years since I thought about how much hard work is involved in producing clean laundry."

"You were very young when the king rescued you. I am surprised you remember anything at all."

"I can still recall how tired my mother was at the end of each day. Making soiled linen clean again is a long and backbreaking process." I moved closer to the tub. "Soaking it is only the beginning."

"Here, you! Leave that be!" My mother stood in the doorway, a basket full of dirty shirts and shifts balanced on one hip and a belligerent look on her face.

If not for her dark eyes, I would never have recognized her. Her complexion, always on the swarthy side and sometimes sunburnt, had turned sallow and unhealthy looking over the years. Her arms were as muscular as ever, from all the hard work she did, but the rest of her had gone soft and fleshy. Even her hair, although she could not yet have passed her fortieth summer, showed signs of age. Where it was visible, hanging in limp clumps that escaped from beneath a greasy kerchief, the brown had gone as grizzled as any crone's.

Her eyes narrowed. "So you've come back, have you?"

"You know who I am?" It was a foolish remark, but the only thing I could think of to say to her.

"It would be hard not to know you with that hair." Abruptly, she turned her back on me, pretending to check on the linens in the buck tub.

Tension radiated from her like heat from the sun, making me wonder if my sudden appearance alarmed her. I had no idea what the king had said to her, or to Dobson, on that long-ago day when he'd given me to John Malte to raise. Had she been paid to relinquish me? Or punished for mistreating me? Or had King Henry simply snatched me away to prevent me from being beaten again?

"I mean you no harm," I said.

"Then go away."

"I have come a great distance to speak with you. I . . . I have questions."

She glanced at me over her shoulder. Slowly, her expression changed. Her gaze swept over me from head to toe, taking in my well-made clothing, my few pieces of jewelry, and the fact that I had both a gentleman and a maidservant in attendance.

I sighed. It was all too obvious that she was calculating my worth. "I can pay you for information."

Father had always been generous with what he called "pin money" and I had saved a modest sum over the years, especially after Bridget married and left the house and could no longer help herself to what was mine. I had been able to pay my own fare, and Edith's, for the tilt boat and afford lodgings at the inn. I still had several gold and silver coins in the purse concealed beneath my kirtle.

Behind me, I heard Edith's familiar mutter of disapproval. Jack reached out to me. The brief touch of his hand on my arm steadied me and gave me the courage to continue what I had begun.

"How much?" my mother asked.

"Two gold angels."

"You have done well for yourself, girl, if you carry that much money about with you."

When I did not respond, she abandoned her work and led us into the little house. It was dark and dirty inside, smelling of unwashed bodies and wood smoke. A fire burned fitfully on the hearth but provided little warmth. She did not offer us refreshment but there was a bench to sit upon. I settled myself there while she plopped herself down on a three-legged stool.

"Nothing but ill luck has befallen me since the king took you away," she said before I could ask my first question.

I considered my surroundings, taking note of the lack of anything that might indicate that the odious Dobson shared them with my mother. "Where is your husband?"

"Long gone. After the king took away his post in the castle, what else was he to do? He blamed me."

"When it was all my fault?" I finished before she could say the words.

Looking sulky, she picked at a chipped fingernail and refused to meet my eyes.

"I want to know what the king said to you that day." That was not all I wanted to know, but it was a place to start.

"He was angry because Dobson struck you." Suddenly defensive, she glowered at me. "A father has a right to deal with a child as he will."

"Dobson was not my father."

"He was your stepfather. It was not your place to defy him."

"Nor the king's?" I took a breath and blurted out the question I most needed to have answered. "Is he my father? Am I King Henry's child?"

The change in her was immediate. Her irritation with me was

replaced by a far stronger emotion, one there was no mistaking. It was fear I saw in her eyes before she averted her gaze.

It had not occurred to me before coming to Windsor that by telling me the truth my mother might place herself in danger. I had not anticipated the possibility that she might have been threatened to keep silent about my paternity. Or bribed. Or both. Did she fear that if she made such a claim about the king, even if she only confided in me and in private, she could be taken up for treason?

"I swear I will not repeat to anyone what you say to me." I leaned forward to take her rough, work-worn hands in mine.

She looked past me at Edith and Jack. "Tell them to go away."

"Leave. Please," I said without glancing over my shoulder. I heard the faint rustle of Edith's skirts and the shuffle of Jack's boots as they honored my wishes. The door closed behind them with a thump.

My mother freed herself from my grip and crossed her arms over her bosom. Even in the dimly lit hovel I could tell that she was glaring at me. "You were never anything but trouble! I should have gone to the village wise woman and done away with you before you ever drew breath."

It hurt me that she hated me so much, especially when it was far too late to change anything that had happened. I rebuilt the shield around my heart and plunged ahead. "Who was my father? What man did you lie with in the year before my birth?"

"I did couple with the king." For a moment Joanna—it was easier to think of her by her Christian name than to regard her as my mother—allowed herself to look smug. The expression faded quickly. She had harbored too much resentment for too many years. "He was mad for Anne Boleyn in those days and she would not let him into her bed. I had something of her coloring in my dark hair and in my eyes. The king wanted to swive her but she held him off.

So he bedded me. Called me Nan once or twice while he was at it. Men!"

"Then I *am* his child?"

I'd thought myself prepared for this moment, but I had not. If the king was my father, why had he never acknowledged me? Why had he given me away? Why had Father—John Malte—*lied* to me? That last was the most hurtful thought. The suspicion was not new, but it pained me that I might finally be obliged to accept the truth of it.

"You . . . might be," Joanna said.

"You are in some doubt? How can that be?"

At the astonishment in my tone, she gave a bitter laugh. "How do you think? The king was not the only one who bedded me. I liked coupling in those days. I went with any man who asked me and a great many did. How do you think King Henry found me, eh? He followed one of his courtiers to my bed."

"Did . . . did you lie with John Malte?"

"I may have. I hear he claimed you were his get."

"He was well rewarded for doing so by the king." This time it was bitterness that laced my words. "But surely, even with so many men, when you discovered that you were to have a child, you must have considered which one was most likely to have fathered me."

"Oh, I had one or two likely prospects—the ones who had money."

"And then I was born and you saw that I had bright red hair. That must have put an end to your doubts."

"Ah, there's the pity of it. The king was not the only redheaded man I let into my bed. There was another."

"Who?"

"Let me see your money first."

I reached through the purpose-cut placket in my skirt and into the purse suspended from my waist, feeling for the shape and weight of the angels. I extracted one. "The other when you answer me."

"Even if you do not like the answer?"

With a sigh, I produced the second coin. I was prepared to pay even more if it would loosen her tongue.

"I do not remember his name. I am not certain I ever knew it. He was a toothsome fellow newcome to court and he was generous with his gifts. He was at Windsor, mayhap, to present a petition to the king. Then he was gone and I never saw him again. But he had a head of flaming red hair, not unlike your own."

Her face gave nothing away. If she had invented this red-haired man out of whole cloth, I had no way to prove it. Fear of what the king might do to her if she named him as my father might have prompted her to lie, but it was equally possible that she had just told me the truth. If she had, I would never have an answer to the question of who had fathered me.

"If he was long gone before my birth, that still left King Henry," I said slowly. "He knew nothing of my existence until he found me crying that day. Why did you not approach him when I was born? Why did he not know about me?"

"The king went away from Windsor, too. And how was I to make my way to him even when he came back again?" She spat. "I am a laundress. I've no business in the king's lodgings. And once I was burdened with a squalling brat, no more courtiers came begging for my favors. I had to settle for Dobson."

All my fault, I thought. Again.

"I regret that your life has been so hard." I rose from the bench, resigned to the fact that I had learned all I would from her.

Unexpectedly, Joanna said, "Malte's a good man. He looks in on me now and again. He even gave me money when Dobson left me and took all that I had saved."

"But is he my real father? He does not have red hair."

"Mayhap he had a red-haired grandmother." She snorted a laugh.

I turned to leave. I was almost at the door of the hovel when she spoke again.

"You have far more already than most girls ever get. It would do you no harm to remember your poor old mother from time to time, or to share your good fortune."

I was a fool to do so, but I detached my purse and handed it to her. Then I left her house without looking back. I did not even wait to make sure Jack and Edith were following me. I kept walking until I reached the waiting tilt boat.

35

Catherine's Court, November 1556

Was the king your father or not?" Hester demanded.

"I was not yet certain." They were within sight of the stable and the horses, scenting hay, perked up and moved faster.

"If he was, then Bridget Scutt is not my aunt at all." Hester sounded delighted by that. "Instead I have two other aunts, and one of them is the queen. Will you take me to court, Mother? I would like to meet Aunt Mary."

"*Queen* Mary," Audrey corrected her, beginning to be alarmed. Hester was too young to realize that the queen might take exception to a claim of shared royal blood. "No more of this, Hester. I would not have us overheard."

The girl had sense enough to obey, but Audrey could see she was bubbling over with excitement. Questions threatened to burst out of her at any moment, no matter who was within earshot.

Audrey dismounted too quickly and had to grasp Plodder's mane to steady herself.

"Is aught wrong, mistress?"

She waved off the groom's concern but reached for Hester's hand.

"Help me into the house, child. I find I am in need of rest after all that exertion."

As soon as they reached Audrey's bedchamber, Hester resumed begging to visit her newly discovered aunts. "If not to court, then let us go to Hatfield. Father has been there often. I am certain we would be welcome."

Audrey was equally certain they would not. Moreover, she was suddenly beset by the conviction that it had been a terrible mistake to tell Hester anything at all about her heritage. The girl was too young to understand the danger.

She eased herself into the cushioned chair by the window and stared out at the landscape they'd just ridden through. She missed the London skyline already. How curious, she thought, since they'd be no safer in Stepney.

Hester flung herself down onto a pillow at her mother's feet. "When, Mother? When can I meet them?"

"You do not even know for certain that those two royal ladies *are* your kin." Audrey's voice was sharper than she'd intended, making Hester wince. She moderated her tone. "Let me finish my tale, my darling girl. Then we will talk about where you can and cannot go and why."

"But—"

"I understand your desire. Believe me, I do. But matters are never as simple as they seem. Will you allow me to tell you what happened next?"

A deep, sulky sigh answered her, but it was accompanied by a nod.

"On the way back to London, I shared with my companions what Joanna Dobson had told me. I was surprised when Edith remarked that Joanna was much to be pitied. She said that before she came to me, she had experienced for herself just how difficult it was to be young and female at the royal court. A noblewoman might not need to fear for her virtue, she said, and most gentlewomen were safe enough, but servants have no powerful relatives or position to protect them. They are considered fair game. Edith had felt safe only so long as she kept close to her mother, and her mother's presence only served to ward off the danger because she was in service to Lady Frances, the daughter of one earl and wife to another."

Hester frowned at this. "I remember that you said your father—John Malte—kept warning you against wandering off by yourself. And that he hired a neighbor to go with you to court, before the king sent Edith to you."

"Even the plainest girl will have the men flocking after her if she is on her own." Audrey smiled a little. "That day, leaving Windsor, Edith's revelations made Jack uncomfortable. He mumbled something about how few women there were at court. Even among the servants, men outnumber women a hundred to one. But he had to admit that perhaps Edith had the right of it. And in the end, I agreed that Joanna might be more to be pitied than reviled. I realized that John Malte must feel the same. Why else would he leave her a bequest in his will? But I still had my doubts about her truthfulness. I suspected her of lying about my paternity."

Hester lifted her head from Audrey's knee. "There must have been a way to learn more. Surely someone among the king's men, someone who was at court before you were born, knew the truth."

"That occurred to me, too, and I said so to your father. My determination to go on asking questions worried him a great deal. He warned me that I must not pursue my inquiries openly, not when they concerned the king. That, I told him, left me with only the king himself to ask."

"What did Father say to that?"

"That if His Grace had meant to claim me, he'd have done so

long ago. I'd once thought the same, but now I was of a different opinion. My memory had been jostled. I found myself recalling more about the day His Grace rescued me. It was the same day upon which Anne Boleyn was created a marquess in her own right. By the time King Henry learned of my existence, he was deeply committed to marrying her. To acknowledge me then would have angered her, and Queen Anne was legendary for her temper. I think perhaps King Henry was a little afraid of her."

"Did you convince Father of your reasoning?"

"I chose not to debate the matter with him. Besides, by then I had begun to realize that something else was bothering him. I'd sensed it throughout our journey to Windsor. I knew that furrow in his brow."

Hester grinned. She was familiar with it, too, and with what its appearance betokened.

"When I tore myself away from my obsession with finding out who'd fathered me and considered Jack's behavior, I realized that he'd been relieved to leave London behind for a few days. But most curiously, now that we were on our way back, he was passing anxious for the journey to end. It was as if he knew something of importance had happened while we were gone."

Within moments of returning to the house in Watling Street, her suspicions had been confirmed. Bridget had already been by to report the latest news from court, relayed to her by Master Scutt.

"Father was on the verge of going to Sir Jerome Shelton's house himself to fetch me home," she told Hester. "The first words out of his mouth when I walked in were: 'Has Lady Hevening-ham been questioned?' My blank stare must have told him I had no notion what had happened. He looked relieved, but then he ordered me to stay away from Mary, and from anyone else I had ever met through the Duchess of Richmond and her brother . . . with one exception."

"Why was he so upset?" Hester asked.

"While I was at Windsor, the Earl of Surrey had been arrested on suspicion of treason. Sir Richard Southwell had laid evidence against him before the Privy Council."

36

December 12, 1546

That Sunday, I went with Edith and Bridget to watch the Earl of Surrey be led through London on his way to the Tower. I vow, every citizen, every apprentice, and every stranger in London turned out to witness his disgrace.

Jostled by the crowd, I soon became separated from the others. I kept one hand on the purse I'd acquired to replace the one I'd given Joanna. The pickpockets were also out in force.

It was not idle curiosity that made me want a close look at the earl. I wished to make certain he was not accompanied by other prisoners, perhaps his sister, perhaps even Mary Heveningham. And, irrational though it was, given that Jack Harington had long since shifted his allegiance to the Seymours, I worried that he might be among them. I'd not heard a word from him since returning to London.

The earl's name was on everyone's lips, along with ever more creative accounts of his arrest. I had heard the true story, thanks to Master Scutt. Ten days earlier, even as I was making my way to Windsor Castle and back, Surrey had dined at Whitehall Palace.

The captain of the king's halberdiers, pretending he had a private matter to discuss with the earl—that he wanted Surrey to intercede with his father, the Duke of Norfolk—lured Surrey away from the crowded hall. Once the earl was separated from his own men, other halberdiers seized him and carried him away to the river stairs. A boat was waiting there to take him to Blackfriars landing and thence to Ely Place in Holborn and the Lord Chancellor, who informed him that he was to be held there, a prisoner, by the king's command.

Now charged with treason, Surrey was being taken from Ely Place to the Tower. He had been stripped of all the trappings of his rank. All his possessions, even his bay jennet, had been seized by the Crown. Thus, even though he was nobly born, the son of a duke, he was being made to walk the mile-and-a-half distance—straight through London itself.

There was no fanfare as he approached the spot where I stood waiting. No silk banners waved. The only entourage accompanying him consisted of a contingent of burly guards.

I breathed a sigh of relief when I saw that he was the only prisoner. If anyone else had been arrested, they had at least been spared the indignity of public humiliation.

Surrey himself was almost unrecognizable. In plain garments undecorated with jewels, he stared straight ahead, his countenance stoic. Onlookers, who had been noisy and boisterous as he approached, fell silent in his wake. It was usual to pelt prisoners conveyed through the city in carts with rotten produce and stones. No one threw anything at the earl.

Here and there, men removed their caps as a mark of respect. Others looked away from the sight of the once-proud nobleman brought low. This was not a day to remember Surrey's drunken rioting and window-breaking. Men instead recalled his role in the French war—his heroism and military prowess. Only the presence of the earl's armed escort prevented them from attempting a rescue. As it was, some shouted out words of encouragement to the prisoner.

Beside me, an old woman began to wail. Others echoed the lamentation, until the entire city seemed to be in mourning for the Earl of Surrey. Suddenly nervous, the guards hustled their prisoner on his way. Around me, the cries died down, but they were taken up farther along the route. Inarticulate sounds close at hand were replaced by muttered words.

"He's bound for the headsman's ax," one man said.

Public executions were a popular form of entertainment, but this fellow did not sound happy about the prospect.

It terrified me. In a panic, I broke free of the press of people and fought my way back through Cheapside. Surrey had been arrested before, but this time was different. This time the charge was treason and he was bound for the Tower, not the Fleet. I could not help but think of what had happened to two other prisoners in that terrible place—Anne Boleyn and Catherine Howard. They had died there, condemned by the same king who had once loved them both. Was Surrey truly about to join his kinswomen in facing the headsman?

I was nearly home, just turning from West Cheap into Friday Street, when Edith and Bridget rejoined me.

"Did you hear?" Bridget's eyes were bright with excitement. "The Duke of Norfolk arrived in London from Kenninghall this morning and now he is also under arrest. He's being taken to the Tower by water even as his son is marched there."

I felt as if a cold hand clenched around my heart. Thinking about Surrey's fate had been bad enough, but this was infinitely worse. "And the rest of the Howards? What of them?" The Duchess of Richmond had been at Kenninghall with her father.

"Mayhap they'll be made prisoners, too. The king has sent troops to seize all of the duke's possessions. They belong to His Grace now, for traitors forfeit all they own."

"The Countess of Surrey is at Kenninghall." There was a tremor in Edith's voice, reminding me that her mother would be there, too, in attendance on the countess's children. "Lady Frances is expecting another child in February."

I reached for Edith's hand and squeezed it.

As is ever the case, no one knew exactly what the Privy Council heard from the many witnesses they deposed, but that did not stop the good citizens of London from speculating. Within hours of her arrival in Lambeth, word that the Duchess of Richmond had been summoned to testify against her brother had reached the market-place. Rumors flew. She meant to have her revenge on Surrey for thwarting her marriage to Sir Thomas Seymour. She was bound for the Tower herself. She had tried to throw herself on the king's mercy—he was her father-in-law, after all—and he had sent her away without an audience.

Edith received a more reliable report from her mother, who wrote from Norfolk to tell her that the Countess of Surrey had been al-lowed to leave Kenninghall for one of the duke's smaller houses, although that one too now belonged to the king. Most cruelly, Lady Surrey's children had been taken away from her. Surrey's heir had been given into the keeping of Sir John Williams while the three girls and the younger boy had been placed with a loyal East Anglian landowner. Edith's mother had been obliged to choose between her much-beloved Lady Frances and the young Howards. In the end, she'd remained with her youthful charges.

Throughout all this turmoil, I waited desperately for some word from Jack. He had to have known what was afoot. Why else had he been so tense during the journey to Windsor and back?

But no message came.

Then a new rumor began to circulate. The king was said to be ill, so sick that he might not have long to live. This was good news for the earl and the duke. If the king died, he could not sign their death warrants. But it was a report that distressed me greatly and made my own need more urgent.

When I heard that the king had returned to Whitehall, I lost no time hailing a wherry and going thither. If he *was* dying, I had little time left.

Once at the king's palace in Westminster, I asked for Sir Anthony Denny. He had been knighted at the time of the invasion of France and more recently had been promoted to the post of groom of the stool, placing him in intimate contact with the king on a daily basis. It had occurred to me that if he did not know the truth of my parentage, he must surely suspect it.

I was made to wait in an antechamber, but after only a short delay, Sir Anthony came to me there, adding strength to my supposition.

"I must speak with the king, Sir Anthony."

"If you have evidence to lay against the Earl of Surrey, you must take your information to the Lord Chancellor."

"Why should you think such a thing?" I was thunderstruck by his assumption. "It is a private matter I wish to discuss—a question I must ask His Grace. I . . . I beg you, Sir Anthony. Help me if you can."

He responded to my plea with a cold look. The temperature in the small chamber, already chilly, seemed to plummet. "Your association with the Howard faction is well-known."

"I have naught to do with factions."

Thawing a trifle, he said, not unkindly, "That is wise of you. You would be wiser still to avoid anyone who might carry the taint of the earl's treason."

Something in his manner alarmed me. "You must speak plainly, Sir Anthony, for I do not understand you."

"You are a known associate of the Duchess of Richmond."

"She has been kind to me in the past. We share a love of poetry."

"And Lady Heveningham?"

Although I knew defiance was unwise, I could not stop myself from blurting out, "She is my friend."

"Sir Richard Southwell is a dangerous man to thwart." Sir Anthony sounded more exasperated than condemning. I thought I detected a hint of sympathy in his eyes.

"I will not be forced into marriage out of fear." I spoke quietly, but with as much firmness as I could muster.

"Not even fear for those you care for? Southwell has already suggested that Lady Heveningham be questioned. It would be a simple matter to add your name to that list. Or even someone who has long since entered the service of the Seymours."

Jack. Sir Anthony knew it had been through Jack Harington that I'd been introduced to the Earl of Surrey's literary circle.

"There must first be evidence of wrongdoing, must there not? If a man—or a woman—is innocent, how can they have anything to fear?"

When Sir Anthony gave a derisive snort, my heart sank. I knew better, too. If the king wished to rid himself of someone, be it wife or courtier, innocence or guilt mattered little. His Grace had always been kind to me. He had saved my life. He had given me Pocket. He had sent Jack to me.

And he had ordered me to marry Sir Richard Southwell's son. I had heard stories of King Henry's cruelty. Of his temper. I knew them to be true, even if I had never witnessed either for myself.

I wondered, for just a moment, if I *did* want to know who had fathered me. But once the king died, I would have no choice but to spend the rest of my life uncertain of my heritage. I had to find a way to ask him before I lost my chance.

"Is His Grace truly ill? Is the king dying?"

Sir Anthony shushed me, his eyes darting from side to side to make sure no one had overheard. "Above all others, that is the question you must not ask."

"Then let me ask another. Who am I, Sir Anthony? Who is my father? If you do not know, then I *must* speak to the king in private."

"That is an extraordinary request from a young woman who has no official standing at court." He tried to sound officious and failed.

My determination did not falter. I waited, holding his gaze, letting him see that I would not be swayed.

He cleared his throat. "His Grace will see no one at present but a few favored courtiers and his doctors. He will admit no petitioners. He has even banned his wife and his daughters from his presence."

"But Yuletide is fast approaching. Surely—"

"Not this year. The queen and the rest of the court have been ordered to spend the season at Greenwich. His Grace means to go to Hampton Court, taking with him only a few trusted gentlemen. Go home, Audrey. There is no place for you here."

37

The king did not return to Whitehall until the tenth of January. Although His Grace did not attend it, the Earl of Surrey's trial was held at the Guildhall on the thirteenth. The proceedings lasted eight hours. When he was sentenced to death, the earl was beside himself. He jumped up and shouted, "The king wants to get rid of the noble blood around him and employ none but low people!"

No one had any doubt that he meant the Seymours, but his words did not help his case. Only a royal pardon would save him, and King Henry continued to keep to himself, still refusing to see anyone but a few select courtiers and his physicians. Even the Privy Council no longer met at court. Instead they convened at the Earl of Hertford's London house.

As no females were allowed into the king's lodgings, not even the queen, I had little hope of seeing His Grace, but that did not stop me from trying. I could scarce haunt the court, although petitioners did flock there every day. A young woman, even one with a maidservant for company, would attract too much attention. I managed an occasional foray, but feared that if Father discovered where I'd been, he would lock me in my chamber. He would be within his rights to beat me for disobedience, although he never would.

Distressing Father was something I wished to avoid. Although he worked every day in his shop with his apprentices, he tired easily. The racking cough that had plagued him a few months earlier had never entirely gone away. And more than once I'd seen him stagger and grasp a table or a chair for support, clinging to it until he felt steady again. I could not tell if he was dizzy or nauseous or both. He would not admit to either.

There were times when I caught Father watching me, as if he had something he wished to say, but he never put his thought into words. I could only guess what stopped him, but my supposition made sense to me. If he had sworn an oath to the king never to reveal my true father's name, then he would not break that vow, no matter how much he might want to.

That January was one of the coldest anyone could remember. The Thames did not freeze solid at London, as it had once when I was eight or nine, but the roads were covered in ice. Winds howled straight up the river from the sea.

Very early on one of those frigid mornings, the Earl of Surrey was taken out of his cell and out of the Tower and up Tower Hill to where the scaffold is. I saw it once, though not in use, since women rarely attend executions. It rose some four feet above the ground, a wooden platform reached by nine steps. I am told it was draped in black on the day Surrey died.

With the Howards in disgrace, I knew that the Seymours must be in the ascendant. If the king died with Prince Edward still so young, someone would have to act as regent. The queen was the most likely candidate, since she had governed in the king's stead when he invaded France. But Edward Seymour, Earl of Hertford, had positioned himself to play an important role in any new government. He was, after all, young Edward's uncle. Sir Richard Southwell, having betrayed the Howards, now stood firmly in Hertford's camp.

I considered appealing to Sir Thomas Seymour for help in reaching the king. Even though I'd still heard nothing from Jack, I was certain he would help me again by speaking to his master on my behalf. But I hesitated to entangle him any further in my affairs, especially if Sir Anthony Denny was not the only courtier to suspect that I had feelings for him. Sir Richard Southwell had betrayed Surrey and tried to convince the authorities to question Mary Heveningham. He'd throw Jack to the lions in an instant if he thought it would help clear the way for his son to marry me.

Instead, I concentrated on wooing Sir Anthony. I wrote to him. I sent him small tokens—a songbook, an artificial flower, and finally a pair of sleeves I had embroidered myself. I'd intended them as a gift for Jack, but winning Sir Anthony's favor took precedence.

I was discouraged when I learned that the Earl of Surrey had also appealed to the king's groom of the stool, dedicating to Sir Anthony one of the translations of the Psalms he had made during his imprisonment in the Tower. It had been accompanied by a groveling prefatory lyric but neither had done him any good.

In contrast to the earl's plea, my persistence was rewarded. Sir Anthony Denny came to Watling Street, just as he had so many years before. He spoke first to Father and then to me. But this time when I set out for Westminster I left Father behind and Edith, too. Sir Anthony proposed to spirit me into the royal bedchamber and he did not want any witnesses.

"The king appears to be having one of his good days," Sir Anthony told me as we slipped through passages I'd never known existed. We were in the "secret lodgings" behind the king's official bedchamber, the rooms where His Grace could be truly private.

"King Henry arose this morning and allowed himself to be dressed, but he is far from well. One of the symptoms of his illness is the rapid shifting of his moods. You will have to be careful what you say. Do not, at all costs, annoy him."

I saw what he meant about the state of the king's health as soon as I rose from my obeisance and got my first good look at His Grace. The king's face was a pale shade of gray. With his slightest movement, beads of sweat popped out on his brow. Although he was seated, I could see that his clothes hung loosely on him, as did his skin. He had lost a good deal of fleshiness during his illness. His leg, in which an ulcer had been cauterized not long before, was propped up on a footstool. It was heavily bandaged and gave off an offensive smell.

"It is well you have come, Audrey," His Grace said. "We are prepared to acknowledge you."

"Your Grace?" I could scarcely believe my ears. Was it to be this simple?

"Your mother was an attractive woman in her day. She . . . reminded me of someone."

I remembered what Joanna had said of her resemblance to Anne Boleyn. I also remembered that the late queen's name was never to be spoken in the king's presence. Father had warned me about that.

"She said nothing of your birth," the king continued, reaching for the box of comfits on the table beside his chair. "A more ambitious woman might have tried—well, no matter. No one could fail to recognize that color of hair for what it is."

I wondered if I should tell him what Joanna had said about the other redheaded man. I decided against it. The king seemed to have no doubt but that he was my father.

"Your Grace, John Malte—"

"Malte is a good and loyal servant. It was best for you that he raise you, for we could not claim you then, no matter how much we might have wished to." He offered me the box. "Take one. Green ginger. Good for settling the stomach."

I scarcely tasted the sweet. And it was my mind that roiled.

With the knowledge I had gained in the intervening years, I understood the king's reasoning. He had been at a precarious point in his relationship with his future queen when he discovered me weeping in the passageway. Anne Boleyn would not have taken kindly to the news that His Grace had fathered another child, especially if she learned that Joanna bore such a close resemblance to herself.

I did not condemn the king for the choice he'd made. I'd had a good life as the daughter of his royal tailor. Part of me wished I truly was Malte's child. If I were simply Audrey Malte, Sir Richard Southwell would never have taken an interest in me.

"Mayhap we will let it be known that you are my child," King Henry said. "We would use our influence on your behalf. What boon would you like, child? What do you desire above all things?"

"To marry where I choose." The words were out before I could stop them.

The king frowned, as if trying to remember something. "Are you not already betrothed?"

"No, Your Grace. There has been no formal contract."

He indicated a floor cushion and I sat. In this position, much nearer the king's bad leg, I had to take shallow breaths to keep from gagging.

"Tell me, Audrey, if you were permitted to choose, what man would you have?"

His kindly demeanor and sympathetic tone of voice lulled me into answering honestly. "Master John Harington, Your Grace—the gentleman you yourself sent to me as a tutor."

In the blink of an eye, the king's expression changed from benign to thunderous. A ferocious scowl replaced the avuncular smile. "Harington? No. He will not do. Fancies himself a poet like Surrey. Traitors all around us," he muttered.

Frozen in horror, I stared at His Grace. Sir Anthony had warned me, but I had never expected the king's mood to shift this rapidly. I dared not utter a word for fear I would once again say the wrong thing.

"We had heard of the earl's musical and literary gatherings. So innocent. Or so they seemed. In truth, he met allies in order to conspire against us." The king leaned forward until his face was only inches from mine. Spittle appeared at the corners of his mouth. "You were part of that circle. You and Harington. Deceitful child! You would use your royal blood to usurp me, just as Surrey tried to claim the throne for himself."

"No!" Horrified by the accusation, I sought the words to defend myself but I had no idea what to say. "Your Grace—"

"You'll get no more from us than you have already. We will never acknowledge you as our daughter. You have betrayed us!"

He seemed on the verge of charging me with treason, and Jack along with me. I do not know what would have happened next if Sir Anthony Denny had not intervened. He had been waiting at a discreet distance but had been near enough to see the sudden shift in the king's demeanor.

He'd had long years of experience dealing with the king. Somehow, speaking in such a low voice that I could not make out his words, he calmed his royal master. When Sir Anthony signaled me to leave, I made my escape.

I was shaking so badly that I could barely manage a curtsey. My legs trembled as I backed out of the royal presence. I collapsed against the wall of the passageway as soon as a closed door separated me from His Grace.

I do not know how long I huddled there, afraid of the king's wrath but also fearful of getting lost if I tried to find my own way out of Whitehall. When Sir Anthony finally came for me, he took me by the shoulders and led me to a small room nearby. He made me sit and sip some aqua vitae.

"The king will take no action against you, Audrey. I promise you that."

"Why was he so angry, Sir Anthony? I am no threat to him. Surely a bastard has no claim to the throne."

"Did your tutors teach you history along with music and dancing?"

I shook my head. I'd read stories of King Arthur and I knew that we'd fought many wars with France over the centuries, but I was woefully ignorant about most of England's past.

"The king's father's claim to the throne came to him from his mother, Lady Margaret Beaufort, and she was descended from a son, born out of wedlock, to one of the sons of King Edward the Third. John of Gaunt later married his mistress and legitimized their children. They and their descendants were barred from the succession, but when the first Henry Tudor enforced his claim by winning the crown in battle, he proved that it was not impossible for the progeny of a royal bastard to gain the throne of England."

"Is *that* why Sir Richard wants me to wed his son? He's mad if he thinks his grandchildren might one day usurp some future king. King Henry has three children born in wedlock and surely they will have offspring of their own."

"Even failing that, there are others in line to inherit, all legitimately born. I do not know what Sir Richard thinks. I can only attempt to explain the king's reasoning."

"His reasoning is faulty!"

Eyes wide, I clapped my hand over my mouth. I had not meant

to criticize His Grace, but it was clear to me that King Henry's mind was no longer as clear as it should be. Was that why the Earl of Surrey had died? Because the king imagined Surrey was plotting against him? Given the irrational outburst I had just endured, I could well believe it. My hands started to shake again and I hastily hid them in my lap.

Sir Anthony cleared his throat. "When you speak of faulty reasoning, I presume you refer to Sir Richard's logic."

I seized upon that interpretation. "Yes. Sir Richard. I . . . I only wish to understand why he is so determined upon my marriage to his son. If it is true that the Earl of Surrey died because he thought he had a legitimate claim to the throne, how can anyone in his right mind wish to admit to possessing a single drop of royal blood?"

"The earl was indeed guilty of treason," Sir Anthony said in a tone that brooked no argument. "He flaunted his remote connection to the throne in the form of a new coat of arms. Nobly born he may have been, and renowned as a poet, but he was ever the fool when it came to reining in his impulses. He overstepped himself once too often and he has paid the price."

With that, Sir Anthony offered me his arm to lead me out of the palace. We had almost reached the water stairs, where a boat was waiting to take me back to London, when he stopped and turned to face me.

"Listen and listen well, young Audrey. You are the king's child, although he will never acknowledge you now. That may or may not matter to Sir Richard Southwell. Thanks to the properties granted to you jointly with John Malte, you are a considerable heiress. No matter whose blood flows in your veins, the man who marries you will be very wealthy indeed."

38

"My grandfather was the king of England." Hester spoke the words in a hushed voice.

Her eyes, so like her father's, glittered with barely suppressed excitement. Although she had listened without interrupting to the rest of the story, her face had been easy to read. She reacted first with awe, then with delight, to Audrey's revelation that the king himself had confirmed her royal inheritance.

"Close kinship to the Crown is a burden, not a gift."

Audrey's severe tone had no effect. Hester's enthusiasm could no longer be contained. She hopped off her mother's bed and danced a jig around the chamber. "I *will* go to court! Could I be one of the queen's maids of honor, do you think? Surely your *sister* could do that much for her niece."

"Half sister," Audrey corrected her, "and you are too young to be a maid of honor even if such a thing were possible."

Where had the child come by such an ambition? Audrey thought back on the stories she and Jack had told their daughter about life at court. Had they made it seem too appealing? Of a certainty, that had not been her own intent when she'd begun her tale in Stepney.

Hester had heard only what she wanted to hear. Audrey supposed she'd been just the same as a girl. No one could have told her, even at eighteen, that the life she envisioned for herself might not be as perfect as she anticipated. Hester was only eight. Was it any surprise that she failed to appreciate the danger?

Audrey leaned back against the bolster, gathering strength to reason with her daughter. In her present state of euphoria, Hester would want to share the discoveries about herself with everyone at Catherine's Court. That could not be allowed.

"Hester," she said severely, "this must remain our secret. You cannot reveal what I have told you to anyone."

"Why not?" She stopped dancing.

"Because, at present, Queen Mary, although she suspects the truth, has no proof of it. Her Grace is no friend to us, Hester. It is to our advantage that she not be reminded of the possibility she might have a second half sister."

"But I want to go to court. *You* went to court when you were only a little older than I am now. I want—"

"Hester!" The girl's mouth snapped shut but there was a mutinous look in her eyes. "Do you remember what happened after King Edward died?"

"Princess Mary became Queen Mary."

"Yes, she did. But not without some difficulty. And after Sir Thomas Wyatt the Younger led a failed rebellion in Kent in an attempt to prevent her marrying the king of Spain, Queen Mary put many people in prison. Your father was one of them."

Hester's voice went very quiet. "I remember. And you went away, too."

"I will tell you more of that in good time," Audrey promised, "but what you must remember now is that Queen Mary is no less dangerous than King Henry was. On a whim, any king or queen can imprison a subject . . . or execute him. A careless word on your part could lead to your father's death. Or mine. Or even your own."

Audrey hated seeing fear replace joy in her daughter's eyes, but it was necessary that she understand the enormity of the secret she now shared.

"I will not tell anyone that I have royal blood," Hester promised in a shaken whisper.

"Come here, then, and give me a kiss." Audrey's limbs felt so heavy that she could scarce lift her hand to touch Hester's shoulder as the child bent to brush her lips across her mother's cheek. She bade her daughter leave her alone to rest awhile, promising to speak with her again when she had recovered her strength.

As soon as Hester had gone, Audrey turned her face toward a corner of the room. There a second door, covered by a curtain, led into the chamber Jack used as a writing room. She was unsurprised when her husband moved out of the shadows. She'd sensed his presence at just about the time she'd been telling Hester what Sir Anthony Denny said to her after the interview with King Henry.

"You told her."

The accusation in his voice stung, the more so because she knew she deserved his censure. It *had* been unwise to burden a child so young with this dangerous knowledge. But what choice did she have? Audrey's sense that time was short increased with each passing day. She had not regained her former health or strength. Despite brief remissions, she was growing steadily weaker.

Aloud, she said only, "It was time she knew."

"She need never have known."

His long strides ate up the distance between door and bed until he was looming over her. She looked up into his scowling face. The expression, though ferocious, had no power to frighten her. She knew full well that Jack would never hurt her, not in any physical way.

"The rest of what I will tell her," Audrey said, "will serve as a cautionary tale. She will come to understand the need for secrecy when I am done."

"Will she? She is eight years old, Audrey. Too young to have any sense of discretion. You accused me of endangering our family, endangering our child, but I vow you have just taken a greater risk than I ever did!"

After Jack stormed out of her bedchamber, Audrey lay very still, staring up at the canopy above her head. Her vision blurred as un-shed tears gathered in her eyes. Jack was right. But he was wrong, too. She herself had gone too long without knowing the truth. Hester had a right to hear it, and from the one person who could share the entire story with her, not just bits and pieces.

Determined to continue her tale on the morrow, Audrey willed herself to sleep.

A nightmare jerked her awake in the wee hours of the morning. She cried out, and Jack's arms came around her, holding her until she stopped shaking.

"What was it?" he asked.

But she could only shake her head. The details of the bad dream were already fading. She did not want to call them back.

She fell asleep the second time with her head resting on Jack's chest, but he was gone when she awoke. By the time she broke her fast and dressed, he had left the house. Despite a steady rain, he had gone out on horseback.

"Have the fire built up in the withdrawing room," she ordered her maid, "and have someone send my daughter to me. Then no one is to come near us for the remainder of the morning."

As soon as Hester appeared, Audrey intended to resume her narrative. She required both warmth and privacy for the telling. Reliving what had happened next would not be easy.

39

John Malte's House, January 1547

I never saw the king again. He died in the early hours of Friday, the twenty-eighth day of January. I did not know that right away. King Henry's death was kept secret for the better part of three days. Even the queen was not told at once. The Seymours were busy putting everything in order for the succession of their nephew, who would reign as King Edward the Sixth. He was nine years old.

On the last day of the month, a Monday, Edward Seymour, Earl of Hertford was created Duke of Somerset and named Lord Protector of the realm. His first act was to dissolve Parliament.

"What about Queen Kathryn?" I asked when Bridget brought word of this to Father and Mother Anne in the house in Watling Street. "I thought she would be named regent."

Father, seated in his favorite chair close to the fire, was wrapped in a blanket against a chill. His cough had worsened with the prolonged cold weather. News of the king's death, although it was not unexpected, had affected him badly. He did not even look up at my question.

"You thought wrong," Bridget said. "The Seymours are in power now."

"Sir Thomas, too?"

"Master Scutt says he's to be created Baron Seymour of Sudeley and Lord High Admiral."

"And how does he know all this?" I demanded. "Your husband has lost his post, has he not, now that there is no longer a queen at court?"

Bridget laughed. "I would not be so certain of that. The Lord Protector has a wife, and she has already commanded Master Scutt to make new clothes for her—rich clothes as fine as any the queen ever had. She's taken possession of Queen Kathryn's jewels, too, those that Her Grace did not have with her when the king died."

The Seymours in power might not be such a bad thing, I told myself. As far as I knew, Jack was still in Sir Thomas's service. If Sir Thomas rose in prominence, so would Jack.

Then another thought occurred to me. "What of Sir Richard Southwell?" Since his betrayal of the Earl of Surrey, he, too, had been allied with the Seymours.

"There's talk of a place for him on the new king's Privy Council." Bridget chuckled. "And how could I forget? Your beloved is back in London, Audrey. Young Darcy, or should I say Master Richard Southwell the Younger, has moved into his father's old chambers in Lincoln's Inn."

"He is not my beloved," I muttered.

Two days later, Sir Richard and his son paid Father a visit.

"My husband is ill," Mother Anne told them. "I'll not have him upset."

"Move aside, woman." Sir Richard pushed her out of his way and entered the hall. He studied Father's shrunken form for a moment before speaking, as if trying to decide whether flattery or bluster would work best.

"You have delayed long enough, Malte." His voice was close to a shout. "I have the marriage contract with me. The details were hammered out months ago. Now is the time to sign, you and Audrey both."

I noticed he did not say "you and your daughter." I took this as more proof, although I did not need any, that Southwell knew I was the king's bastard and wanted me for his son for that reason and that reason alone.

I placed myself between the angry knight and the man who was, in all ways that were important, my father. "I do not intend to sign, Sir Richard. Not ever. And I cannot be forced into marriage."

"I would not be so certain of that."

I glanced at the younger Richard. He would not meet my eyes, but I knew that he did not want to marry me any more than I wanted to wed him. I wished I could count on him to stand with me and say so, but his craven manner convinced me that he would never disobey his father.

"Give me a little more time, Sir Richard." This feeble whisper came from Father. He did not lift his head to look at any of us as he spoke.

"You've had more than enough time already. This business has dragged on for years. Everything is in place. Sign and we'll complete the formalities as soon as the banns can be called. Better yet, I'll secure a special license and Richard and Audrey can wed at once."

Father abruptly stood, as if to defy Sir Richard face-to-face, but the effort was too much for him. He staggered, then fell forward to land hard on the hearth. Sir Richard was closest to him, but he made no effort to catch him or to break his fall.

Mother Anne and I rushed to Father's side and helped him to sit up. Dazed, he looked at me as if he did not know who I was. With an effort, we got him to his feet. Sir Richard still did nothing to help. At least his son, after one agonized glance in his father's direction, stepped in to take Father's weight from us and help him shuffle into his bedchamber.

Sir Richard followed at a leisurely pace and watched in stone-faced silence as we got Father into bed. Mother Anne sent a servant for a posset. Only after she'd coaxed Father into swallowing a few sips of the healing brew did Southwell speak in a low, menacing rumble of sound.

"This is not finished, Malte. The king's death has changed nothing. In truth, I have even more influence in this new reign. You might think on that while you recover."

Having uttered that vague but very real threat, he turned on his heel and left the house. Young Richard rushed out after him.

The slam of the door in the shop below us made Mother Anne jump it was so loud. I winced. Father's eyes flew open and he reached for my hand.

"I want you to be safe after I am gone, Audrey." His pleading gaze broke my heart, as did the lack of strength in his grip. His fingers slid away from mine, too weak to hold on. "Southwell looks after his own."

"And when I am no longer useful to him? I'll not be safe then." I thought of the Earl of Surrey and a shudder ran through me.

"You must marry someone, child," Mother Anne put in. "And that boy is not his father. There is kindness in him. Wed him, bed him, bear a child or two, and your life will be your own again."

"No, it will not. Once I have a husband, he will own everything, even the clothes on my back. A wife is no better than a slave. The only hope I have of happiness is to marry a man who truly cares for me. You have had that happiness with Father. How can you ask me to accept anything less?"

"You still want Jack Harington," Father whispered, "but the man has no estate and no fortune of his own. He is a good man, Audrey, but he cannot provide for you or protect you."

"Nor have you seen him for some time," Mother Anne put in. "He has accepted that his pursuit of you is futile. You must do the same."

I nearly blurted out that I *had* seen Jack, and not so very long ago, either. Only two months had passed since our journey to Windsor Castle. I caught myself in time. It would only distress Father to learn of that trip, and to know that I had sought Jack out at Seymour Place. I let him continue in his belief that it had been years since we'd last met.

"Whatever man marries me *would* have the wherewithal to protect me. He'd have control of *my* inheritance."

"You will never be able to tell, Audrey, if such a man loves you for yourself or only wishes to wed you for the land you will inherit when I die."

Fighting tears, I dropped my gaze to my hands. They were clenched so hard that the knuckles showed white. I could say no more without causing Father greater distress, but that was not the only reason I wanted to weep.

I loved Jack Harington, but he had never once said that he loved me, only that he would wed me if he could. It did little to soothe my troubled thoughts to remember that he had behaved nobly, refusing to ask for my hand for exactly the same reasons Father gave—his poverty and lack of prospects.

And what of the other, I wondered—my royal inheritance? That strain of Tudor blood, tainted though it was, had value only if it was acknowledged by the king and now His Grace was gone without ever revealing my true identity to the world.

I frowned in confusion. If there could never be any proof of my parentage, then why was Sir Richard Southwell still so intent upon my marriage to his son?

"My lands will make me a considerable heiress," I said aloud, "but there are other heiresses far more wealthy than I am. Why has Sir Richard not pursued one of them for his son?"

"He wants *you*." Father's whisper was weak but still audible.

"Why?"

"What does it matter? He will not give up. The more you resist, the more determined he will become to have his way."

Was it that simple? A craving for power over others? I swallowed convulsively, remembering that Sir Richard Southwell had brought down one of the most powerful families in England. The Duke of Norfolk was still a prisoner in the Tower and under sentence of death.

As if she read my thoughts, Mother Anne said, "Sir Richard will leave us in peace once you agree to marry the boy."

Abruptly, I stood. "I must be alone. To think."

Responsibility weighed heavily upon me. I did not believe that Father had long to live. Once he was gone, who would protect those he left behind? Mother Anne and the servants and the apprentices would be almost as vulnerable as I was. My actions could bring disaster down upon us all.

I fled the sickroom and the house, pausing only long enough to don my warm cloak. I dashed into Watling Street, catching Edith off guard. By the time she gathered her wits and tried to follow me, I was already out of sight.

Desperate to get away from everyone, I had no destination in mind as my running steps slowed gradually to a fast walk. Oblivious to my surroundings, deaf to the noise and confusion all around me, I pushed my way through the throngs of people clogging London's streets. I paid them no heed, but I tried in vain to ignore my own chaotic thoughts.

40

At length, when I stopped and looked around, I realized that my feet had carried me into East Cheap and then north along Bishopsgate Street. The former priory of St. Helen's was within sight.

The servant who answered the door of Sir Jerome Shelton's house radiated suspicion. I suppose that was only natural, given the events of December and January. Deciding that he would not be likely to tell me if Lady Heveningham was staying there, even if she was within, I contented myself with asking if he would deliver a message to her. With obvious reluctance, he agreed. I gave him my name and asked that she be told I wished to speak with her. Then I left.

I had walked no farther than the Merchant Taylors' Hall before another servant came running to fetch me back. Mary Heveningham welcomed me with open arms.

We cried together over the fate of the Earl of Surrey.

After she roundly cursed Sir Richard Southwell for his part in the downfall of the Howards, I admitted that Sir Richard was the reason I had sought her out. My story did not take long to tell. She had guessed most of it already.

"Do you *want* to claim royal blood as your inheritance?" she asked me in her familiar blunt fashion.

"No!"

"That is wise. But consider that it is also true that your dowry is sufficient to make Sir Richard determined upon the match. And for a certainty, that wretched man does not like to be thwarted."

"Let him find some other heiress!"

"Young Richard is baseborn, Audrey. That counts against him with some girls' fathers."

"But a bastard is good enough for a bastard? Is that it?" I let my bitterness show.

"Still," Mary said thoughtfully, "there may be some advantage to continued resistance. I have not done so badly refusing to be rushed into marriage."

"But Tom Clere died," I objected.

For a moment, her eyes swam with unshed tears. She hastily brushed them away. "He did. And I will grieve all my life for him. But I have a good husband and a fine healthy daughter and am about to return to them. I only came to London to fulfill a promise to the duchess."

I was suddenly ashamed. I had not even thought to ask after the Duchess of Richmond. "Where is Her Grace?"

"At Reigate in Surrey, not so very far away. She has been granted the care of her brother's daughters."

"And their governess?"

"Your Edith's mother? Yes. She is with them. They're safe enough, and have sufficient funds to live upon, although all of the duchess's possessions were confiscated by the Crown at the same time they took everything that belonged to her father and brother.

She was fortunate the king allowed her to keep the clothes on her back."

"Will they execute the duke?"

Mary shook her head. "I wish I knew. That is why I came here—to present a petition to the new Privy Council to spare Norfolk's life. The Lord Protector granted me a few minutes of his time, but he was not encouraging. I very much fear that, at the least, the duke will remain a prisoner so long as young Edward is king."

"I pray the king will spare the Duchess of Richmond's father," I murmured, acutely aware that it had been my own father, who even now still lay in state in Westminster, who had imprisoned Norfolk and wanted him dead.

"And I will pray that God spare yours." At my startled look, Mary said, not unkindly, "John Malte, Audrey. Perhaps he is not as ill as you think. Has a physician been called in?"

"He will not have one. He consulted a doctor the last time he was seriously ill and the treatments the fellow prescribed were so distasteful, and so ineffectual, that he lost all faith in medical men."

"A healer then? Some wise woman skilled in the use of herbs?"

But I shook my head. "He'll take possets from Mother Anne—his wife—but naught else. And those do little but ease his pain. I fear he is dying, Mary. He grows weaker every day. I . . . I think he has lost the will to live, especially after word reached him of the king's death." As Mary had, I swiped at my tears before they could fall. Fishing a handkerchief out of my pocket, I blew my nose.

"I am saddened by your grief, my friend, and you will not like me much for saying this, but it will serve you best if John Malte does not recover."

At first I did not think I could have heard her correctly, but she repeated this outrageous statement, adding, "You know already that one of the few rights a girl has is to refuse a marriage that is distasteful to her. There is another part of the law you may not have heard. I suspect that men keep silent about it for their own advantage. It is this: a girl who is fourteen or older and not yet betrothed to anyone at the time of her father's death can inherit in her own right. So long as she remains unmarried, she keeps control of her property and her person. You must not, no matter how great your desire to ease John Malte's mind, allow him to extract a deathbed promise from you. Stand fast, my friend, and you will soon be free."

I swallowed hard. This was good news, but it brought with it a terrible sense of guilt. How could I wish for Father to die the sooner? I loved him. I wanted him to live as long as possible. And I was certain that, unlike Mary's father, John Malte would never force me into accepting a betrothal against my will.

I returned home in an even greater perturbation of mind than when I'd left.

I do not like to remember the days that followed. Father was in pain and I made it worse by refusing to countenance a betrothal. Without Mary's warning, I might well have thought to ease his suffering with a lie, making a promise I had no intention of keeping. Had I done so, my fate would have been sealed. Such a vow, before witnesses, is binding.

The funeral cortege taking King Henry's body to Windsor for burial left Westminster on the fourteenth day of February. On the fifteenth, John Malte breathed his last.

We were all at his bedside. Mother Anne and I had been in nearly constant attendance for weeks. At the end we were joined by Mary, Elizabeth, Bridget, and Muriel and their husbands.

"I've named you executor," Father said to John Scutt, although he had to pause for breath between words. "You and Bridget together. Anne will give you my will when the time comes."

Bridget looked so pleased that I wanted to kick her.

"Take care of Audrey. She has no one else."

Scutt frowned but promised.

Then Father turned to me. I feared he was about to ask me once again to agree to marry Sir Richard Southwell's son, but he only smiled a little sadly, closed his eyes, and died.

Mother Anne and I clung together, weeping, for a very long time. By the time I recovered myself enough to pay attention, Bridget had Father's will in hand and was working herself up into a fine fury over the provisions.

"Listen to this!" she exclaimed. "To Joanna Dingley, otherwise Joanna Dobson, twenty pounds. Five pounds to the foundling child left at my gate. To Audrey Malte my bastard daughter begotten on the body of Joanna Dingley, now wife of one Dobson, the manor of Andesay otherwise Nyland in Somerset." She stopped reading, her face purpling with rage. The list of manors in my inheritance, I supposed, went on and on and on.

"Father was generous to all of us," Muriel said in a futile attempt to cool her sister's temper.

"But he loved *her* best. It was ever so!"

I knew from long experience that it was no good trying to reason with Bridget. I ignored her outburst and concentrated on comforting Mother Anne as best I could. Of all of us, she would feel Father's loss most deeply. Adding to her grief was the responsibility of running the tailor's shop and seeing that Father's apprentices finished their training. She would have to decide whether to take over, as was her right as a widow, or sell out to another member of the Merchant Taylors' Company.

The new king's coronation took place a few days after Father died. The entire city turned out for his procession through London to the Tower. They celebrated with bonfires and fireworks when he was duly crowned. Although King Edward was just a little boy and

England would, it seemed, be ruled by his uncle, the Duke of Somerset, most ordinary citizens looked upon the change in the monarchy as a reason for celebration. King Henry had not been as popular in his last years as when he first came to the throne. Many hoped the new regime would be better.

I simply hoped that Sir Richard Southwell had less influence with the new king than with the old one. In this I feared I was to be disappointed. He sent word through John Scutt that he awaited my agreement to the marriage contract he and Father had negotiated.

"I am past the age of fourteen," I informed Bridget's husband. "I am of age to inherit on my own and to decide my own fate, as well. Tell Sir Richard that I will not marry his son and that I will never change my mind."

That son left his studies at Lincoln's Inn to come to the house and ask to see me. I refused to speak with him.

Master Scutt delayed submitting Father's will for probate, which meant I had no ready money of my own and no way to claim the lands bequeathed to me. I therefore also lacked the wherewithal to do anything but stay on in Watling Street with Mother Anne.

Although she was still deeply sunk in her own grief, she kept a watchful eye on me. I could tell that something worried her. That suspicion was confirmed when she took me aside and warned me to guard myself well anytime I ventured out of the house.

She looked as if she wished to say more but was unsure whether she dared voice her thoughts.

"What have you heard?" I took both her hands in mine and willed her to meet my eyes.

"Nothing."

"Then what do you suspect?"

She pulled free of my grip and went to stand by the window. "What do you see from here, Audrey?"

"John Scutt's house."

"The day you turned Southwell's son away, he left here and went directly there."

I considered that. As executor of Father's will, Master Scutt had already shown himself willing to delay handing over my inheritance. Such meddling did not alter my rights. I could not be forced into marriage. Indeed, if he continued to withhold my property, I could take him to court.

Confident that, in time, any legal issues would be settled in my favor, I counted my blessings. I had a roof over my head and food in my belly. And even though he was now a very old dog, I had Pocket to cuddle when I needed comfort.

41

February 27, 1547

On the first Sunday in Lent, we went to church as we always did. The congregation included my sisters and their husbands, all of us still wearing mourning for Father, as we would be expected to for some months to come. Mother Anne would wear black for him for the rest of her life.

I avoided Bridget and Master Scutt, but Mother Anne spent some little time talking with them before we returned to the house. Her worried frown warned me she had more bad news to impart.

"Does he still refuse to fulfill his duties as executor?" I asked. "Mayhap it is time to consult a lawyer."

"It is more than that." Unaware that she did so, Mother Anne twisted her hands in the fabric of her skirt, clenching and releasing, clenching and releasing.

I took her arm and led her to the window seat with its view of the street below. "Tell me. Together we will deal with it, whatever it is."

"You are a good girl, Audrey, but it is yourself you must have a care for, not me. Bridget has never made any secret of her resentment of you. I fear she has let envy rule her. And now Sir Richard seems willing to make it worth her while to conspire with him—"

"Conspire? To do what? No one can force me into a marriage I do not want."

"I do much fear you may be wrong about that. Heiresses have been kidnapped ere now. And priests bribed." She seized me by the shoulders, her fingers biting into my arms. "There is no denying that men are stronger than women. You could easily be carried away against your will. Imagine yourself in some remote spot, all the doors locked and guarded by Sir Richard's men. If, then, his son forced himself upon you to consummate the marriage, there could be no possibility of an annulment."

"But if there is no marriage, no betrothal, that would be rape."

"You could be beaten into submission. Thrashed until you signed the papers."

The picture she painted was an ugly one. I wanted to say she was imagining things, but it was all horribly possible. What recourse would I have if I were subjected to such treatment?

Best to avoid any chance of being captured by such villains, but if Bridget was in league with Sir Richard . . .

I slept little that night. With both Father and King Henry gone, I had only myself to rely upon. I'd heard not a word from Jack Harington since the day he'd brought me back from Windsor Castle. I thought he was still with the new Baron Seymour of Sudeley, but I was not even certain of that.

I needed the protection of someone more powerful than I was if I wished to keep my freedom. There was only one person I could think of who might be persuaded to take me in.

In the very early hours of the next morning, I ordered Edith to pack my belongings and hire a cart to take my boxes to Paul's

Wharf. I told the boatman where I wished to go and in short order we were headed westward on the Thames. It was bone-chillingly cold. The waterman said there was ice-meer in the water—cakes of ice that floated up from the bottom of the river, where it was frigid enough to freeze. Stones and gravel came up with it, making travel by water more hazardous than usual.

Halfway to my destination, we passed Norfolk House in Lambeth, only it was not Norfolk House any longer. It had been seized by the Crown and then King Henry had granted it to Queen Kathryn's brother. I wished him joy of it.

A bit more than an hour after embarking, I stepped ashore at the royal manor of Chelsea. The gardens stretched down to the river, but in February there were no colorful blossoms. Even the evergreens looked dull and lifeless.

The house itself was built of brick, with small turrets and many chimneys. It had been designated the dower house of the queen dowager, Kathryn Parr.

I took a deep breath and, leaving Edith to see to my possessions, boldly approached the liveried guard at the gate. A few minutes later, I was shown into Queen Kathryn's privy chamber.

"Mistress Malte," she greeted me. "How unexpected to see you here, and at such an early hour."

My obeisance was as deep as I could make it without tumbling over. "Your Grace, I have come to ask a boon."

"Have you indeed. I was under the impression that the king had been most generous to you."

She knew, I thought. She knew for a certainty that I was King Henry's daughter.

"His Grace was most generous to *my father*," I said, stressing the relationship to John Malte, "because of Father's long years of service to the Crown," I added. "But I fear there are unscrupulous persons who wish to prevent a good man's last wishes from being carried out."

A flicker of interest showed in the queen dowager's hazel eyes. One of her carefully plucked eyebrows lifted. "Tell us more."

I told her *almost* everything. Since she knew the truth, she could surmise the rest. Aloud I said only what I was content for the world to know—that Sir Richard Southwell pursued me for his son because I had a goodly dowry and, now that I had the freedom to refuse, was plotting with my half sister to force me into an unwanted marriage.

I did not realize that Princess Elizabeth was also at Chelsea Manor until a rustle of brocade gave away her presence. She had heard all I'd said to her stepmother.

If there was anyone who could understand a half sister's jealousy, it was Elizabeth Tudor. From an early age, she and Mary, King Henry's daughter by Catherine of Aragon, had been at odds, simply because Elizabeth's mother had replaced Mary's as queen. Elizabeth remembered me from that long-ago progress. And I remembered that, at the time, I had wondered if it had been a question about my parentage that had been responsible for the king's decision to send his daughter away.

The queen dowager, too, seemed to find something in my plight that she could sympathize with. "You fear and despise the young man's father," she said. "Knowing Sir Richard, I can understand your feelings. But is there more to your reluctance to wed an otherwise unobjectionable young man? Is there another, mayhap, you'd prefer to take as your husband?"

I hesitated. "I thought there was. I . . . I think he has been frightened off."

Some strong emotion flickered across the queen dowager's

features but it was gone again so quickly that I thought I might have imagined it. I did not imagine her compassion.

Pocket chose that moment to poke his head out of the placket in my skirt. He was no longer overweight. Indeed, he reminded me a little of Father at the last, shrunken and wasting, but he still held a place in my heart and he loved me unreservedly.

"Why, it is the little dog the king gave you!" Princess Elizabeth exclaimed.

I drew Pocket out. "He is very old now for his breed, but I could not abandon him."

"Nor will we abandon you, Mistress Malte," the queen dowager said. "For as long as is needful, you shall have a place in my household."

42

Chelsea Manor, March 1547

*T*he queen dowager's entourage at Chelsea was not unlike that she'd maintained as queen consort. A number of her ladies remained with her and she'd been joined not only by her step-daughter, Princess Elizabeth, and Elizabeth's household, but also by her sister Anne, the wife of Lord Herbert. He used Baynard's Castle as his London residence, and since Lady Herbert's three-year-old son was there, she spent much of her time traveling back and forth on one of the small row barges at Queen Kathryn's disposal.

Within days of my arrival, another familiar face turned up at Chelsea, bringing a message to the queen dowager from the Lord Admiral. Jack Harington's eyes widened when he caught sight of me among the women in the queen's presence chamber, but more than an hour passed before he was able to seek me out in private.

"What are you doing here, Audrey?"

We were alone in a quiet gallery and he had me pinned between his arms, one on each side of me, his palms resting against the wall that supported my back. I was hemmed in. Surrounded by him. And yet nowhere did his body touch mine.

I glared at him. "Keeping myself safe. And you?"

Taken aback by my blunt reply, even though it was in direct response to his own rude question, he dropped his arms and stepped away from me. "Safe?"

"Yes, safe." I stayed where I was. "Did it not occur to you that I'd need protection after my father died?"

"Whi—? You mean John Malte?" He took off his bonnet, slapping it against his thigh, and raked his fingers through his hair until it stood up in disordered peaks. "I was saddened to hear of his death, but with the king so recently dead . . . That is no excuse, and well I know it. I should have sent a message of sympathy. I should have attended the funeral. I do most sincerely beg your pardon, Audrey."

"I suppose your employer keeps you busy."

I do not know why I wanted to ease his conscience by making excuses for his neglect. Who can explain the attraction that draws one person to another or the urge to defend one's beloved? I knew full well that Jack Harington had flaws, but from very nearly the first moment I saw him, when I was still a child, I had felt a powerful bond with him. As I grew older, the need to have him in my life had blossomed into desire. It no longer mattered to me that my feelings for him were so much stronger than his for me. This was the man I would have for my husband, or I would take no husband at all.

"I am Lord Seymour's man," Jack said. "I do as he bids me. Of late, that has meant that I am here at Chelsea as often as I am at Seymour Place."

For a moment, I did not grasp his meaning. I'd been so absorbed in reacquainting myself with his physical appearance—his tall, muscular form, his thick brown curls, those brown eyes with their amber flakes in the depths—that his words had made little impression. I shook myself free of carnal thoughts and sent him a hard look of another sort.

"Why *are* you here?"

He laughed. "Can you not guess? The Lord Admiral Sir Thomas Seymour is most assiduously courting our widowed queen, as he has been ever since he received word of the king's death."

I must have looked shocked, because he laughed again.

"Why do you find that surprising? They are in love. They have been since before Kathryn Parr caught King Henry's eye. It was the Lord Admiral's interest in her, back before he *was* Lord Admiral, that prompted His Grace to send Seymour abroad on one mission after another. Anything to get him out of the country and keep him far away from court."

"Is that why Sir Thomas did not pursue a marriage to the Duchess of Richmond?"

Jack nodded. "One reason, at least. His feelings for the queen have been one of the worst-kept secrets at court. I am surprised you were unaware of them."

"I did not go to court all that often," I reminded him. "And of late the only news I've heard has come through my sister's husband."

It was cold in the long, nearly empty room. Drafts seeped in through the many windows. But when Jack indicated that I should sit on a padded bench in front of one of them, I was willing enough to oblige. I caught his hand and pulled him down beside me. Knee to knee, his gloved fingers clasped in mine, I told him everything that had transpired since the last time I'd seen him.

When I got to the part about Sir Richard Southwell's plan to kidnap me with Bridget's help, he let out a low whistle. "I always knew she hated you, but such wickedness is beyond belief."

"Believe it, Jack, for I do." I marveled that he, who had lived at court so long, could be surprised by anything. Perhaps it was that a woman was involved.

"Does Sir Richard know where you have gone?" he asked.

"Not yet, but he is sure to learn of my whereabouts eventually. When that happens, I pray that the queen dowager can keep me safe."

"You are of age and—"

"Merely having the law on my side may not be enough to save me, not if Sir Richard is high in favor in the new regime."

His face a solemn mask, Jack confirmed my worst fear. "He is on the Privy Council, and he is one of the Lord Protector's favorite toadies."

"There must be something more I can do to protect myself."

Jack stared out at the bleak landscape beyond the window. "The Lord Admiral is not without influence. He's the new king's uncle, too. I will speak to him, Audrey. And I can ask the Marquess of Dorset and his wife for help. I was kindly received by them when I carried messages back and forth concerning the Lord Admiral's plan to advance the interests of their eldest daughter at his nephew's court."

I frowned, trying to sort out what family he meant. I was not familiar with every title, and several noblemen had been advanced in the peerage in the new reign, thus changing the names by which they were known. "Who are they?" I asked.

"Lady Dorset was born Lady Frances Brandon. Her mother was the late king's younger sister."

My *cousin*, I thought. We'd never met and I wondered if she had ever heard of me and if it would make a difference if she had.

"After the negotiations I conducted on the Lord Admiral's behalf, Lady Frances's daughter, Lady Jane Grey, went to live at Seymour Place in the care of Lady Seymour, the Lord Admiral's mother." Jack was already speaking softly, but he lowered his voice still more. "If all goes according to the Lord Admiral's plan, the Lady Jane Grey will marry her cousin the king."

This scheme was of little interest to me. I was only concerned with one thing—would the Dorsets lend their support to my cause. "Will they help me if you ask them to?"

"I think they will. Their influence, added to that of the Lord Admiral and the queen dowager, should be sufficient to keep you safe from Southwell's machinations."

"If you are so certain of that, then why do you still look worried?"

His frown smoothed out as if by magic. "It is nothing."

I sighed. Jack now sat as far away from me as the window seat allowed, careful not to touch me even in the most casual way. And yet I did not think it was because I repelled him. I was certain the most obvious solution has already occurred to him, and if he would not voice it, for whatever reason, then I knew I must. "I would be truly safe from Sir Richard Southwell once I wed someone else."

My words hung between us. Jack took a long time to respond to them. Too long. I tried to take comfort from the fact that he did not react with surprise or distaste or even discomfort. It was that he did not react at all that defeated me.

"Say *something*," I begged him, "even if it is to tell me that you cannot bear the sight of me."

"My dearest Audrey! How can you think such a thing?"

"How am I to think otherwise? You said once that you would marry me if you had land and wealth, but you have never said that you loved me. You are a poet, but you have never made me the subject of one of your poems! And now that I am truly free to choose my own husband, you still say nothing."

"I still have nothing to offer a wife."

"You do not *need* anything. I am an heiress."

"Unless Scutt contests the will. Or destroys it."

"I would still come into a considerable fortune in land. I have the right of survivorship in the king's grant—a manor called

Kelston in Somerset, a house called Catherine's Court, and four hundred ewes."

"Sheep?"

"Yes, sheep. Will you marry me for my ewes, Jack?"

"I will marry you for you, Audrey."

And then, *finally*, he gathered me up in his arms and gave me a proper kiss.

43

Chelsea Manor, April 1547

ir Richard Southwell did not quite dare threaten the queen dowager, but he made it clear he was not leaving Chelsea until he had spoken with me. "She is my son's betrothed," he insisted.

"I am no such thing," I assured Queen Kathryn.

She addressed Sir Richard in a stern voice. "Have you signed a pre-contract?"

Sputtering, on the very verge of swearing in Her Grace's presence, Sir Richard finally had to admit that he had not. I breathed a little easier. I had been afraid he'd counterfeit one. It would not have been difficult to forge my signature, or my father's.

"A word with the young woman, Your Grace? In private."

"I cannot permit you to hound her, Sir Richard. Her maid will accompany her and at least one gentleman, and that is only if she agrees to speak with you."

Since I had a thing or two I'd like to say to Sir Richard, now that I felt he'd been put in his place by the queen dowager, I consented.

"Are you certain this is wise?" Jack asked. He'd been at my side throughout Sir Richard's audience with Queen Kathryn. He'd followed at once when he'd learned from one of the Lord Protector's servants that Sir Richard was on his way to Chelsea.

"You will be with me. And Edith."

"Best take Pocket along, as well. If all else fails, your little dog can bite him." Pocket had, quite sensibly, taken an immediate dislike to Sir Richard the first time he'd caught a whiff of him.

We adjourned to an antechamber. Sir Richard sent Jack a baleful look, having no doubt by now about who his son's rival was. How long he'd known, I could not begin to guess, but it scarce mattered any longer.

"Ever the knight-errant," he sneered.

"Jack and I intend to wed. You can do nothing to stop me from choosing my own husband. I know the law on marriage."

I did not like the way he was smiling.

"I cannot stop you," he agreed, "but there is one who can. The king is your half brother, Audrey. You know it and I know it and soon the king will know it."

I could not see what difference that would make, but the pressure of Jack's hand on my arm warned me not to speak, not even to deny that King Henry was my father, until Sir Richard revealed what he had in mind.

"His Grace has two half sisters already, Mary and Elizabeth. Legally, both of them are also bastards, since the late king's marriages to their mothers were annulled. King Edward would regard your situation as no different from theirs." He paused, to make sure I was following him. I was not, but when I said nothing, he continued, his tone that of a teacher speaking to a dull-witted child. "A king's kinswomen are subject to his control in the matter of their marriages, no matter how old they are."

This threat had teeth, but I had been intimidated by this wicked man for far too long already. "You are mistaken, Sir Richard, in thinking that King Henry fathered me. He did not."

"Can you prove it?" He laughed, certain I could not.

I had the good sense not to answer him and, after a moment, still chuckling to himself, he left.

"*Can* you prove it?" Jack asked.

I threw my arms around him. "Yes! The wording of John Malte's will proves I am *his* merry-begot, not the king's. He even names my mother."

"But Audrey, for all you know, John Scutt destroyed your father's will. It has not yet been probated."

"We have to convince him to produce it. Failing that, those who have read it must be forced to come forward."

"Bridget?"

The reminder earned him a scowl but did not dent my certainty. "I will find a way. I cannot believe Master Scutt would destroy the will. There were too many witnesses to its making. And besides, it contained generous provision for Bridget and her son. If the estate has to be divided among Father's heirs, as it will if Father is declared to have died intestate, then Bridget could well end up with less."

"I will ask the Lord Admiral to lend his support. And you must talk to the queen dowager. She still uses Master Scutt's services, does she not?"

"She's had little need for them, being in mourning, but that will not last forever. In the meantime, the Lord Protector's wife is his patron. She is the Lord Admiral's sister-in-law. Perhaps—"

Jack cut me off with a short bark of laughter. "I would not look for help from that quarter. The Lord Protector and his wife have refused to return Queen Kathryn's jewelry, even those baubles she owned before she married the king. For that reason alone, there is no love lost between the brothers."

"Still, you will try, will you not?"

"I will do my best," he promised, "but we must proceed with caution. The last thing you want is to remind Sir Richard of the existence of that will."

I resolved to bide my time, but others saw no point in waiting for what they desired. The plans Jack and I had made were thrown into confusion by love. Not my love for Jack, but the Lord Admiral's for Queen Kathryn and hers for him. Too impatient to let a respectable period of mourning pass, they wed in a private ceremony shortly before April turned into May.

The secret was ill-kept, at least at Chelsea. The servants and the ladies who attended the queen dowager knew that the Lord Admiral spent his nights in Queen Kathryn's bed. Rather than be thought a whore, she told a select few of her household the truth and they spread the word. By mid-May everyone knew.

"You should follow our example," Queen Kathryn advised me. "You are free to wed whatever man you choose, just as I was as a widow. Why not do so? Let the legal matters sort themselves out later."

I saw the sense in what she said even as I recognized the irony of her words. There was a storm coming over her hasty marriage. At court, her new husband was just waiting his chance to speak with King Edward in private so that he might ask the young king's blessing for their union. Without it, should the news break too soon, the Lord Admiral might even find himself in the Tower for having had the audacity to wed a royal widow without prior permission. Queen Kathryn, whether she was willing to admit it or not, was bound by the same law that controlled the marriages of the king's half sisters. It was treason to marry one of His Grace's kinswomen without first securing royal approval of the match.

"What *would* happen if we married now?" I asked Jack when he returned to Chelsea with a message from the Lord Admiral to his wife—a report that, as yet, he'd had no success in meeting with the king.

"I have been thinking about that. It is possible that the very fact of our marriage might push Master Scutt into producing the will. He knows I have powerful friends. I just wish we knew whether or not Sir Richard has had anything to do with Scutt since you slipped out of their clutches."

"Mother Anne might know." I felt a pang of guilt. I'd left a note telling her I was going somewhere safe, but I had not been in touch with her since taking refuge at Chelsea. For all she knew, I could be dead.

Jack went in secret to the house in Watling Street. He returned with Mother Anne's blessing on our union and the news that Bridget had complained long and loud about Sir Richard's failure to do as he had promised and send new business Master Scutt's way.

"Southwell openly snubbed Scutt at court," Jack reported, "acting as if he was too good to be seen associating with a mere artisan. He made a mistake there."

"Bridget will never forgive him," I agreed. "She'll help me now, if only to spite him."

As soon as the banns could be read in Chelsea church, Jack and I were wed. It was a quiet ceremony, with only the queen dowager and the Lord Admiral as witnesses. The next day, we paid a visit to my sister and her husband to announce the happy event.

Bridget looked down her nose at us. To her mind, I'd married a nobody. Jack had no profession and no fortune of his own.

A few minutes of conversation made it clear that Master Scutt knew nothing of Sir Richard's latest threat.

"Once probate is complete," Jack reminded him, "Audrey will be in a position to reward you for your services as Malte's executor, and your own wife will be able to claim her inheritance."

Scutt sent a fulminating glare Bridget's way, making me think she had been the one responsible for the delay. She smiled sweetly back at him.

"I'll see to it," Scutt promised.

I hid my elation, lest Bridget turn against me again. If Scutt kept his word, there would be no more claims that I was King Henry's daughter. Once John Malte's will was properly entered into the official record, I would have documentary evidence to the contrary.

We went next to Mother Anne to announce our marriage, then visited my other sisters and their husbands. By the time we left London for Kelston, the largest part of my inheritance, I was at peace with all my kin.

We planned to live quietly in Somersetshire. Kelston was an idyllic setting for newly wed couple. Edith was with us, and little Pocket. Although the house had not been lived in for some time, it had been in the care of an industrious housekeeper. We settled in to wait for all the legalities to be settled.

The first good news to arrive was word that the will had been probated, thus rendering Sir Richard Southwell's latest threat impotent. When he learned how he'd been thwarted, his first reaction would be anger and a desire for revenge. We resolved to rusticate awhile longer, giving his temper time to cool.

In July, news of the queen dowager's remarriage became public. The Lord Protector was furious with his brother the Lord Admiral. Fortunately for the Lord Admiral, he had already succeeded in obtaining the young king's enthusiastic approval.

"They are safe," Jack reported, looking up from the letter that brought us this news.

"Thank the good Lord. They deserve their happiness."

"As do we."

I smiled at him. The weeks just past had been the most blissful of my entire life. Having established beyond a doubt that I was Audrey Malte, I was now quite content to be, only and forever, Audrey Harington.

44

Catherine's Court, November 1556

The fire in the withdrawing room had burned down to ashes by the time Audrey stopped speaking, but she did not call for a servant to build it up again. It would do no good. She felt the cold deep inside herself where no flame could warm it. It was as she had feared. It hurt almost as much to relive moments of great happiness as it did to remember those filled with grief.

Hester stood and stretched. "I wish we could acknowledge being kin to the queen, but I am glad you and Father were able to wed." She grinned. "I should not be here if you had not." She headed for the door.

"Where are you going?"

At the sharpness of Audrey's question, Hester turned in surprise. "To the hall. I want to look at the portraits."

They lined the walls—Audrey and Jack, King Henry, King Edward, Queen Mary. There were even small ones of the Lord Admiral and the queen dowager, a gift on the occasion of Audrey's wedding to Jack.

With an effort, Audrey hoisted herself out of the chair and

followed her daughter. There was more she needed to tell her, and perhaps seeing the likenesses of those she'd talked about would enhance her words.

Hester stopped first in front of the picture of Queen Kathryn. "I know what happened to her. She died in childbirth."

In her innocence of such matters, she said the words easily. She had no idea how many good women perished just as they achieved their greatest triumph. Audrey herself had almost succumbed. After Hester was born, the midwife had told her she was unlikely ever to conceive another child.

Audrey indicated the likeness of Thomas Seymour, Lord Admiral of England. "It was not long after his wife's death that Seymour attempted to break into the bedchamber of his nephew the king. He killed one of the king's dogs, lest it sound an alarm."

This elicited a horrified gasp from Hester, who was as fond of dogs as she was of horses. Audrey, too, had been appalled by the Lord Admiral's act, the more so because, at the time, she had just lost, to old age and infirmity, her own longtime companion. She'd buried Pocket in her garden just a few days before news of the Lord Admiral's arrest arrived at Kelston.

"You were not yet a year old when he was executed for treason by his own brother, the Lord Protector. As I told you, your father was in the Lord Admiral's service. He delivered messages for him and therefore was privy to many of the Lord Admiral's plans."

The worried look in Hester's eyes told Audrey that her daughter had an inkling what she would hear next.

"Jack was arrested, too. He was in prison for over a year."

"But he was released. It all ended well." Hester moved on to the portrait of King Edward and frowned.

"The young king reigned only a few years," Audrey said. "Upon his death, the country was very nearly plunged into civil war. That was averted, but more plots against the new queen, Mary, were quick to surface."

"I remember," Hester said. "I was old enough by then to know something of what was happening. You and father were both taken away. Did Father conspire against Queen Mary?"

"Never! No more than he knew of the Lord Admiral's plans to kidnap King Edward. But innocence does not guarantee safety. You will remember that I spoke of Sir Thomas Wyatt the Younger?"

Hester nodded.

"He attempted to march into London and capture Queen Mary to prevent Her Grace from marrying Philip of Spain. People were in great fear of Spanish rule in those days."

And of the return of Catholicism to the land, Audrey added to herself. That fear had been well founded. They were all good Catholics now, under the rule of Mary and Philip, no matter what they believed in their hearts.

"The Duke of Suffolk was to raise the Midlands," she continued. "That was the Marquess of Dorset, Lady Jane Grey's father. He'd been elevated in the peerage two years earlier, when his wife's brothers died. Poor Lady Jane was already in the Tower of London, for she'd been a pawn in an earlier scheme to keep Mary Tudor from claiming the throne. At the time of Wyatt's uprising, your father was at Cheshunt. He had just delivered a letter to Princess Elizabeth at Ashridge when two of the duke's brothers, on their way to join Suffolk, stopped there for the night. They tried to convince Jack to join with them. He refused, but the mere fact that they'd spent the evening together was sufficient to condemn your father in the queen's eyes."

"Did Wyatt mean to put Elizabeth on the throne in Mary's place?"

"Some say he did. No one really knows."

From what Audrey had heard since, the leaders of the rebellion had been a confused lot with conflicting goals and little in the way of organization. Any well-trained housewife could have mounted a better campaign.

"It scarce matters what his goal was," she continued. "Queen Mary was suspicious of her half sister and that suspicion extended to everyone associated with her, including your father. He was accused of being a conspirator and imprisoned in the Tower of London. Then the queen ordered Elizabeth to come to London and lodged her, under guard, in a secure corner of Whitehall Palace near the privy garden."

Hester listened attentively, her eyes wide. Audrey prayed for the strength to make her understand what the rest of her story meant. Hester had not asked again to go to court and meet her royal aunt, but that did not mean she had given up her ambition to be a maid of honor. In telling her daughter the next part of the story, Audrey hoped to dissuade her, once and for all, from ever trying to trade on her royal inheritance.

She drew in a strengthening breath. She needed her wits about her now more than ever. When she'd begun, her only goal had been to make certain that her daughter did not grow to adulthood in ignorance of her heritage. Audrey would not have wished that fate on anyone. But now there was more she must do. The simple truth was out but it was not enough. Now she must shape her remaining memories into a cautionary tale, to prevent Hester from misusing her newfound knowledge.

45

When word came that Jack was back in the Tower, I at once made plans to leave Somerset for Stepney. We'd acquired our house there some three years earlier. Even though he'd just spent many months imprisoned for no greater crime than being one of the Lord Admiral's loyal retainers, he'd laughed when he first noticed that we had such an excellent view of his former prison. Then he'd recited the epigram he'd written on the subject of treason:

> *Treason doth never prosper. What's the reason?*
> *Why if it prosper, none dare call it treason.*

That was how he passed his time while incarcerated for the first time—writing. He translated Cicero's *The Book of Friendship* and composed verses, including a sonnet to the Lord Admiral that, had anyone seen it, would most likely have added to the length of Jack's imprisonment. The poem ended with a couplet:

Yet against nature, reason, and laws
His blood was spilt, guiltless without just cause.

I did not like to think what new verses my husband might be composing. He was temperate in speech, but he seemed to believe that expressing his thoughts as poetry gave him license to say what he would. The day after my arrival in Stepney, I applied to visit him. When that request was denied by the constable of the Tower, I presented myself at court and begged an audience with Queen Mary.

King Henry's eldest daughter had been at Ashridge the one summer I went on progress with the court but I had never been presented to her. I did not think she had noticed me. For the most part, I had stayed well in the background, even though I was made welcome in Queen Kathryn's household.

When I arrived at Whitehall Palace with my petition for Jack's release I expected to spend days, if not weeks, awaiting the opportunity to plead my case. I was not the only suitor hoping to see the queen on behalf of a loved one. Between those who'd been involved in the futile attempt to put Lady Jane Grey on the throne in Mary's place when King Edward died and the rebels who'd joined with Sir Thomas Wyatt the Younger and the Duke of Suffolk in this more recent rebellion, a great many men were currently locked away.

It was already too late for some. The Duke of Suffolk had been executed. So had his daughter, Lady Jane Grey, despite the fact that she'd had naught to do with this latest uprising. Wyatt yet lived, no doubt because the queen hoped to persuade him to implicate her half sister, Elizabeth, in his treason.

On the second day of my vigil at court, one of the queen's ladies, recognizable by her russet and black livery, came for me. She led me into the queen's privy chamber, where Queen Mary sat not on a throne, but on an ordinary chair, her hands busy with needlework.

She was beautifully dressed, in a gown of violet velvet. Her skirt and sleeves were embroidered in gold. At first glance, all this magnificence disguised the fact that in her person she was rather plain.

Filled with trepidation, I approached Her Grace. Now that the moment was upon me, I was terrified that I would say the wrong thing and make things worse for Jack.

She squinted at me when I rose from my curtsey—she was notoriously shortsighted—and bade me come into the light shining through the window beside her. Even though the queen was seated, I could tell that she was of low stature, much shorter than I was. I tried not to stare, but I could not help but think that she had not inherited much from her father. Her hair was a dull reddish brown instead of the true "Tudor" red. She did have King Henry's fair skin, but her face was as lined as that of a much older woman—she was thirty-eight at that time—and her lips were thin and bloodless. Her eyes were her most prominent feature, large and dark.

When she spoke it was in a powerful, almost mannish voice. "We are told, Mistress Harington, that you have a petition for us."

"Yes, Your Grace. I have come to beg you to release my husband from the Tower. He has done nothing wrong."

"Has he not? We have met John Harington, madam. He is a most pernicious fellow. This is not the first time he has attempted to meddle in the succession. He acted as a go-between when the late Lord Admiral conspired with the Marquess of Dorset, as he was then, to marry the Lady Jane to King Edward."

"I know nothing of that, Your Grace."

I lied with a straight face. I knew all about the messages he'd carried back and forth between the two men, and that Lady Jane Grey had been sent to Seymour Place and the keeping of the Lord Admiral's mother in order to be closer to court and the young king. Shortly after I married Jack, the Lady Jane had gone to live at Chelsea with the queen dowager. She'd remained with Queen Kathryn until Her Grace's death and had served as chief mourner at her funeral.

The queen continued to stare at me, making me so nervous that I burst into speech. "My husband spent nearly a year in the Tower for no other reason that he was one of the Lord Admiral's gentlemen, but in the end he was freed and pardoned."

"Pardoned for what crime, madam?" She leapt on that like a dog on a bone. "To have been pardoned, he must have been guilty of something. Come, we know he played a role in the Lord Admiral's schemes. And then there is his faith. He composed a certain scurrilous hymn that the late king our father did like to sing."

"He was a very young man when he wrote that, Your Grace. At the time, the Church of Rome had been banished from the land."

My fervent defense caused an ugly red color to suffuse the queen's face. I bit my lip, wishing I had kept silent.

Queen Mary leaned forward to peer more closely at my features. "You seem familiar to us, Mistress Harington. Have you been at court before?"

"My father was John Malte, the royal tailor."

The queen jerked back as if she had been struck. In that instant, I knew that she had heard the old rumor about me. I'd have suspected Sir Richard Southwell of repeating it to her, except that I'd already heard that he'd fallen out of favor in the new regime. Uncertain what to say, I said nothing. The queen was silent, too. Then she waved me away.

"Return on the morrow. We will speak with you again then."

I backed out of the privy chamber in a state of profound confusion.

I was no less befuddled when I returned the following day. Another of the queen's ladies was on the lookout for me. She escorted me to a small room furnished only with a prie-dieu and the large, ornate cross on the wall in front of it. She instructed me to wait there.

Obedient, I stood and stared at the low desk. It had a space for a book above and a cushioned kneeling pad below. Once every home had had one of these, but they had gone out of fashion after King Henry broke with Rome in order to end his marriage to Catherine of Aragon. Queen Mary, Catherine's daughter, had steadfastly refused to give up her faith. Now that she was on the throne, she intended to restore the religion her father had tried so hard to replace.

Tentatively, I knelt. The cushion felt odd beneath my knees but I folded my hands in front of me and bowed my head. If ever I had needed my prayers to be answered, this was the day, but no words came to me. I did not know what to pray for. That Jack be innocent? I feared he was not. That the queen would pardon him? Would that be enough? While I was still wrestling with this quandary, the door behind me opened and closed.

When I tried to stumble to my feet, the queen's gruff voice ordered me to remain on my knees. Having shifted onto the bare floorboards, I froze, half turned away from the prie-dieu.

"It is good to find you at prayer," Queen Mary said. "Do you accept the true faith?"

"I . . . I am in need of instruction, Your Grace. Much has been forgotten. Even the priests do not seem to remember what to do."

She nodded, accepting the truth of that assessment. Her religious practices had been outlawed for more than fifteen years. "Instruction will be provided for you. And for your daughter."

I swallowed convulsively. It frightened me that the queen knew about Hester but I thanked her for her consideration. Then I waited, so nervous of what she would say next that I could scarce hold still.

"There are some who say you are not John Malte's daughter at all."

I had tried to prepare myself for this line of questioning. I knew I must continue to deny that I had any trace of royal blood. Furthermore, I must make the queen believe me. I cleared my throat.

"It is clearly stated, in both John Malte's will and in a royal grant given him for loyal service, that I am Malte's bastard daughter by Joanna Dingley. On the one occasion when I spoke to my mother about rumors to the contrary, she assured me that John Malte had fathered me."

"So you did have doubts?"

I managed a weak smile. "I heard the rumors, too, Your Grace. But I am satisfied that they are untrue."

"You bear a strong resemblance to the Lady Elizabeth."

"A coincidence only, Your Grace." My nervousness increased at the form of address the queen chose to use. Not *Princess* Elizabeth but the Lady Elizabeth. What did it mean that the queen would not call her half sister, the heir to her throne under King Henry's Act of Succession, by her rightful title?

"There are many red-haired men at court," the queen murmured.

"Yes, Your Grace."

She nodded, as if I'd just confirmed something she'd thought for a long time. Belatedly, I realized what it was. She did not believe King Henry was my father because she did not believe he had fathered Anne Boleyn's child, either. The claim that Elizabeth was not the king's child had been made before, when Queen Anne was tried and executed for adultery, but most people did not believe it. One had only to look at Elizabeth Tudor to see King Henry.

It was not to my advantage to point this out. I kept my mouth shut.

"You wish me to release your husband, Mistress Harington. In good time I will do so, but freedom must first be earned."

"Your Grace?" I could not imagine how Jack could earn his freedom so long as he was locked up.

"You will earn it for him," the queen explained, "by entering the service of the Lady Elizabeth and reporting back to me everything she says or does that is the least suspicious."

What choice did I have? I agreed.

46

Tower of London, March 18, 1554

I was thrust upon the Lady Elizabeth on what must have been one of the worst days of her life. It was Palm Sunday, when almost everyone was in church, that she was taken forth from confinement in Whitehall Palace and escorted to a waiting barge. I was already aboard and I had known for some days what our destination would be. Her Grace had no warning, although she must have feared this outcome from the moment she arrived in London. To make matters more difficult still, her guards waited until the last moment to tell her that most of her ladies must be left behind. She could not help but resent anyone chosen as a replacement.

That she recognized me was not in doubt, but she had other things on her mind. She did not bother to demand an explanation for my presence. No one save her sister the queen could have selected the attendants who would wait on her during her coming incarceration.

We were rowed rapidly downstream. Since the tide was low, we could pass beneath London Bridge without danger of being dashed to bits, but once on the other side, I had an unobstructed view of what was about to become my prison, too.

Small clouds of kites and other carrion birds flew up in front of the barge, an evil omen. But at least, given the state of the tide, we were unable to enter by water through the Traitors' Gate. I counted it as a small blessing when we landed at Tower Wharf instead. We walked into the massive fortress by means of a drawbridge.

Sir John Gage, Constable of the Tower, came forward to escort the Lady Elizabeth to her lodgings. She maintained a stoic fortitude until she saw that there were armed guards standing all along the way she must pass.

"What? Are all these harnessed men here just for me?"

"No, madam," Gage assured her. "They are present at all times."

"They are not needed for me," she said with an attempt at irony. "I am, alas, but a weak woman."

Some of the guards doffed their caps as she passed by. One knelt and cried out, "God save Your Grace!"

The way was narrow in places, and there were more drawbridges. We were in the middle of one of them when a terrible sound rent the air. It was so loud and so unexpected that it made me jump. One of the other ladies turned pale and another let out a squeal.

"You have nothing to fear," Sir John assured us. "That is just one of the lions in the royal menagerie."

I remembered Jack telling me that there were four of them and two leopards. Kept behind wooden railings, he'd said. Poor things. They were prisoners, too.

The Lady Elizabeth faltered only once, when she passed beneath the Bloody Tower and caught a glimpse of the scaffold erected at the far side of the court. It was the one where her cousin—my cousin— Lady Jane Grey had so recently been executed. No doubt it stood in the same spot as the earlier scaffold Anne Boleyn had mounted to meet the headsman specially imported from France to sever her neck with a sharp, merciful sword instead of an ax.

Sir John hurried us along past the grisly sight and through Coldharbor Gate, the main entrance to the inner ward. He led us not to some dank dungeon, or even to a single cell, but into the royal apartments—the same ones where Anne Boleyn had lodged before her coronation and again when she awaited execution.

There were four chambers—a presence chamber, a dining chamber, a bedchamber with a privy, and a gallery. The latter adjoined—although that door was now locked—the king's apartments. Beyond there was also a bridge across another moat that led in turn to a privy garden. The whole was comfortably furnished and the Lady Elizabeth would be attended by a full dozen servants, but it was still a prison. The door through which we entered had two great locks in it. Sir John kept the heavy keys that fit them.

"Your hall and kitchen staff will be accommodated on the other side of the Coldharbor Gate," he told the princess. "Your meals will be brought to you here."

"And for exercise?" the Lady Elizabeth asked. "Are there leads upon which I may take the air? Am I to be permitted to venture into the garden?"

"For the present, my lady, you must remain within." He backed hastily out of her presence. The sound of the keys turning in the locks sounded as loud as cannon fire.

In silence, my half sister explored her prison. The bedchamber was large and well appointed. A fire warmed it and tapestries had been hung on every wall to keep out the drafts.

"Leave us," she instructed the few women she'd been allowed to keep. "All except Mistress Harington."

When we were alone, I flung myself to my knees in front of

her. "I am not here by my will, Your Grace. The queen gave me no choice."

Elizabeth's dark eyes, so like my own, bored into me for a long moment. Then she gestured for me to rise. "What threat does she hold over your head?"

"It is my husband, Your Grace. You know him well, I think. He is here in the Tower, on suspicion of complicity with the rebels."

"Was he complicit?"

"I . . . I do not know. I do not think so. It seems to be the fact that he is known to have delivered a letter to Your Grace that brought him to the queen's attention."

A rueful smile played about her lips. "Ah, yes. But the queen can prove nothing, can she? There is no evidence of wrongdoing."

Sir Thomas Wyatt might still be tortured into implicating others, but I kept that thought to myself.

"You have been instructed, I presume, to spy upon me."

"Yes, Your Grace."

"And will you tell the queen everything you hear and observe?"

"No, Your Grace, although I must tell her something."

She nodded, accepting that. "I will be careful to say nothing incriminating in your presence." And then she laughed. "If you are to pretend to serve me, you may begin at once. Fetch my other ladies. Then you must unpack the few belongings I was permitted to bring with me. At least I am allowed my books and paper and ink."

I wondered if she meant to write poetry, as Jack had during his last imprisonment.

Elizabeth Sandes, one of the Lady Elizabeth's most faithful servants, sent me a hate-filled look as she swept past me. "Lady Harington," she sneered. "We know all about you."

I could not fathom what she meant, but I accepted that my

presence was resented. The princess might trust me, but even she would not befriend me when anyone could see us. I was resigned to being shunned. I told myself there would be compensations. In the end, Jack would be freed. The queen had promised it. And in the interim, I would be permitted conjugal visits.

In the days preceding the first of these, Mistress Sandes took to falling abruptly silent whenever I passed by, as if she had been talking about me. When she tired of that, she made a point of asking if my husband had ever written a poem in my honor.

He had not, but I lied and said he had.

"Master Harington penned poetic tributes to six of the princess's maids of honor when we were last at Hatfield."

"He is inspired by many things, Mistress Sandes."

"One of those pretty young women had the honor of receiving two poems written to praise her beauty and her virtues . . . and perhaps more." Her smirk left unclear whether she meant more poems or just . . . more.

"How lovely for her," I said, and walked away. Either interpretation meant that Jack had favored another woman over me. That was a bitter pill to swallow.

The very next day, I found a scrap of paper among my possessions. On it was written a poem. The verses shook me to my core, for I could not help but read the worst possible interpretation into them.

> *Oh! most unhappy state,*
> *What man may keep such course,*
> *To love that he should hate*
> *Or else to do much worse:*
> *These be rewards for such*
> *As live and love too much.*

It was Jack's work, to be sure, and enigmatic in many ways, but I took his words to mean that he had never loved me—that he was close, indeed, to hating me. And that now he loved another. The mysterious maid of honor at Hatfield, I presumed.

On Easter Sunday, after the mass celebrated in the Lady Elizabeth's rooms by a priest the queen had sent, I was taken to see my husband.

Jack was lodged in far less sumptuous quarters in the Broad Arrow Tower, a squat structure two stories high that could only be entered by way of a staircase in the north turret. His cell was not as bad as it might have been. He had a pallet and bedding, candles, a brazier and coals to burn in it, a table, and a chair. And he had books and papers and pen and ink, which I suspected were more important to him than food or drink.

"Audrey?"

Under other circumstances, the astonishment in Jack's voice would have been insulting. Clearly, no one had warned him to expect a visit from me. Nor, it seemed, did he know that I, too, now resided in the Tower of London. I lost no time apprising him of the situation.

"Queen Mary trusts you? Are you certain?"

"They both do, I think. The queen expects me to do what I must to free you. The princess accepts my word because she trusts you and knows I would never betray her."

"Truly, I do not deserve you," Jack murmured.

"What I deserve," I told him, "is the truth. I could not answer the queen's questions because I did not know what you had been up to at Ashridge and elsewhere, but I assured Her Grace that you are innocent. Are you, Jack?"

"I did nothing more than take a letter to Ashridge from the Duke of Suffolk in which he advised the princess to leave there for the greater safety of Donnington Castle. She'd already been given the same advice by others who had some inkling of what was afoot. She may even have been considering following it, but the queen's ministers learned of the rebels' plans before she could do so."

"Her Grace was questioned about Donnington in my hearing," I told him. "Members of the Privy Council came to the Tower to interrogate her. At first she said she could not remember owning a house by that name. Then she recalled the property but pointed out that she had never visited it. Finally, she agreed that there might have been talk among her officers of going there but she turned the tables on the councilors by asking why they should question her right to travel to any of her own houses at any time."

"How did they react to being challenged?"

"One or two looked skeptical, but others were won over. The Earl of Arundel, upon leaving, threw himself to his knees and begged Her Grace's forgiveness for having troubled her."

"Is Her Grace well? In good spirits?"

I assured him she was. "She is to be allowed to walk for exercise twice a day in the privy garden and also in the great chamber adjacent to her lodgings."

Jack sent a scornful look at the four walls that contained him. "Then she is fortunate indeed. Fresh air is a luxury here, as is open space. And for everything there is a fee. Have you money?"

"A little. A purse hidden beneath my skirt."

"Keep it for now, but if I send to you for it, do not hesitate to give it to the guard who brings the message. I have all but exhausted what I had. First I had to pay to be unshackled, then to have all this brought to me." His gesture encompassed everything in his cell.

I was appalled by the notion that had he not had a few coins with him at the time of his arrest, he'd have been chained to the wall. Now that I looked, I could see the bolts that secured unfortunates there. Then I glanced again at the table.

"I see that you paid for pen and ink, as well."

"Those are not luxuries, but rather a necessity, if you would have me emerge from prison a sane man."

I picked up one of the sheets of paper and read the poem he had been composing.

> *When I look back and in myself behold*
> *the wandering ways that youth could not descry*
> *and see the fearful course that youth did hold*
> *and met in mind each step I strayed awry*
> *my knees I bow and from my heart I call*
> *O Lord forget youth's faults and follies all.*

"Faults and follies," I murmured. Choosing the wrong cause to follow? Or the wrong woman to wed?

"The princess's women tell me you have written several poems in praise of the ladies who serve Her Grace. The few who were allowed to come with her to the Tower are most impressed by your skill with words."

"Which gentlewomen are here?"

When I told him their names, his relief was palpable.

"Who is she, Jack?"

"I do not understand you."

"You understand very well. I am told that one of the princess's maids of honor inspired you to write more than one poem in her honor."

"A poet must have a muse," he protested.

I nodded encouragement, even though my heart was breaking. "Tell me about her."

"Her name is Isabella. Isabella Markham. She was in attendance on the princess not long ago. Do you know where she is now?"

"The queen sent her sister's maids of honor and waiting gentle-women back to their families."

He must have heard the anguish in my voice, or seen something in my expression. He seized me by the shoulders and waited until I met his eyes. "Audrey, Isabella is not my mistress. Only my muse. She is the lady on a pedestal, in the old tradition of courtly love."

But he loved her, as he had never loved me. I'd always known that Jack had married me for what I could bring him. I could not fault him for that. Marriages are rarely made for love. And to give Jack credit, he had never claimed to be passionately in love with me.

He did love our daughter. I had no doubt of that.

And he was my husband, and would be until death parted us.

That being the case, I meant to do everything in my power to free him from the Tower . . . so long as it did not also endanger the princess.

Although I had served Elizabeth for only a short time, I had long been aware of the connection between us. That our appearance was so similar was only part of that bond. She had inherited King Henry's presence, and his ability to inspire loyalty. Not even the continual backbiting of her other attendants could turn me against Her Grace.

Sir Thomas Wyatt was loyal to his princess, too. He went to his death on the eleventh day of April, marched out of the Tower and up Tower Hill. On the scaffold, he proclaimed her innocence, denying as he had all along that Elizabeth had been complicit in his treason.

A priest came to her chambers afterward, the one sent by the queen to witness Wyatt's execution. He tried to shock the princess into betraying herself.

"He met a traitor's death, madam—beheaded first. Then his body was quartered on the scaffold. His bowels and private parts were burned and the head and quarters went into a basket to be taken by cart to Newgate Prison. There they will be parboiled before being nailed up as a warning to all who would betray the queen. The head will go on top of the gibbet at St. James's Palace."

His graphic description sickened me, but if it affected the Lady Elizabeth, she did not let her revulsion show. Disappointed, the priest left. The councilors who came the next day likewise failed in their attempt to persuade Her Grace to admit she'd supported the rebellion. The only time I ever saw my princess show any reaction at all was when, in early May, she heard that she was to be placed in the care of Sir Henry Bedingfield.

"Is the Lady Jane's scaffold still standing?" she asked in a shaken voice.

47

*T*wo months after she'd been brought to the Tower by
water, Elizabeth Tudor left it the same way. We traveled
on a row barge accompanied by smaller craft carrying armed guards.
Crowds gathered to watch from the shore and cheer for the princess,
thinking she'd been freed. As we passed the Steelyard, where the
merchants of the Hanse have their depot, guns fired a salute.

My longing gaze picked out familiar sights along the way. I could
not see my old home on Watling Street from the river but St. Paul's
sat on a hill and dominated the skyline. We passed Seymour Place,
the property of a new owner. And Durham House, where I had met
the Earl of Surrey, the Duchess of Richmond, and Mary Shelton so
long ago. Whitehall sprawled on one side of the Thames and Norfolk House stood on the other. I did not know who now lived in the
latter. Queen Mary had taken it away from Queen Kathryn's brother
when he backed the attempt to put Lady Jane Grey on the throne in
her place. Only days after being pardoned for that treason, he'd been
arrested again for complicity with Sir Thomas Wyatt the Younger.

As far as I knew, he was still a prisoner in the Tower.

So was Jack.

We disembarked at Richmond Palace, more than a dozen miles upstream from London. Sir Henry Bedingfield and his men surrounded the princess the moment she set foot onshore and allowed no one to come near her. She was escorted directly to the chamber where she would spend the night. Contrary to the rumors in the city, Elizabeth had not been set free. She was on her way to Woodstock, there to be held under heavy guard at the queen's pleasure.

When I started to follow the princess and her guards into the palace, a hand caught my arm. "Not you, Mistress Harington."

I did not know the man who'd stopped me, but he wore Queen Mary's livery.

"I must go with—"

"Your services are no longer needed."

My "services" had been of little help to Queen Mary. I had duly reported on the Lady Elizabeth's activities. Her Grace read, she embroidered, she played cards with her ladies, she ate, and she slept. She walked for exercise as often as it was permitted. Sometimes other prisoners in the Tower called out to her, but I did not repeat those words of encouragement.

I did not object to being dismissed. I was not cut out to be a spy. But I did mind being left in limbo. "What about my husband?"

"I know nothing of him." The fellow released me and turned away.

"Wait! How am I to reach Kelston?"

Somersetshire was a considerable distance from Richmond and I had no servants and little ready money. I had sent those who'd escorted me to Whitehall home when the queen ordered me to join the Lady Elizabeth's household.

"That is not my concern," the queen's man said, and he kept walking.

At first I despaired. I stood on the river stairs, buffeted by a light wind and spray from the Thames, and could not think what to do. I was not accustomed to being completely on my own, but neither was I helpless. I squared my shoulders and counted my money. The only sensible thing to do was book passage on the next tilt boat bound for London.

During the journey, I had to endure bold stares from the men on board. They saw a woman traveling without a maid or a gentleman escort and thought the worst. Ignoring them as best I could, I set my mind to thinking what my next step would be. Those to whom I once would have turned first for help—Mother Anne and my sister Muriel and Sir Anthony Denny—were no longer alive. I dismissed at once the idea of asking assistance from Bridget and Master Scutt. My faithful Edith was still in Somersetshire, for I'd trusted no one else to look after Hester in my absence.

That left only my sister Elizabeth. From her husband I obtained an escort to take me safely to our house in Stepney. We'd left a few loyal retainers there. Within a week, I was back at Kelston and re-united with my precious daughter.

The strain was terrible during the months that followed. I did not sleep through a single night in all that time. I had no way of knowing what the queen would decide to do with Princess Elizabeth or with Jack. If my husband was charged with treason, all he owned, including everything I had brought to our marriage, would be for-feited to the Crown. Hester and I would be destitute.

Another fear haunted me, too. The queen, for all she wanted to believe that the Lady Elizabeth was not her sister at all, could not deceive herself forever. Elizabeth's resemblance to King Henry— a resemblance I shared—was too pronounced. If Elizabeth was a threat to the throne, then so was I. In Mary's mind, we were both the king's bastards.

In January, Jack came home to us. He had spent more than eleven months a prisoner, a shorter incarceration than the last time, but not by much. It had been more than eight months since I'd seen him last. He was thinner, and more somber. He swore to me that he was a changed man.

"We will build a new life for ourselves," he promised. "You and I and Hester will rusticate here in Somerset, far from the royal court, free of intrigue and in no danger."

The year of our Lord fifteen hundred and fifty-five, spent at Kelston and Catherine's Court, was the happiest of my entire life.

48

Catherine's Court, March 1556

I went to stand beside Jack as he stared up at the night sky. The comet was there again, as it had been all week. It looked like a star with the long tail and many people were frightened by it.

"Is it an omen?" I asked.

"Some believe comets foreshadow future events, but whether those events are good or evil, who can tell?" Then he laughed.

"What amuses you?"

"If this comet augurs well for the future, then perhaps it is time I returned to London."

"If you think you can ingratiate yourself to Queen Mary, you are much mistaken. She will be too suspicious of your motives to allow you anywhere near her."

Even in Somerset we'd heard rumors of yet another plot against the queen. I imagined Her Grace's councilors would look askance at anyone new arrived at court, especially someone like Jack, who had twice before been arrested because he'd had ties to enemies of the Crown. That nothing had ever been proven against him would matter little.

He followed my thoughts without difficulty and answered the question I had not dared ask. "I have had no dealings with any conspirators, nor do I have seditious books or papers in my possession."

Failure to conform to the teachings of the Church of Rome was as dangerous in Queen Mary's England as fomenting rebellion. Those who clung to the church King Henry had established soon found themselves in gaol. If they would not recant, they were burned at the stake for heretics. Many people had fled into exile, vowing to remain abroad until Elizabeth succeeded to the throne.

So long as the queen and her Spanish husband did not produce a child of their own, Mary's half sister remained her heir. Our hope that Elizabeth Tudor would eventually reign, restoring the New Religion to England, was one of several things about which Jack and I were in perfect agreement. Our opinions on other matters diverged. I opposed his return to Stepney.

"Why go there when you have no hope of being given a place at court?" I asked.

"But to be seen to hover on the fringes, supporting the queen," he argued, "can do me no harm. And to have you and Hester with me in Stepney would provide most excellent proof of my sincerity."

"And when you are not at court?" I was beginning to have a bad feeling about this. "Will you stay with us there?"

He grinned unrepentantly at me. "Part of the time. Then again, it is but a short ride to Hatfield." Princess Elizabeth, after a long incarceration at Woodstock, had been allowed to return to her own house.

"Hatfield is at least twenty miles from Stepney."

"I can ride that distance in one day."

"To see the princess? Or is that just an excuse to visit your muse?"

"But that's the beauty of it!" he exclaimed. "To all those who have read my poetry, it will seem that I go there to see Mistress Markham. No one will suspect that I carry messages of support to Elizabeth Tudor."

The smug satisfaction in his voice made me want to strike him.

"How many people do you suppose have read your poems, since they have never been published?"

"Rumor is enough to carry out the ruse. The ruse of the muse." He chuckled, delighted with his own cleverness.

"Rumor will not call her your muse, Jack. Everyone will think you have abandoned me for your mistress."

His smile turned to a frown. "I will remind them of Surrey and Fair Geraldine." At my blank look, he laughed again. "Have you never read the poem the earl wrote to Elizabeth Fitzgerald? She was a child at the time. He felt sorry for her, alone at court and blighted by her Irish father's treason. The verses singing her praises were intended to remind men of her noble heritage and help her to a good marriage."

"So you wrote poetry to Mistress Markham only to help her find a husband?" The words were so sweetly said that honey should have dripped from my lips.

Jack lapped them up. "I wish her well, as I do all of the ladies who serve the princess or have served her in the past."

I knew better. As they had in the Tower, his features softened whenever he spoke of Isabella Markham. She was more than a muse to him. More than a young woman he sought to help to a marriage with someone else. He desired her. If he had not committed adultery in the flesh, he had most assuredly sinned in his thoughts about her.

It is always better to face the truth than to deceive one's self, even when the truth is so painful that it hurts to take the next breath.

We left for Stepney within the fortnight.

49

Stepney, August 1556

*I*t was some five months later that the summer fevers came.
I fell ill, so ill that I feared I would die. To be so near to
death forced me to think about my life and whether I would have
done anything differently. I decided that I would not, but as I began
to recover, it worried me that my daughter lived in total ignorance
of her connection to the royal family, even more so than I had for so
many years.

Ignorance is never wise.

I had no desire to claim a royal inheritance. It was far too dangerous. I wanted to be John Malte's bastard rather than the king's and I
had fought to back that claim with legal documents. But since both
Queen Mary and Princess Elizabeth knew the truth, I no longer believed I could protect my daughter by keeping her uninformed.

I quarreled with Jack about telling her my story. He forbade it.
That ended the discussion for a time. I felt too weak to argue further.
But as the weeks passed and I did not regain my former good health,
my sense of urgency grew stronger. When fortune presented me with
an opportunity, I took it, and so began my tale.

50

here was silence in the hall. The portraits on the walls looked down on Hester Harington and her mother, seated side by side on a padded settle before the hearth. Audrey had her arm around her daughter's shoulders, holding her close.

She had told Hester everything now, Audrey thought, all except the reason they were presently rusticating in Somerset. Her daughter appeared to be mulling over what she'd learned. Physically spent, mentally exhausted, Audrey could not think of anything more to say. Had she convinced Hester to keep silent about her royal blood? The girl was so young. Did she truly understand the danger?

A voice spoke from behind them. "It is very late. You both should be in bed."

Hester abruptly disentangled herself and ran to greet her father. Jack hugged her tightly in return, then gave her a little push in the direction of her bedchamber. She made a face, but she went.

"I wish she would obey me as readily as she does you," Audrey murmured.

Jack said nothing.

"I've told her everything. It will be up to you to guide what she does with that knowledge."

He frowned. "What do you mean? You are her mother."

Audrey rose slowly, attempting to compensate for the dizziness she knew would come. The spells did not pass as quickly as they once had. By the time she felt steady enough to take a step, Jack was at her side, his face ashen.

"There are learned physicians in London. We could return there."

"My fate is in God's hands. Have we not been taught that, Jack, by both the New Religion and the old?"

In his face she saw the confirmation of her fears. She had never fully recovered from the fevers of the summer just past. She grew weaker with each passing day, not stronger. She might have weeks left, perhaps even months, but her days were numbered.

Jack helped her from the hall. Slowly, they made their way toward Hester's chamber. By the time they reached her bedside, she was already soundly sleeping, one hand curled under her cheek.

Audrey smiled. She had finished what she'd set out to do. For better or worse, with or without her mother's presence, Hester would not have to go searching for the truth. She knew what her royal inheritance was and she knew why it was better to make no claim to it.

A glance at her husband reassured Audrey. That Jack would remarry when she was gone seemed certain. No doubt he'd wed his muse. But his feelings for Hester would never change. As they stood together, looking down at the sleeping child, his eyes were full of his love for their daughter.

NOTES FROM THE AUTHOR

Although this is a work of fiction, all the characters except Edith, Mistress Yerdeley, and Dionysus Petre the dancing master are based on real people. You will find mini-biographies of some of them in the next section. These may also contain spoilers.

Many of the things Audrey experiences really happened, although she may not have been present when they did. We do not know exactly when she died or where, but there was an outbreak of fever in the summer of 1556 and many who were ill then but survived were carried off by a second outbreak that took place during the winter of 1556–57.

The names Audrey and Hester may strike readers as unusual for the times. Audrey was a nickname for Ethelreda (don't ask me how, but I'm told there is a linguistic explanation). Many girls were named after this English saint who lived in East Anglia from 630 to 679. It has been suggested that Audrey was named for her because she was born on St. Ethelreda's Day, June 23. As for Hester, I think it likely that something happened circa 1548 to call attention to Queen Esther's story in the Bible, perhaps the publication of a popular version of the tale. In addition to Hester Harington, there were at least two other Hesters born at about that same time, Hester Saltonstall and Hester Pinckney.

The glove or pocket beagle is a real breed and King Henry is known to have kept a pack of them for hunting.

Audrey's mother is said to have been a laundress at Windsor Castle. I didn't want to include an information dump in the novel, but for those who are interested in what the life of a laundress was like, what follows is a description of how you'd get your linens clean in the sixteenth century. The process would start on a Saturday by soaking the laundry in a thick green mixture of water and summer sheep's dung. This took three days. On Monday, Tuesday, and Wednesday, each item had to be dipped repeatedly in the river. After the last rinsing, it was beaten out and left to soak until Thursday morning, when it was finally allowed to dry. On Friday the laundress put everything into a buck tub. This sat up on a stool with an underbuck beneath it for the lye to drain into. A laundress would spread a buck sheet over the linen and then spread a thin paste of dog's mercury, mallow, and wormwood over the sheet. Finally, she'd pour strong, boiling lye over the whole thing, cover it up, and leave it to stand overnight. In the morning, she'd take the linens out and spread them on the grass and water them all morning. This business with the buck sheet and the lye and the watering would be repeated twice more before the laundry was dropped into a vat of lye and urine and soaked to bleach it. Then, on Monday morning, each piece would be laid out and watered. This process was repeated daily until the laundry was considered to be white enough. Sometimes that required another week or more.

As for Princess Elizabeth's incarceration in the Tower of London, my account contradicts some popular beliefs about her stay there. I've relied for details on the information in David Starkey's 2001 biography, *Elizabeth: The Struggle for the Throne*, which points out several factual errors in earlier accounts.

WHO WAS WHO AT THE
ENGLISH COURT
1532-56

ANTHONY DENNY

Anthony Denny was one of King Henry VIII's most trusted servants throughout the period of this novel. He was a yeoman of the wardrobe by 1536, as well as a groom of the privy chamber. In 1539 he became chief gentleman of the privy chamber and deputy groom of the stool. He was knighted in 1544. In October 1546 he was named groom of the stool and was also keeper of the "dry stamp" with the king's signature. In other words, he could authorize documents in the king's name. This made him a very powerful figure at court, despite the fact that he was not a nobleman. His wife was a lady-in-waiting to all six of Henry VIII's queens. He died in 1549.

JOANNA DINGLEY

Nothing is known about Joanna Dingley or Dyngley other than that she was said to have been a royal laundress. Her natural or "base" daughter, Audrey Malte, was raised as the child of John Malte, Henry VIII's tailor, but was later said to have been the king's child. Joanna was married to a Mr. Dobson by the time Malte made his will on September 10, 1546. It refers to her as "Joane Dingley, now wife of one Dobson" and as "Joane Dyngley, otherwise Joane Dobson." He left her twenty pounds. Joanna does not seem to have played any part in her daughter's life and the identity of Mr. Dobson remains elusive.

EDWARD VI

Not yet ten years old when he became king, he was a devout follower of the New Religion and favored his Protestant half sister Elizabeth over his Catholic half sister Mary. Modern scholars seem to agree that it was Edward's own idea to pass over both Elizabeth and Mary in favor of making his cousin, Lady Jane Grey, his heir. He died in 1553.

PRINCESS ELIZABETH

Elizabeth was at Ashridge in August 1543 with her half siblings, father, and new stepmother. She went with the royal progress to Ampthill but was abruptly sent back to Ashridge. The supposition is that she asked the wrong question, probably about her mother. Speaking the name Anne Boleyn in the presence of King Henry was not permitted. In 1554, when she was briefly imprisoned in the Tower of London, one of her attendants was John Harington's wife, Audrey. Elizabeth did consider fleeing to France in 1556–57, but decided against it, remaining in England until she succeeded Queen Mary, peacefully, in 1558. She reigned until her death in 1603.

HESTER HARINGTON

Hester was the only child of Audrey Malte and John Harington. The date of her birth is uncertain, but could have been no earlier than 1548. At one time there was a portrait of her, described as showing a child holding a book. She was still living in 1568 but after that disappears from history.

JOHN HARINGTON

A gentleman of the Chapel Royal early in his career at court, Harington later entered the service of Sir Thomas Seymour, most often serving as a messenger. He helped arrange for Lady Jane Grey to join the household at Seymour Place. When Seymour was arrested for treason, Harington spent more than eleven months as a prisoner in the Tower of London. He was there once again in 1554, suspected of conspiring with the Duke of Suffolk during the uprising known as Wyatt's Rebellion. It is not known how he met Audrey Malte, but they were married by 1548 and through her he became a considerable landowner. They had one child. By 1549, he is believed to have fallen in love with Isabella Markham, one of Princess Elizabeth's ladies, to whom he wrote poetry. She later became his second wife. Harington died in 1582.

HENRY VIII

King of England, known for having six wives and numerous mistresses. In fact, the only two women who were certainly his mistresses were Elizabeth Blount and Mary Boleyn. Did he have a child with a laundress? We'll never know for certain. He died in 1547 and was succeeded by Edward VI.

HENRY HOWARD, EARL OF SURREY

Known as the poet earl, Surrey was a loose cannon. He did go rioting through the streets with his friends. He did suggest, in public,
that his sister would do better to become the king's mistress than Sir
Thomas Seymour's wife. Was he guilty of treason? Probably not, but
there was just enough doubt about his intentions to send him to his
death in 1547.

MARY HOWARD, DUCHESS OF RICHMOND

Mary Howard was the daughter of Thomas Howard, third Duke of
Norfolk. She was a maid of honor to her cousin Anne Boleyn, and
was married to King Henry VIII's illegitimate son, Henry FitzRoy,
Duke of Richmond, at Hampton Court on November 26, 1533.
They never consummated the marriage. Following her husband's
death in 1536, Mary lived primarily at Kenninghall when she was
not at court. She was at the center of a literary circle that included
her brother, Henry Howard, Earl of Surrey, and Lady Margaret
Douglas. She was a lady-in-waiting to Catherine Howard but was
sent back to Kenninghall in November 1541 when the queen's
household was disbanded. There was talk of a marriage with Thomas
Seymour, Queen Jane's brother, as early as 1538 and the idea was
broached again in 1546, but Surrey was violently opposed and Mary
does not seem to have liked the plan much herself. In December
1546, when Mary's father and brother were arrested on charges of
treason, she was forced to give evidence against them but managed
to say very little of use. After Surrey was executed, Mary was given
charge of his daughters. She established a household at Reigate and
employed John Foxe to educate them. Unlike most of the rest of the
Howards, Mary adopted the New Religion, which meant she fell out
of favor when Queen Mary came to the throne. She remained close

to her father and when he died in 1554 he left her five hundred pounds. Mary died in 1557.

ANNE MALTE (MAIDEN NAME UNKNOWN)

Anne Malte was the second wife of John Malte, the king's tailor. On October 16, 1548, Anne Malte purchased the manor of Hickmans in the Hamlet of Haggerston and about one hundred acres in the northeast part of the parish of Shoreditch. Anne left this property to her daughter Elizabeth and Elizabeth's husband, Thomas Hilton, who were also named executors of her 1549 will.

AUDREY MALTE

Audrey Malte, also called Ethelreda and Esther in various documents, was officially the illegitimate daughter of John Malte, Henry VIII's tailor, by Joanna Dingley or Dyngley. The late-sixteenth-century book *Nugae Antiquae*, written by John Harington's son by his second wife, is the earliest source for the claim that she was the natural daughter of the king and this may be a complete fiction. What seems to support it is the fact that the king gave a large grant of land jointly to John Malte and Ethelreda Malte. This document is very specific in identifying Ethelreda as Malte's bastard daughter. John Malte's will, dated September 10, 1546, and proved June 7, 1547, is also clear on this point, leaving a generous bequest to "Awdrey Malte, my bastard daughter, begotten on the body of Joane Dingley, now wife of one Dobson." She was to inherit most of his property in Berkshire, Hertfordshire, and Somerset. One wonders why both documents were so careful to point out both her illegitimacy and the fact that she was Malte's child. How old she was at the time Malte died is unclear, but there were already negotiations under way for her betrothal to an illegitimate son of Sir Richard Southwell. At some point between September 10, 1546, and November 11, 1547, however, she married John Harington of Stepney instead. There is no indication of when or where they first met. They had one child, a daughter they named Hester. In 1554, Audrey was one of Elizabeth Tudor's attendants during the princess's incarceration in the Tower of London. She was still living in early 1556 but had died by 1559.

BRIDGET MALTE

Bridget Malte was the daughter of John Malte, the king's tailor, and his first wife. Most accounts call her his youngest daughter. By 1545, she had married John Scutt, a much older man, and given birth to a son, Anthony. Bridget and John Scutt were named overseers of John Malte's will. After the family moved to Somerset, Scutt gained a reputation for mistreating his wife. When he died suddenly, there were whispers of poison. The whispers grew louder when Bridget remarried a fortnight after her husband's death, taking as her second husband Edward St. Loe, the son of a local landowner. Later it came out that Bridget was three months pregnant with St. Loe's child at the time of the marriage, but two months after they wed, on November 30, 1557, it was Bridget who died suddenly. Six months after that, Edward St. Loe married her stepdaughter, Margaret Scutt. All this gave rise to suspicion but no proof of murder. The inquisition postmortem was held on August 9, 1558. In the Chatsworth House Archives there is an account of a lawsuit in which Bridget is described as "a verye lustye yonge woman."

ELIZABETH MALTE

Elizabeth Malte may not have been a Malte at all. She was certainly the daughter of Anne Malte, second wife and widow of John Malte

(d. 1547), royal tailor, because Elizabeth and her husband were executors of Anne's will. Elizabeth is not, however, mentioned in John Malte's will. By then, Elizabeth was probably already married to Thomas Hilton (Hylton/Hulton), usually identified as the illegitimate son of William Hilton, who served as the king's tailor before John Malte.

JOHN MALTE

John Malte was the king's tailor until late 1546. The Malte house was in Watling Street in the parish of St. Augustine at Paul's Gate. In 1541, Malte's worth was set at two thousand marks and he was assessed £33 6s 8d in the London Subsidy Roll for Bread Street Ward. John Malte wrote his will on September 10, 1546, and it was proved June 7, 1547. He left bequests to his two married daughters, his two married stepdaughters by his first wife (I reduced this to one), his unmarried bastard daughter, and the foundling child left at his gate. His second wife, Anne, survived him.

MURIEL MALTE

Muriel Malte was the daughter of John Malte, the king's tailor, and his first wife. In 1545, she married John Horner. In 1544, his father had purchased Cloford, Somersetshire, and John Malte purchased the manor of Podimore Milton, Somersetshire. Both properties were given to the young couple on their marriage. They had three sons: William, Thomas, and Maurice. Muriel died on March 9, 1548.

KATHRYN PARR

Henry VIII's last queen attempted to reunite all the royal children at Ashridge during the summer progress of 1543. After the king's death, she moved to her dower house at Chelsea Manor, where she maintained her own household. I have no evidence that she even knew Audrey Malte, but she certainly knew John Harington. As one of Thomas Seymour's gentlemen, he would have been party to Seymour's courtship of Kathryn and their later marriage. The queen dowager died in 1548.

JOHN SCUTT

John Scutt or Skutt was one of the royal tailors from 1519 to 1547, making clothing for all six of Henry VIII's wives and also for private clients. Scutt was master of the Merchant Taylors' Company in 1536. He was a widower with a young daughter, Margaret, when he married Bridget Malte, who appears to have been his neighbor in Bread Street Ward (parish of St. Augustine at Paul's Gate). His worth was recorded at two thousand marks in 1541 and he was assessed £33 6s 8d. Scutt was granted arms on November 12, 1546. After the death of Henry VIII he retired to the manor of Stanton Drew, Somerset. He died in 1557. There was some speculation that his wife might have poisoned him.

THOMAS SEYMOUR

It is believed that Henry VIII was aware that Thomas Seymour and Kathryn Parr had tender feelings for each other after Kathryn's second husband, Lord Latimer, died and that the king deliberately sent Seymour out of the country on diplomatic missions. Seymour's hasty marriage to the queen dowager, his inappropriate behavior toward Princess Elizabeth, and his clumsy attempts to influence his nephew King Edward VI, and possibly to kidnap him, led to his downfall. He was executed for treason on March 10, 1549.

MARY SHELTON

Mary Shelton was the daughter of Sir John Shelton of Shelton, Norfolk, and Anne Boleyn, the sister of Queen Anne Boleyn's father. A number of scholars argue that Mary Shelton was the king's mistress in 1535 and also a candidate to become Henry's fourth wife. I find the logic of this unconvincing. The mistress of 1535, known to history as "Madge," was more likely to have been Mary's older sister Margaret. The single mention of Mary Shelton as one of two ladies in whom the king was interested in 1538 comes in a letter that says nothing about marriage. The comment could as easily refer to the king's choice of one of the two as his next mistress. What we do know to be true about Mary is that she was friends with Lady Margaret Douglas, Lady Mary Howard, Duchess of Richmond, and the duchess's brother, Henry Howard, Earl of Surrey. She contributed to and edited the "Devonshire Manuscript," a collection of poems, some of them original, that was passed around among members of their circle. Two of the poems suggest that Sir Thomas Wyatt pursued Mary and was rejected by her. Of course, Wyatt was married at the time. Mary may have been in attendance upon Queen Catherine Howard. After Catherine's arrest, she spent most of the next year with her friends Mary Howard and Margaret Douglas at Kenninghall in Norfolk, Mary Howard's home. She fell in love with Thomas Clere, one of the Earl of Surrey's close friends. They intended to marry but were prevented by Clere's death on April 14, 1545. Clere made her his principal heir and she is mentioned in the elegy Surrey wrote to Clere. Sometime in 1546, Mary wed Sir Anthony Heveningham, by whom she had several children. It is as Lady Heveningham that Surrey wrote to her while she was staying at the house of her brother, Jerome Shelton, formerly part of the priory of St. Helen, and this letter led to the suggestion that she be questioned after Surrey was arrested for treason. After Heveningham died, Mary wed Philip Appleyard. She was probably the Lady Heveningham at court in 1558–59. She died in 1571.

SIR RICHARD SOUTHWELL

Sir Richard Southwell is the villain of this piece. I can't say for certain how he behaved toward Audrey Malte, although he did negotiate with John Malte for her marriage to his illegitimate son, but he did murder a man in 1532 and he did give evidence to the Privy Council that led directly to the Earl of Surrey's arrest and execution in 1547. He also had a hand in the downfall of two other important figures at the court of Henry VIII—Sir Thomas More and Thomas Cromwell. His weak chin is immortalized in a sketch and portrait by Hans Holbein the Younger. Southwell fell out of favor at court after the death of Edward VI. No earlier than 1559, he married his long-time mistress and had one more child by her. This child, although legitimate, was a girl. Richard Darcy, alias Richard Southwell the Younger, remained his father's principal heir. Southwell died in 1564.

RICHARD DARCY, ALIAS SOUTHWELL

Sir Richard Southwell's illegitimate son studied at Cambridge and later entered Lincoln's Inn. His betrothal to Audrey Malte was thwarted by her marriage to John Harington. He later married twice, the first time around 1555, and had numerous children. He died in 1600.

For more information on the women on this list, please see their entries at http://www.KateEmersonHistoricals.com/TudorWomen Index.htm.

ROYAL
Inheritance

BY KATE EMERSON

About This Guide

This reading group guide for *Royal Inheritance* includes an introduction, discussion questions, and ideas for enhancing your book club. The suggested questions are intended to help your reading group find new and interesting angles and topics for your discussion. We hope that these ideas will enrich your conversation and increase your enjoyment of the book.

Introduction

This new novel from Kate Emerson, the critically acclaimed author of the Secrets of the Tudor Court series, centers around Audrey Malte, an illegitimate daughter of King Henry VIII who grows up at court thinking that her father is the king's tailor.

When Audrey reaches marriageable age, she begins to realize, from the way certain people behave toward her, that Malte is keeping secrets from her, and she sets out to discover the truth. Her quest brings her into contact with some of the best and worst of Henry's courtiers, among them a man with whom she falls in love.

Unfortunately, Malte has already entered into negotiations for her betrothal to someone else. It is up to Audrey to navigate Henry's court so that she may marry the man she loves.

With the rich, lush detail that has become a trademark of Kate Emerson's novels, *Royal Inheritance* is a wonderful picture of a young woman trying to find her own legacy at the Tudor court.

Topics and Questions for Discussion

1. As *Royal Inheritance* begins, Audrey has decided to tell her daughter, Hester, the truth about her own background. Why does she think that she has a duty to do so? Do you agree with Audrey's decision to tell Hester the truth? What does Audrey mean when she tells Hester, "Close kinship to the Crown is a burden, not a gift" (page 257)? Discuss the ways that Audrey's statement manifests itself in her own life.

2. Audrey says, "It is always better to face the truth than to deceive one's self, even when the truth is so painful that it hurts to take the next breath" (page 327). However, when she first begins to have doubts about her parentage, she delays in finding out more. Why do you think she does so? Are there characters you encounter in *Royal Inheritance* who hide important truths from themselves? Who?

3. Audrey refers to her hair as having a "too-bright color" (page 133). Why does she think it is too bright? What other clues about the true nature of Audrey's parentage are there?

4. The first time Mother Anne meets Jack Harington, she greets him with a "friendly kiss . . . as is the custom when greeting those who are truly welcome," leading Audrey to believe that he "must have desirable connections at the royal court" (page

53). What are your initial impressions of Jack? Do they change throughout the course of the novel? In what ways and why?

5. When Audrey is an adolescent, she says, "I did not often remember that I was a bastard myself. Even Bridget did not taunt me about it" (page 66). Why do you think that Bridget refrains from ridiculing Audrey? Discuss the relationship between the two sisters. Compare and contrast it to that of Elizabeth and Mary.

6. Mary Shelton says, "It is the fate of wives to be unhappy" (page 93). Do you think that Audrey is happy in her marriage? Do you agree with Audrey's assessment that "any woman takes a great risk when she gives herself to a man" (page 167)? What does Audrey give up by getting married?

7. After Audrey meets Elizabeth for the first time, she says, "The encounter left me feeling strangely vulnerable" (page 127). Describe the encounter. Were you surprised by the way that Elizabeth reacts to Audrey when they are in the Tower of London together?

8. When Audrey reconnects with her mother, she says that "it was easier to think of her by her Christian name than to regard her as my mother" (page 230). Why do you think that this is the case? Describe their encounter. Were you surprised by Joanna's treatment of Audrey? Why or why not? Why does Edith think that Joanna should be pitied rather than reviled? Do you agree with her?

9. Joanna tells Audrey that Malte is a good man. Why do you think that Joanna chooses to tell Audrey this at the end of

their encounter? Do you agree with Joanna's assessment of Malte? Why do you think that Malte agrees to raise Audrey as his own? How do they make Audrey feel that she is part of their family?

10. When Audrey criticizes Jack for spending his money on pen and ink while imprisoned in the Tower of London, he responds, "Those are not luxuries, but rather a necessity" (page 318). Why is writing important to Jack? Poetry is also important to the circle of friends that Audrey meets through Jack, including Thomas Clere and Mary Shelton. Discuss their meetings. What role does poetry play?

11. Malte tells Audrey he wants her to marry Southwell's son Richard Darcy because "I want you to be safe after I am gone . . . Southwell looks after his own" (page 266). What reasons does Audrey give for refusing to do so? Do you think that Audrey will be safer married to Richard Darcy? Or do you think that she is correct to distrust Southwell?

12. Jack tells Audrey, "Far more dangerous are the animals that live indoors, wearing fine clothing and smiling" (page 226). In what ways is the court a dangerous place? Discuss the shifting alliances that occur throughout *Royal Inheritance*.

13. When Audrey says that Henry is the head of the Church of England because of his reforms, Mary Shelton responds, "There are reforms and then there are reforms" (page 192). What does she mean by this statement? Discuss it in the context of Elizabeth's and Mary's reigns.

14. After being told Anthony Denny's title, Audrey says that it "sounded very important, although no more so than 'royal

tailor.' I was too young yet to grasp the difference between a gentleman born and a merchant whose wealth allowed him to rise into the ranks of the gentry" (page 17). What is the difference? How is it apparent in the betrothals that occur in *Royal Inheritance*? Why is Richard Darcy seen as a better partner for Audrey than Jack Harington?

Enhance Your Book Club

1. Henry VIII's royal court serves as the backdrop for *Royal Inheritance* and many historical figures appear as characters in the book, including Lady Jane Grey, Queen Mary, and Queen Elizabeth. Learn more about these historical figures by visiting the official website of the British Monarchy at http://www.royal.gov.uk/HistoryoftheMonarchy/KingsandQueensofEngland/TheTudors/TheTudors.aspx.

2. Audrey finds herself in the Tower of London serving Elizabeth, who has been incarcerated by her sister, Queen Mary. Take a virtual tour of the Tower: http://www.londononline.co.uk/towerguide/ and discuss the conditions in which Elizabeth and Audrey may have lived while they were staying in the Tower.

3. To learn more about Kate Emerson and find out more about her Secrets of the Tudor Court series, visit her official site at http://www.kateemersonhistoricals.com/.

4. Read more depictions of life in the Tudor court. Suggested reading: *The Red Queen* by Philippa Gregory, *In a Treacherous Court* by Michelle Diener, *Royal Mistress* by Anne Easter Smith, *The Last Wife of Henry VIII* by Carolly Erickson, *The Queen's Gambit* by Elizabeth Fremantle, and *At the King's Pleasure* by Kate Emerson.